# THE
# GAPS

## LEANNE
## HALL

TEXT PUBLISHING MELBOURNE AUSTRALIA

textpublishing.com.au

The Text Publishing Company
Swann House, 22 William Street, Melbourne Victoria 3000, Australia

Published by The Text Publishing Company, 2021

Book design by Imogen Stubbs
Cover images by Shutterstock and Stocksy
Typeset by J&M Typesetting

Printed and bound in Australia by Griffin Press, part of Ovato, an accredited
ISO/NZS 14001:2004 Environmental Management System printer.

ISBN: 9781922330482 (paperback)
ISBN: 9781925923933 (ebook)

A catalogue record for this book is available from the National Library of
Australia.

This book is printed on paper certified against the Forest Steward-
ship Council® Standards. Griffin Press holds FSC chain-of-custody
certification SGS-COC-005088. FSC promotes environmentally
responsible, socially beneficial and economically viable management of the world's forests.

## PRAISE FOR **THE GAPS**

'Haunting and beautiful. At first it has the page-turning addictiveness of a thriller and then it evolves into a captivating exploration of grief, guilt and resilience in the face of fear and uncertainty. Hall's characters are meticulously drawn, brave, fierce and vulnerable. A stunning achievement from an Australian treasure.'

**WAI CHIM**

'A powerful, compelling read about the fragility, resilience and fierceness of girlhood. Unputdownable.'

**LILI WILKINSON**

'Hall's writing is breathtakingly good. *The Gaps* is a lightning bolt of a novel about power, privilege, race, art and identity.'

**NINA KENWOOD**

'A creeping psychological thriller about loss and fear and guilt and the fractured relationships that are left behind. Brilliant.'

**ROBERT NEWTON**

Leanne Hall is an author of young adult and children's fiction. Her debut novel, *This Is Shyness*, won the Text Prize for Children's and Young Adult Writing, and was followed by a sequel, *Queen of the Night*. Her novel for younger readers, *Iris and the Tiger*, won the Patricia Wrightson Prize for Children's Literature at the 2017 NSW Premier's Literary Awards. Leanne works as a children's and YA specialist at an independent bookshop.

*For Penny, Hannah, Emah and Tash*

# *Chloe*

**DAY 1**

There's a photo of a schoolgirl next to the newsreader's head, emblazoned with the word ABDUCTED. The orange-and-green check of the girl's dress is unmistakeable.

'Yin Mitchell,' I say to myself. A cold feeling races through me.

The photo on the screen is at least a few years old—Yin has stubby ribboned pigtails, round cheeks. She wears her hair longer these days, with a feathery fringe she pushes to the side.

I stab the volume button on the remote and my sketch-book slides to the floor. The newsreader's voice is flat, but laced with an appropriate amount of sorrow.

'The armed assailant broke into the Sandpiper Drive house in the early hours of this morning via a ground floor window. The victim's mother, Chunjuan Mitchell, intercepted the intruder, but was forced into a downstairs bathroom and tied up. The alarm was raised around dawn when Stephen Mitchell, who had been sleeping in a separate part of the house, heard his wife's cries and discovered that their sixteen-year-old daughter was missing.'

Yin. Yin. Hangs out with Claire and Milla. Was in my English class in first term, but switched out later, I'm not sure why. Wears liquid eyeliner to school on the sly. Quiet, smart, deep into the orchestra scene.

It can't be true. Not again.

'Turn it down, Chlo. We'll get another note under our door.'

Mum points to the thin wall we share with our elderly neighbours, leans against the doorframe to put her earrings in, her hair hanging like a silk sheet. Everything about her is tiny and neat and pretty; she always looks immaculate in her work uniform.

'Someone else has been abducted from Balmoral.'

'Oh my god.' Mum comes closer and we watch grainy footage of a suburban street, cordoned off with striped plastic tape and swarming with shadowy figures searching for clues. Rosy-dawn-tinged, police-light blue. In the background a curious neighbour lingers in a pink dressing gown, hand clamped over her pixel mouth.

'Is she in your year level?' Mum sits next to me and grabs my hand.

My brother Sam slinks into the room and crouches in the shadows next to the couch. Our Jack Russell, Arnold, lifts his head from the rug to look disapprovingly at him.

'Yeah. Not in my class though.'

The scene doesn't look real.

It looks like a Bill Henson photograph, one of the barely lit landscapes I saw at the National Gallery on first term's Art excursion. I'd never seen photos that looked so painterly.

They featured beautiful young bodies and ancient sculptures and mammoth rocks and the ocean sliding in and out of shadows, night-time scenes barely lit in ways that made them unsettling, enticing, mysterious.

I stayed and looked at the exhibition for so long the bus almost returned to school without me. I drank in the photos like they were water. I wanted life to be something like those pictures: dark, raw, significant.

But not like this.

When I decided to take the scholarship to Balmoral Ladies College, my Morrison High friends called it the Kidnapping School.

This isn't the first time this has happened.

'When?' Mum says.

'This morning.'

'Ransom?'

'Don't think so. Not yet.'

I catch myself playing with the dangly jade charm on Mum's bracelet, a childhood habit.

The Mitchell family property has a six-foot-high wall, and a video intercom on the front gate. It's a fortress—so how did someone break in?

'Her parents must be frantic.' Mum always gets upset when bad things happen to other people, even though she never gets that upset for herself.

The view switches to a helicopter shot, showing the blue and green shapes of swimming pools and tennis courts, driveways as long as airport landing strips, avenues of trees and cream-and-yellow Lego mansions. So this is where my classmates live. I've never been to a Balmoral girl's house; I've never been invited.

'I'll cancel my shift. Where's my phone?'

'No.' I nudge her phone under a cushion.

I'm not scared to be at home alone. Not very, anyway. Not enough to lose money over.

'I'm not leaving you by yourselves.'

'No, Mum!'

Mum's manager is a real knob. He hates giving her time off or letting her swap shifts. It's probably because he asked her out in her first few weeks at the hotel and she said no.

An identikit portrait fills the screen—a man wearing a balaclava and sunglasses, his whole face covered. A ridiculous thing to show because it could be anyone. Generic bad dude.

'Whoa,' says Sam. 'Freaky.'

Mum starts like she's only just realised he's in the room.

Sam crawls closer, his mouth rapturously open in the television glare. It's probably the same as the opening scenes of *CSI* to him. Arnold pedals his tiny legs against Sam's encroachment and whines.

Mum reaches over and switches the telly off. She hasn't got the memo yet that Sam isn't a baby anymore.

'I'm still watching!' Sam balls his fists.

'You're not watching anything,' Mum tells him. 'Keep your phone on and beside your bed,' she says to me. 'I'm going to text you every half hour. If you don't get back to me straight away, I will jump in a cab immediately.'

'Don't worry, Chlo, I'll protect you,' Sam says.

'Actually, Sam, he'd tie you up and then take me. Easy as that.'

Sam flinches and I regret my words. He's wearing shrunken Star Wars pyjamas that he refuses to admit he's grown out of. Sam still believes in superheroes and the Force.

Mum corrals us into a family hug, holding on a little bit longer than normal. My chin sits on top of her head; our long black hair gets tangled together.

'You're both getting so tall,' Mum murmurs.

Arnold huffs and rolls over. He puts his head on his paws and looks up at me, angling for a walk. I look away, over Mum's head, trying not to get strangled.

'Arnold will protect us,' I say, to make Sam, and maybe Mum, feel better.

I decide to leave the hallway light on all night, and put the outside porch light on as well. Mum's asked the landlord more than once for a security light along the driveway. It's one of the few things we agree on with Ron and Pearl next door.

For a moment I push the front curtains aside and look over at the car spots opposite. The only time ours is used is when Dad visits, which is hardly ever. The porch light is feeble; beyond our block of units the leafy darkness quickly takes over. It makes no sense that light makes humans feel safer, when it doesn't protect us at all. Fear has a steady grip around my throat and I regret telling Mum to go to work.

My phone beeps for the billionth time tonight, since the first news reports, and my nerves jangle afresh.

Liana.

*babe you need to leave that school n come back!!!!!*

My old school friends are losing their minds. My phone goes off again.

Katie.

*dont get killed x*

I send the knife emoji and the scream face and then put my phone on silent. I was already wondering how I was going to survive my first year at Balmoral, this is just adding to the sick joke.

At ten o'clock I watch the late news with the volume down low. It's mostly a rehash of what's been said in the earlier reports—they show the same outdated photo of Yin, the same identikit drawn from Yin's mum's description, and the same aerial footage that shows us how improbable it was that anyone broke into the compound.

There's still no ransom demand; no one has seen anything or anyone suspicious in the area. The reporter mentions that Yin's eight-year-old twin brothers were spending the night at their grandparents' house. I try not to think about how distraught her brothers must have been when the news was broken to them. They're barely old enough to understand.

My phone vibrates again and this time it's a relief to answer.

'Babe. Oh my god.' Liana's voice echoes. I'm sure she's

calling me from her backyard. 'Do you know her? Are you okay?'

'I'm okay. I don't know her that well.' I hate saying that, as if Yin should matter less to me because I'm not in her friendship group. 'She's in my year but I've only talked to her a few times.'

'I'm freaked out Chlo. What if it was you who got taken?'

'It wasn't me. I'm at home and I'm fine.' Liana's voice is a balm, though, and I want to keep her on the line as long as possible.

'Please, please come back to Morrison. It's not safe there.'

'L, I'm not rich, we don't live anywhere near Glen Park, I've only been at Balmoral for three terms…it's like, minimal risk.'

'I don't know what I'd do if you went missing.'

That silences me. I believe her, but this is probably the first time she's called me in two weeks.

'Do you know anything?' she asks. 'Like, insider info?'

'No. I only found out watching the news earlier. I know as much as you do.'

After I finish speaking to Liana I search online for reports about the first Balmoral girl who was kidnapped, three years ago.

Karolina Bauer was a fourteen-year-old exchange student from Düsseldorf. Her host family were the Sheldons—they had a daughter, Maddie, in Year Twelve at Balmoral at the time. Karolina was abducted from her hosts' home while the parents were at the next-door-neighbour's house; Maddie was left behind. Karolina was eventually returned after a few days, unharmed and wearing nothing but a plastic rain poncho. Even though it had happened way across town, to a girl who was nothing like me, it was easy to picture.

How cold you would be, how goosebumped your bare skin under the thin plastic. Walking down the street, shivering and rustling. Numb inside, knowing nothing would ever be the same. Trying to pick the right house, a safe house with good people in it who would rescue you and call the police and give you hot tea.

Could two students from the same school be a coincidence?

Later, close to midnight, I check on Sam. He's asleep on top of his covers, with his football boots still on and Arnold slumped across his legs. His doona cover has rockets and planets and stars on it. He's only two years older than Yin's brothers.

If anyone ever did something bad to him or Mum, I'd hunt them down and kill them. Adrenaline swirls in my arms and legs and gut when I think about it. I'd destroy anyone that hurt my family.

I leave Sam as he is. Mum likes to come home from the hotel and tuck him in, no matter the hour. Arnold opens one eye triumphantly as I leave; he isn't usually allowed on our beds.

The washing machine cycle has finished, but I can't bring myself to walk outside into the dark space behind our house and hang it out. I leave the wet clothes in a basket on top of the machine. Tomorrow morning.

One last patrol of our brick unit takes around twenty seconds and ten steps. Sam's bedroom, my bedroom and our tiny, plant-filled bathroom huddle in one corner. The lounge is separated from the kitchen by the bench, and beyond that, the door to Mum's bedroom.

From my bed I stare at the photos and drawings and magazine pages I've blu-tacked to my bedroom walls in one big chaotic collage. Normally I love to lie here and look at it. Maybe this is what the contents of my brain would look like if you tipped it out. Colours and patterns and shapes and faces. Memories and wishes and plans for the future. Like the answer to me, the sum of me, is up there on the wall.

Tonight, though, I can't stop my eyes from sliding left, to the window. It's fitted with a flimsy plastic handle that winds it open and closed. There's no lock.

I think through the logistics.

Force the window open, drag me out. The window opens onto a narrow side passage. You'd have to haul me past Ron and Pearl's unit, but they're ancient and no threat. Then I'd have to be dragged over the low dividing wall, kicking and screaming, into the front yard. It'd be difficult. Not impossible, but maybe not easy enough.

The detective that spoke on the late news seemed to be deliberately avoiding mentioning Karolina Bauer.

When I was deciding whether or not I was going to take the scholarship to Balmoral, Karolina's kidnapping was mere trivia. I was more interested in poring over the school prospectus, reading about subjects and results and awards, trying to understand what it all meant in real-life terms.

Trying to decide if I should do my final three years at a brand new school.

None of it prepared me for the harsh and dizzying reality of Balmoral Ladies College.

I'd actually talked to Yin in my first week. She was one of the first girls to pay me any attention at all.

I had been in the bathrooms near the science labs, in a cubicle. Not to pee, but to buy time away from the maelstrom of new faces and hard-to-find classrooms. I wasn't the only new student. Lots of families couldn't afford the full six years at Balmoral, so plenty of girls started in Year Ten. But those families at least paid three years' tuition. I wasn't supposed to be there at all.

I'd gone into the bathroom alone, but soon several pairs of feet came in and set up at the mirrors and sinks. The taps turned on and off, and I remained deathly quiet. Someone used the hand dryer, there was quiet chatter interspersed with silence. I held my breath.

'Gimme that,' someone said. Laughter followed by spray-can sounds.

'Wang is better than Doolan.'

I was in Mrs Wang's form but I had no idea who was speaking. Now that I'd waited those extra moments I couldn't come out of the cubicle. I'd been too quiet; it was obvious I wasn't in there to use the toilet.

'Liz says Scrutton is the best form teacher. He lets you do anything as long as you don't bother him.'

'There are four new girls in our form, including two scholarship students. That's a lot, right?'

'It's so funny how we're not supposed to know who the charity cases are.'

'God—so obvious. Can I borrow some?'

'First,' the loudest voice said, 'there's the uniforms. Second-hand and huge. And also the shoes, those ugly Mary Janes they recommend even though no one wears them.'

'To be fair, some Year Sevens have them.'

'Secondly,' the lead hyena continued, 'they're such try-hards. They join literally everything—orchestra, choir, volunteer squad, debating...'

'But they have to be good at everything or they'll lose their scholarships. And then where would they be? Back in the ghetto.'

'I feel sorry for them,' a new voice says. 'No one has told them yet how shit Balmoral is.'

There was laughter before the bell rang, and everyone cleared out.

I waited until the bathroom was quiet, already worried about being late to Maths. I was sure I was alone, but when the door swung open, Yin was there, a Ventolin puffer in her hand.

We looked at each other in the long mirror that stretched from window to wall. Me in my too-big uniform, carrying my new textbooks, a highlighted map of the school sitting on top. My face was bright red in some parts and ghost-white in others. Tears had made two obvious tracks down my cheeks.

Yin handed me some paper towel.

'I think we had English together first period. Do you need help finding your next class?' she asked.

I shook my head.

'Are you sure? This place is huge. It takes a while to learn your way around.'

Even though taking up her offer would have made my life easier, I refused again. Humiliation had glued my mouth shut.

Yin gathered her things and left, smiling sympathetically at me on the way out.

I splashed my face with cold water, patted it dry, and forced myself to go outside into the corridor. Like I've been forcing myself ever since.

I'm always nervous walking into school on a Monday morning, but today it's especially weird. There's a sick buzz flowing through the Year Ten corridor, and it's littered with whispered scraps:

*I didn't sleep*

     *I worked out where to hide*

*I can run next door*

     *Piss yourself and he won't rape you*

Small groups huddle—there are tears, hugs, wide rabbit eyes.

I have to fill five gaping minutes before form room, so I sit in front of my locker and colour in my knee with black texta to hide the hole in my opaque tights. I imagine a clear, wobbling bubble, separating me from everyone else.

No one comes to talk to me, to ask if I'm scared, did I sleep, how I'm feeling, and I'm relieved. Yin was—Yin is—a Junior Schooler, and some of these girls have known her since they were six years old. Nothing I'm experiencing could possibly compare with what they're going through.

I only lift my head when I hear the traditional morning bitchnami crashing down the hallway. You'd think they'd take the day off, but no.

Natalia *et al* march four across like teen witches in a movie, and everyone gets out of their way, as usual. People refer to them collectively as The Blondes, for obvious reasons. They didn't get the memo that it would be politically correct to include some ethnics in their group. Not that I'm applying for the job.

I draw my legs in, but not quickly enough.

'Out of my way, new girl,' says Natalia. But her expression is empty; her heart's not in it.

I don't mind what she calls me: it's the truth. Six months at Balmoral still makes me the new girl. I don't go skiing with them in winter; we didn't ride ponies together as kids. A lot of the new girls in my year are boarders and they bonded quicker than survivors on a desert island. The ones that aren't boarders still have the right parents, live in the right postcodes.

Sarah, always a step behind Natalia in every way, gives me the finger as they pass.

'Goth,' Sarah mouths. Her hair, straightened this morning, swings beautifully behind her. There's a lot of maintenance required to be a Blonde. The other two betas, Ally and Marley, look sheepish. Their foursome is simultaneously beautiful and ridiculous, like an ad that you know is airbrushed to hell but you still can't look away.

My bubble breaks open and corridor noise spills back in. Someone's left a banana in their locker over the weekend and the smell spreads far and wide. I spin my combination lock.

'Fingernails, Chloe!' a teacher barks. 'Gone by recess.'

My nails are chipped metallic blue; a hangover from the weekend. If I wanted to answer back—and I don't—I wouldn't be able to, because Mr Scrutton is already nothing but a distant speck.

✦

Instead of normal morning assembly with the whole school in the Great Hall, they quarantine Year Ten in the Performing Arts Centre. Our teachers hover at the end of rows, their faces tight. Mrs Wang and Ms Nouri have clearly been crying. I think they're aiming for a 'safe space' vibe, but instead it feels like punishment. The whole year level is infected.

The principal, Mrs Christie, is belted tight in forest green and booming as usual.

'...some of you will want to speak to the school counsellor or the chaplain, and we encourage you to do so.'

I tuck my blue nails inside my jumper sleeves as our year level coordinator, Mrs Benjamin, sweeps the gathering with her laser eyes. Someone in the row behind me is swallowing sobs.

'Miss Starcke will be available all day. You can sign up at reception. Mr O'Connor will be running a pastoral care session at lunch.'

Miss Starcke stands before us and nods, but seems seconds away from bolting. Mr O'Connor, on the other hand, looks good and ready to ram a little Jesus down our throats.

'We have been reassured that the police are making extraordinary efforts to ensure your classmate is returned safely.'

A crackle rises at the mention of the police. Mrs Christie meets it head-on. She grips the edges of the lectern in full power-stance mode.

'You would have seen the media at the gates this morning. I don't need to tell you that we expect *every student here* to demonstrate their maturity and refrain from talking to reporters. If you have any important information, you are urged to talk to the police. Reception will take your names, and they will contact you directly. LET. US. PRAY.'

Hundreds of heads drop. Mrs Christie prays in the same voice she uses to talk about skirt length and bags left out in the corridors. She hasn't said Yin's name once. I suppose she wants to keep us under control, more than anything. As if we'll erupt into hysteria at any moment. Which we might.

I keep my head up and my eyes open as the prayer drones on.

Most girls lower their heads and close their eyes, even though I don't believe for a second that all of them are religious. The fence-sitters drop their heads but keep their eyes open. Only a small number rise above the crowd, and they're not the popular girls or the chronically rebellious. They're the nerdy girls and the quiet girls, girls who practise other religions and atheists like me. Yin was one of us.

I glance down my row and see Petra's lips moving frantically. Her eyes are squinched shut; she's praying as if her life, not someone else's, depends on it. Even though I'm not a believer, there's something beautiful about how her faith shows in her face, like there's a small light inside her. If it wasn't completely inappropriate and intrusive, I'd like to take a photo of her now, capture that look.

I try not to act surprised when Petra speaks to me in the corridor, as if she somehow sensed me watching her during prayers. The first bell rings around us. Our lockers have been side by side all year, yet we've never done much more than nod hello.

'They didn't even like Yin,' Petra whispers around her locker door. 'I don't know why they have to make such a scene.'

The scene is most of 10S sitting on the floor in a red-eyed, sniffling heap. Teaghan is hiccup-crying loudly. They look genuinely upset, although I notice one or two girls looking up occasionally to check that everyone is noting their distress.

I wedge my foot under my locker door to stop it from swinging too far open. My phone jitters on the top shelf. I don't even need to look at the screen to know that it's yet another episode in the Morrison High meltdown. Liana and Katie have even got the boys messaging me, telling me to come back.

'They never paid any attention to her,' Petra says. 'And now they're carrying on as if she was their best friend.'

I don't know enough about school politics to judge if what she says is true.

The inside of Petra's locker is plastered with timetables, flyers for school societies, inspirational quotes, a list headed 'Yearly Goals', and a photo of Ruth Bader Ginsburg. Her textbooks are stacked neatly in a tower, from largest to smallest.

'Are you friends with Yin?'

'I guess. We're in orchestra together. She's first clarinet and I'm second, so we sit next to each other.'

'Do you think she'll get released?' I ask. 'Safely, I mean?'

I mean alive. Petra might be the only person I get to talk about Yin with today, so I may as well ask.

'Karolina Bauer was returned after twenty hours.' Petra clutches her textbooks to her chest and speaks fast. She's the same height as me, but she hunches.

'The exchange student, right?'

Petra nods. 'It's now over twenty-four hours since Yin was taken, give or take a few hours because they don't know the exact time, but that doesn't necessarily mean anything bad has happened.'

'So you think it's the same guy? They wouldn't say on the news last night.'

'Almost definitely.' Petra lowers her voice. 'The *modus operandi* is very similar. I've been comparing. In both cases, entry was through a ground-floor window, and family members were tied up. And if I'm right, then the weapon he carried was a gun.'

I try not to raise my eyebrows. Petra is intense. The second bell rings, setting off a chorus of slammed locker doors.

'Karolina survived because she kept quiet and did what she was told,' Petra continues when the bell stops. 'She memorised important details about her surroundings, even though none of it ever got released to the public. Do you know why the police never reveal all the evidence? They keep it under wraps so they can use it to verify—'

Petra breaks off as her best friend Audrey joins us.

'You ready?' Audrey doesn't look at me. If I was asked to name the most aloof girl in our year level, Audrey would win, hands down. She is so above everything I almost admire her for it.

'Sure.' Petra gives me a brief, polite smile. She wrestles a music case out of her locker.

'I need help with Chem.' Audrey all but clicks her fingers as she walks off, Petra at her heels. The boarders stick together, and Petra especially sticks to Audrey. She's undeniably the suckerfish and Audrey is undeniably the shark.

Day three of Yin missing, and the student distribution in the quadrangle is out of whack. Normally groups of Year Tens spread out to every part of the courtyard, but today we huddle close on the steps. Even those who are pretending not to take part sit close enough to eavesdrop.

We're not supposed to have our phones out during school hours, but that's not possible now. Not when there's rolling news coverage online, comments and theories and prayers and wishes. Some girls haven't stopped crying yet, and none of us look like we've slept.

My usual lunch spot is the low brick wall above the steps, putting me higher than the rest of the quad, with the dangling branches of a willow screening me. Claire and Milla, Yin's closest friends, are the epicentre of the gathering. They look incomplete without Yin, a triangle with one of its sides missing. I'd seen them walking around school, heads together, in the library, hauling their musical instruments from one place to the other.

'They were wearing normal clothes, not police uniforms,' says Claire. 'We talked in the lounge room and my parents had to be there.'

Teaghan sits close to them. 'What did they say? Do they have any leads?'

'It doesn't make sense. I mean, if I did have something to tell them, a secret, I wouldn't do it with Mum and Dad there.'

'Did I miss anything?' Lisbeth slides onto the wall beside me. I shake my head and move over so we can both see.

Lisbeth and I have joint custody of the quad wall;

sometimes we lay our sandwiches between us and swap halves. I don't have that much in common with Lisbeth, but she's always been friendly to me, and that counts for a lot. She doesn't seem to have many friends and I think it's because her family are Pentecostal Christians, the full speak-in-tongues type. Even her sandwiches taste religious.

Claire looks stunned by the attention. Her face is blotchy and her eyes puffy. Teaghan pokes her until she answers the question.

'They asked if Yin had been upset recently, or if she'd had any fights with her parents or teachers or anyone else.'

'See? I told you. They think she's run away,' says Sarah.

The Blondes, normally in their own secluded corner, sit on the bottom step. Sarah lies on Ally's lap; Ally is wedged up against Marley. With the tree masking me, I can watch Natalia unseen. She sits slightly apart, touching no one, drawing biro patterns on her bare legs. She seems oblivious to everything around her, but something tells me that she's listening intently. She's still wearing her summer dress, even though we were meant to have switched to winter uniform at the beginning of the term. It's entirely possible that cold blood runs through her veins. Natalia is like one of those ships that power through the polar ice caps. Good at every-thing, with zero effort. An A-student, makes sporting teams, gets leads in school plays, rules the roost.

'And has she run away?' Teaghan mimics a current affairs reporter. 'Is there something you're not telling us?'

'They asked me if she ever talked to strangers online.' Milla's eyes aren't as puffy as Claire's but I notice her nails are bitten down so far they're bleeding. She chews on them now. 'One theory is that she has a secret boyfriend.'

That makes Sarah snort into her juice. She has the unusual good grace to turn it into a cough. I want to speak up, to say that doesn't make any sense—because who trapped Yin's mum in the bathroom?—but I don't.

'Has she been acting worried or scared recently? That was another question.' Milla's voice drops and the whole year level leans in. I almost topple off the wall. 'Was she scared of anything?'

Everyone is quiet for a few seconds, running through, I imagine, the old monsters and bogeymen of their childhoods, and the new teenage ones as well. Serial killers, rapists, paedophiles, pornographers, public masturbators, flashers, angry guys we ghosted, creepy uncles, online stalkers.

'The woman asked a lot of questions about her phone,' Claire adds. 'I thought maybe it's missing?'

'Yin had that silly cover she bought on Etsy, remember?' Milla ventures a private smile to her friend, but something else is occurring to Claire.

'Mil, did you message her that night?' she says. 'I did. I was asking about orchestra practise.'

Milla nods with wide eyes.

'Imagine if *he* read your messages.' Teaghan can barely hide how titillated this new idea makes her. 'The kidnapper, I mean. He could be reading your private, personal messages, *right now* on Yin's phone. Or looking at photos of you.'

Fresh horror on Milla and Claire's faces. If I had a history of participation at Balmoral this is probably where I'd step in and tell Teaghan to stop being such a vulture. I look across at Lisbeth, and can see she's thinking a similar thing. Natalia stabs her biro into the ground.

Teaghan must sense the tide threatening to turn against her, because she adds, 'I mean, I'm just so *distressed*. Mum says we're going to have PTSD from this.'

'I've been thinking,' someone says. 'The man that's keeping Yin has his hands full at the moment. So, in a way, we're safer than ever.'

'I heard that they were using GPS to track where she went,' chimes in someone else.

'Where did you hear that?' Natalia sits up sharply, instantly alert, alert all along. Her eyes flash. I'm reminded of a predator moving into position. I lean as far forwards as I can without falling off the wall, Lisbeth too. Something awful builds in the quadrangle.

It's easy to want something to happen, anything, even a fight. Something to break the tension, a wave to crash over us, letting us know that, yes, disaster has really struck.

The girl who made the comment—Tara or Kara or something like that—clearly regrets speaking. One word from Natalia, one look even, can cut some of these girls to ribbons.

'Online,' Tara/Kara mutters eventually. 'Someone set up a private group. People are saying what they know, what they've heard. The teachers have been told not to talk to us, so how else are we supposed to figure out what's going on?'

'Did you write that email?' someone calls out.

The girl closest to Lisbeth and I says in a low voice to her friend, 'I'm going to walk home a different way every day. In case I'm being watched.'

'Say whatever you want in your group.' Natalia stands. 'Send around those pointless chain emails, I don't care. She's not coming back.'

More than a few mouths are open. A gust of wind tears through the trees, jangling leaves, jangling nerves. I haven't heard anything about a chain email, but it doesn't surprise me that I'd be left out of the loop.

'How would you know, Natalia?' Teaghan demands. 'Have you got some special line to the police?'

Natalia may be short and slight, but she commands everyone's attention easily. 'The GPS thing doesn't make any sense. If police knew where she was, they would have rescued her days ago, they wouldn't wait. If they knew anything, they'd be talking. Do you know how long it's been? She's not coming home.'

'We know how long it's been!' Claire manages to get these last words out before dissolving into tears.

Milla cradles Claire's head on her shoulder, her face crumpled. 'Why are you such a bitch, Natalia? Why can't you be nice?'

Sarah gasps at that, gasps so hard I almost laugh at the melodrama of it. People talking back to Natalia: it was like a solar eclipse. It hardly ever happened.

Natalia's voice is calm but her hands are clenched. 'You're all thinking exactly the same thing. Don't pretend you're not.' She stands up and her friends stand with her. 'Eighty-eight hours and counting. That's too long. Time to face facts. I'm the only person with the guts to say it.'

No one speaks.

I can see Natalia's chest rising and falling, even from here.

The wind does a lap of the quadrangle, scattering plastic wrappers and paper bags. Sarah clamps her hands over her shiny hair.

The anger melts off Natalia's face and something else, another expression, is visible for a split second before she covers it up. Then her face hardens and she mutters to herself and turns away.

'Huh,' says Lisbeth.

Even though Lisbeth has cochlear implants in both ears, she still lip-reads at times. I don't ask her what she's seen. If she wanted to tell me, she would.

The bell rings.

Everyone disperses slower than usual. I jump off the wall and brush off my skirt. There's a strange sensation in my mouth, like it's full of words I might actually let out at school.

Lisbeth says, 'It doesn't seem real, does it? It's like a nightmare. I've been praying a lot.'

I can't think of a reply to that, so I ask a question. 'Do you think she'll get released?'

'I read about something that happened in America. Three girls were held in a basement for eleven whole years before they escaped, all of them alive. It gave me some hope.'

I'm not sure that being imprisoned for eleven years is preferable to being dead and at rest, and I don't even believe in heaven. Lisbeth and I drift towards the breezeway door, waiting for a flood of Year Eights to pass through.

'Do you know what email they were talking about?' I stop for a moment, to speak face to face. Lisbeth has told me that noisy, open places don't work for her.

'I got it last night, I'll send it to you.' Lisbeth holds onto her red lunchbox and smiles. 'See you in Japanese, Chloe.'

I say goodbye and dump the rest of my sandwich into the bin. On the way to English I count how many people would notice if I never showed up to school again. I do not need to use more than one hand.

Lisbeth is true to her word. Halfway through English an email comes through. I drop my iPad into my lap, using the desk as a shield.

> Dear chloe, I don't believe in chain emails but some of these points do seem quite sensible. liss x

> **WARNING!!! You must forward this email to five people in the next five days or someone close to you will be kidnapped!! Do not ignore this warning!**

> IN THE UNLIKELY EVENT OF AN ABDUCTION

> 1) Become an unappealing target. Deviants have fantasies about the innocence of schoolgirls so ruin that by making yourself seem older and experienced. If you have no personal sexual experience to draw on, you can channel a promiscuous character from a TV show.

> 2) Urinate. Experts recommend peeing yourself to prevent rape. It has never been reported that prior victim Karolina

Bauer was raped, but statistically speaking that's what these perpetrators usually do.

3) In the event that you can't avoid abduction, remain calm and alert. Mentally record evidence and information. Some examples are: what kind of vehicle are you in? How many minutes was it to your destination? Did the car sound old or new? Did it smell of anything?

If you are taken to another location take note of your surroundings: stairs, paving, grass, type of doors, number of lights. Pay attention to outside noises: cars, trains, buses, trucks, planes, school bells, birds, lawnmowers and other people living nearby.

4) Do not look at the attacker or attempt to see his face. Identifying him is a death sentence.

5) If the attacker ties you up, breathe in as deeply as you can to expand your torso, and tense your muscles to make them bigger. When you exhale and relax, hopefully the binding will have loosened enough for you to free yourself.

6) You should try to be a good girl, obedient and well behaved, and make the attacker like and/or pity you. You shouldn't try to escape. (This advice makes no sense in relation to points 1) and 5) but this is what the experts say, and it's all we have to go on.)

## DAY 4

I sigh, even though I really want to rip everything to shreds. Another photo ruined. The watercolour bleeds everywhere, turning the paper into a crinkly mess. I dab at it with a tissue, but I can't save it.

Our final folio has to include a self-portrait, and it's the one piece I've been avoiding. I can do still lifes and landscapes and portraits of other people very happily, just don't ask me to look too hard at my own face.

Painting over my school photo was the easiest way I could think of to meet the requirement. I had the idea after I stumbled across an interesting photo of a young geisha. The portrait was from the late 1800s, so before colour photography, but it had been hand-painted so well it almost looked real. The geisha's cheeks were flushed pink, and the floral pattern of her kimono was meticulously coloured, with daubs of red and yellow and green.

I thought it would be a relatively easy effect to replicate, but I've ruined five prints so far. It's hard to concentrate on anything today. I couldn't settle in bed last night, and when I look around at my classmates' faces, I don't think they slept well either.

I fold the latest botched photo in half and thumb through my sketchbook instead, trying to remember a distant era when I had one good creative concept. At Morrison our Art teachers would give us very specific themes and assignments we had to complete, but Balmoral takes a much looser approach. You'd think that would be good, but actually it is a form of torture. My ideas start solid and sure in my brain, but quickly turn wispy when I try to get them out into the real world.

What I should do is complete my self-portrait, accept its mediocrity, and then free myself to focus on my major project. But I don't. Instead, I start eavesdropping on Ms Nouri's consultation with Audrey at the table behind me.

'I was inspired by the work of early female video artists,' Audrey says. 'I want to use my own body and face to explore ideas about connection and place, but also keep a surrealist edge to it.'

I want to roll my eyes, but the fact is, I'm intimidated. I have never made a video good enough to call art; it's difficult not to look amateur, even though we have access to all this equipment. Balmoral has ten art studios, a photography studio, three darkrooms, a printing room, a dedicated woodwork space, this massive pottery kiln, and a tech studio full of 3D printers and computers loaded up with the latest software.

'I've collected images from all the places around the world my family has lived and projected them onto my skin...'

It would be nice if Audrey was all hot wind, but she's not. She's good. Her certainty about her art underscores my complete lack.

'Remember to move beyond technique and fully explore your idea,' says Ms Nouri.

I realise she could be speaking directly to me about my self-portrait. All I've got is the technique of using paint to hand-tint a photo, but no idea behind that.

The art-room door opens.

'Ms Nouri, could I have a quick word?'

Ms Nouri excuses herself and stands in the corridor with Ms Baker, my Biology teacher. Almost immediately, the speculation starts, as if there has been a river of chatter flowing beneath the surface all this time. It's painfully obvious that things are going on that we're not being told about. Teachers keep getting called out of class, extra security guards roam the campus and serious men in suits walk the corridors.

'I told you, it's the dad.'

Sarah's voice is crystal clear, even from the other end of the room—she's obviously under the mistaken impression that her easel has created a floor-to-ceiling sound barrier.

'My mum finds it hard to believe that he slept through the whole thing.'

I can't tell who the other voice is, but it will be one of the Blondes. They only take Art because they think it's an easy A, which shows they don't know Ms Nouri very well.

'Not the stepdad, he's ancient. I mean Yin's real father, the Chinese guy. Apparently he runs an importing business and spends a lot of time overseas. He could easily be involved in organised crime.'

'I saw something on YouTube about the Triads once.'

'Also, the custody battle for Yin when they divorced was nasty, so she could already be back in China being forced to marry some old man, and she'll never be heard of again. They don't have proper laws or protection over there.'

Over in the boarder section of the room, Jody says to Brooke, 'My mum says there are way too many Asians at Balmoral these days. It wasn't like that when she went here. My parents are thinking of sending me somewhere else.

If they wanted me to be around this many Asians, we'd move to Bangkok or something.'

I lean around the edge of my easel to shoot a filthy look in Sarah's direction for starting up the conversation. The Blondes have set up their easels in a semi-circle, right next to the radiator, with Natalia at the centre. Sarah has her phone angled above her head, ready for a pouting selfie.

The international students—from Hong Kong, Mainland China, Malaysia, Taiwan—have a habit of keeping to themselves in another corner, but there's no way they can't hear what's going on. I can't believe they have to live in the boarding house with people like Jody. My heart speeds up.

Sarah clocks me staring at her and pauses, her mouth an ugly slash. 'What? Have you got something to say to me?'

Ally and Marley lean out further for a better look, smelling delicious conflict.

'You were being a bit racist, don't you think?' I want my voice to sound strong, but instead it wobbles.

'How is what I said racist?' Sarah's genuinely confused.

'Well…automatically assuming that Yin's dad is a gangster, like a walking stereotype from a John Woo movie and—and the forced marriage to an old man thing. And they do have laws in China, they're just different from the laws here.'

I struggle to order my thoughts. There's plenty to be said about the rule of law in China and human rights, but that's way too nuanced for this conversation.

'I don't even know who John Woo is.' Sarah hits back straight away. 'And anyway, stereotypes are there for a *reason*.

They've have to be a bit true or how do they even start?'

'We don't mean you, Chloe,' says Ally in her baby-soft voice. I'm surprised she knows my name. 'You're not a *real* Asian, you know what I mean? You're from here.'

Her eyes shoot over to the international students, as if I won't get it. In her eyes I'm slightly more acceptable because I was born here and I don't have an accent.

'I don't think that's relevant.' I'm already regretting having broken my rule to always fly under the radar. Natalia's eyes settle on me. 'It's offensive to anyone. But you are actually half talking about me, okay?'

It's more than that. It's more than half of me. Because I take after Mum so strongly, the world sees me as Asian, therefore I am. It's not like that for Sam, who looks more like Dad.

'Lighten up, girl. Really.' Sarah returns to her pose, but Natalia stands up and snatches Sarah's phone right out of her hand. She has her predator face on again.

'Sarah, did you know I've got a special name for your selfies?' She pauses. Every head in the room turns to her. 'I call them *Insert-Dick-Here* photos. Maybe you should change your handle to that.'

There's stunned silence. Sarah looks cut to the ground.

'What? You've always got your mouth wide open, what am I supposed to think? Lighten up, girl. *Really.*'

Natalia sits down and smiles at me, secretly, conspiratorially. I look away. I don't need her to defend me.

'Way too harsh, Tal.' Ally sounds thrilled and impressed.

'It's got nothing to do with Yin's dad, anyway, it's the

same guy who took that German girl.' Brooke would never normally join in a conversation with the Blondes, but people have been talking all day, to anyone. She's on tiptoes, trying to see the two teachers in the corridor. 'Did you see those two men outside reception? I bet they're plain clothes detectives. Ooop!'

Brooke makes it to her stool as Ms Nouri slips back into the classroom.

Natalia raises her hand. 'Ms Nouri, why did the life model get cancelled? Sarah was looking forward to seeing a naked dude.'

Sarah's expression doesn't even change. She's still shell-shocked from the first takedown. Natalia looks at me again, and this time I stare back, trying to figure her out. *I don't need your help*, I try to say with my eyes. But maybe that's not it, maybe she's randomly lashing out at her own friends for no good reason. There's no sign of the desperation I glimpsed on her face in the quad yesterday.

'We thought it best to reschedule.'

'Is it because he's a suspect?'

Ms Nouri sits on the edge of her cluttered desk. The art rooms are the only places at school that aren't unnaturally neat. She's wearing a black dress and tights that look like smashed-up stained-glass windows.

'Let's discuss the art prize,' she says. 'The deadline is the week before your major project is due. So you should all consider finishing your project early and entering the prize. This year I want to make a proper exhibition out of it—Mrs Christie has already agreed to let us use the main hallway.

Most of you have been working hard, and I think it would be great for other students to see what you've done. We're going to award a separate prize for the student vote.'

Ms Nouri seems to stare hard at me in particular as she says this. I let my head drop, and my hair closes around my face. How could anyone *not* know about the art prize, given the entire school is plastered with posters about it?

At the beginning of the year I looked up Ms Nouri's website. She's a real artist, with a painting degree from the best art school in Tehran. She's done commissions and exhibitions, and is way too talented to be stuck at Balmoral. I want to impress her so much it's crippling. And the $500 first prize would be handy.

'How can we think that far ahead when we don't know if we'll survive this week?' Ally's voice is plaintive.

'I know it's difficult right now, Ally.' Ms Nouri is known as one of the most genuinely sympathetic teachers at school. 'Do your best, that's all. You've got roughly two months to go, keep that in mind.'

Brooke raises her hand. Ms Nouri doesn't like us to do that, but habits are hard to break. 'Miss, who were those men in the lobby earlier?'

Ms Nouri combs her fringe flat with her fingers, looking nervous. She never talks down to us, and that's why everyone likes her.

'I was told they were gentlemen from the Sexual Crimes Squad.' Her face takes a funny turn; she regrets being so honest. It shuts everyone up.

✦

Arnold and I run our usual route, along the Renfrew Street strip of shops, past the mini-mart, the servo and the medical clinic. Most places are preparing to close.

I move onto the gravel shoulder of the road. There's still peak-hour traffic rushing past, and it's not the safest place to jog, but I keep going. The more my legs hurt the more I can forget that train wreck of a conversation in Art class. Broken glass from bottles and old car accidents hides among the small stones, and I have to ignore two guys in a ute, who slow down beside me and whistle and try to get me to look at them.

'Nice dog!' one of them yells.

It's unclear whether they're referring to Arnold or me.

My legs ache but I'm already enjoying the rhythmic *huh-huh* of my breath, and the cold pinching my cheeks. I'm so glad to be back in crappy Morrison Heights and far away from school. The entire year level has been suspended precariously between crying and hysterical laughter all week. Every time the PA crackles we all jump a mile, like we're about to receive the worst news.

The most difficult thing is that there hasn't been any news about Yin at all.

A car screeches loudly behind me, and then shoots past, a leering face pressed against the rear window. Arnold strains at his leash. I pretend I'm one of Sam's superheroes, the kind that can achieve full invisibility.

By the time we reach the park, my tracksuit pants are rubbing against my sweaty thighs. I used to walk Arnold in my school uniform, before I accepted that he has one speed only: full tilt. So now I wear my oldest pair of tracky daks and my sneakers. Arnold goes wild the moment I pull his lead out of the cupboard.

At the entrance to the park I almost collide with another jogger—a guy my age in high-tech leggings and earphones.

'Hey!' he says, not bothered by our near-collision. 'Evening!'

I frown in return. He's not puffing at all, while I sound like a malfunctioning steam train.

The jogger is a park regular, I see him out most evenings. He's cute too. Not my type—too sporty—but cute. Once I'm sure he's crossed the road, I turn and check out his springy stride. The leggings cut his muscles into defined areas.

The park is emptier than usual. The light is fading and the grass is already wet with dew. It was a mistake to do my homework first. Sometimes I run with earbuds in, but not tonight. If someone comes up behind me, I want to hear them.

We pound the train path, down the hill and across the creek. I think about how the jogger probably plays football (deal breaker), and how Brandon from my old school is ruining his near-genius brain with pot, and how the Grammar boys on the tram are way too clean-cut and not inclined to slum it, not that I need anyone's pity lust anyway.

'You'll marry me, won't you, Arnold? If I get to thirty and don't have anyone?'

Arnold gallops and pants inappropriately and doesn't answer, as usual.

This is what I know about this park: no one has ever

been raped in it, but there was a flasher here when I was in Grade Six.

Arnold doesn't mind the way the trees crowd thickly on either side of the path, creating shadows where a person could hide. Hide and then leap out, pulling an arm tight against my throat, feet kicking against air.

The bridge clangs as we thump over it. I squint into the distance. A figure crests the hill ahead. I can't tell if it's a man or a woman.

Normally the park brings me a small sense of peace, even though it's pretty basic as far as parks go. The train line runs the length of it at the top of a high embankment, and to the right is a lumpy paddock criss-crossed with paths and the creek. The park sits on top of a waste site: rusted barrels and broken concrete blocks still poke through the green. Some of the blocks look like grey french fries scattered among the ti-trees.

I consider turning back, but the view from the top of the hill makes the pain of running worth it. If I let myself get scared, then it means another victory for the evil people of the world. Still, I fish my keys out of my waistband pocket and grip them so they poke out for maximum stabbing potential.

Stop being irrational, I tell myself. You're in no greater danger today than before Yin was taken.

As we get closer I can see that the mystery person is a man in a suit, probably on his way home from work. Not many men wear suits around here. Suit-wearers are supposed to be respectable, but more importantly, they sit at desks day after day and are probably unfit.

When the man gets within ten metres I draw myself up to my full height and lift my feet, making sure I look care-free and energetic, as if I could run at this pace for hours. I consider spitting on the ground to gross him out.

Out of nowhere, Arnold growls. He never growls.

The man—balding, white, dad-aged—assesses me below the neck, but never meets my eyes. We pass each other. I continue up the hill, he continues down. The moment passes. Even Arnold relaxes.

At the top of the hill, I pause to catch my breath. Arnold lifts a leg to pee and scratches in the dust.

I practise looking and seeing, like I always do. Across the valley, past the vacant lots and teeming highway, to lit-up construction sites topped with cranes. I make a square-ish frame with my hands and hold it in front of my face. I've been wondering if I have the skills to do something photo-graphic for my major project.

The truth of this scene is beer bottles mixed in with weeds, a wire fence falling down, fluoro traffic cones, the word CONPLEX painted along the boom of a crane.

The truth is cars scuttling like beetles, neon-painted streaks, a mysterious glowing civilisation across the highway, a hushed park where lovers meet under pooling lights. It's all in my power to make this ugly or beautiful, gritty and real, or not.

But I can't stop my mind turning towards the ways you could trap someone in a park. You could use people's kind-ness against them and pretend to be hurt, setting up a fake bike accident. You could blend into the environment, dress up as one of the council rangers or rail workers. Or you could carry a tricycle or a children's backpack, pretending you were a dad. Fathers appear more trustworthy than childless men, even though I know that's not the case.

At my back, there's a rumble and a rush of wind as a train screams past. A streak of light in the dusk, people flashing by, all of them strangers.

Mr Mitchell's face looks like a sunken cake. Yin's mum keeps her face turned away. The reporter says Mr Mitchell is a 'prominent Melbourne lawyer'.

I was going to have a shower and change out of my sweaty running gear straight after dinner, but the police are finally having another press conference after being silent for days. Yin's parents and two detectives sit in front of a crowd of journalists. I sip on my custom blend of Milo and instant coffee.

'That's Yin's mother?' Mum says. 'She was the one that was nice to me at that Mother's Day thing. Did you know she's a neurosurgeon?'

Mum has the night off work and I'm secretly relieved. Her hands travel over my woollen school tights, darning the holes. Sam is safely in his bedroom playing games on Mum's phone. We've had to ban him from watching any more news reports about the abduction.

'Remember, Chlo? She was the only one that would talk to me. Oh, that's even more awful now.'

I remember. Mum said that she'd felt like a fish out of water at the Balmoral Mother's Day breakfast. Apparently the rich blondes huddled on one side of the room and the rich Asians on the other side, and she hadn't fit into either group. It sounded scarily similar to my own experiences.

Sometimes I want to launch myself at the international students and beg to be adopted into their group, even if I can only speak English. The boarders from East Asia hang together, but they overlap a lot with the East Asian day girls. There are hardly any South Asian boarders, but there are lots of South Asian students and they seem to form their own friendship groups.

There are so many exceptions to the rules though, and I can't help wondering if it's only me that's hung-up. Melody is biracial too, but she grew up in Hong Kong and can speak Cantonese. Anjali is swim-squad royalty and hangs out exclusively with jocks, and Anusha and Sunita form a four with Bridie and Ming-Zhu and I couldn't draw a Venn diagram of all of it if I tried.

Maybe I'm making up divisions in my head that don't really exist. But then Jody carries on about there being too many Asians at the school, and I know I'm not making all of it up.

'I consider Yin to be my own daughter,' Mr Mitchell says on the telly. 'I have been very lucky to find myself with this family, long after I thought my time for it had passed.'

Even though he must be used to speaking in front of people, his voice during the press conference is tissue-paper thin. His white hair and wrinkled skin explains why Yin copped so much at school about how old her dad is. It's good that Mum doesn't want to get involved in anything at Balmoral. It's best not to provide the ammunition.

'Our house is very quiet without Yin, too quiet,' Mr Mitchell continues. 'Usually I have to tell her to turn her music down every night. Yin, if you are listening to this, when you come home you can play your music as loud as you want. Your mum and brothers miss you very much.'

Mum kicks her legs, as if she's trying to get rid of pins and needles. 'The worst thing is, I'm sure he's the first suspect on the police's list. And look at him. He's devastated.'

Mr Mitchell looks straight down the lens of the camera. 'This is a plea from our family to everyone in the community. Please think carefully and consider if you know anything that could be related to my daughter's disappearance. Cast your minds back to the weekend. You might have seen something that you thought unimportant at the time. Nothing is too small to report.'

A police hotline number sits at the bottom of the screen.

I still have the sourness in my gut that's been there since I saw the very first news report. It's a queasy, guilty feeling because I'm not sure if I'm genuinely worried about Yin, or if I'm more worried about myself. I can't remember the reasons why I thought it was a good idea to transfer to Balmoral, and now the universe has presented me with a great big reason to not be there.

Mum knots the thread and breaks it between her teeth. She moves onto the second hole in my tights. 'By the way, your dad called.'

I raise one eyebrow. When I was twelve I spent a whole summer practising this new expression for my new cynicism.

Mum and Dad separated when I was eight and divorced when I was ten, but when I was twelve Dad went to Western Australia to work on the mines and didn't come back for three years. He said he was doing it for Sam and me, to save for our futures, but instead he bought a house on the other side of town with his mate Jarrod, and I don't see how that benefits us. The house has been the source of a lot of fights between Mum and Dad, but Mum seems to have let it go now.

'Don't give me that look, Chloe. Call him and have a quick chat. It won't cost you a thing.'

'Okay. Ma, okay.' I wave Mum's fussing away. Dad and I spoke on my birthday, which wasn't that long ago. The senior detective is being questioned onscreen and I don't want to miss it.

'Are the police treating this case as linked to the Karolina Bauer abduction?' asks a journalist.

'That's the exchange student who was taken a few years ago,' I say.

The lead detective looks like the kind of man you'd see in a department store catalogue modelling clothes for older men, not a hunter of psychopaths. 'At this early stage we're examining all angles, including looking at previous cases.'

'Early?' says Mum. 'It's been four days—that's way too long. The first 48 hours are crucial.'

Mum consumes a solid and unvaried diet of crime fiction—it's her main hobby. She could probably have a decent stab at heading up a police investigation based on that alone.

A different journalist speaks up. 'So you admit there are startling similarities between the two abductions. Is the investigation focussing on people with a connection to Balmoral Ladies College?'

The detective doesn't take the bait. 'We're conducting a methodical and thorough investigation, as we always do. We'll be able to bring you more information in the next few days.'

I think back to my conversation earlier with strange, intense Petra. 'The police don't tell the public all of the details, did you know that, Mum? They keep the important stuff to themselves.'

'Yeah, that's classic methodology, hon. The police use the unreleased information to eliminate suspects.'

I want to ask her how that can be fair—what if there's information that could keep more girls safe, if only they knew it? But I swallow the question, because the last thing I want to be, or look to be, is scared.

'I've got a bad feeling,' Mum admits. 'It reminds me of those Bayer kids. Before you were born. They got taken from their beach house. Never seen again. Vanished into thin air.'

They're showing Yin's photo again on the TV screen while the newsreader talks.

'She doesn't look like that now, you know,' I tell Mum. 'That photo is from Junior School, grade six or something. Why would they use an old photo?'

'I don't know…maybe it was the first one they could find? Her parents probably weren't thinking straight.'

'But if a witness sees her in the back of a car, or in a window, they might not recognise her.'

'Maybe the public will be more sympathetic if she looks young and cute. If she looks older or closer to being a woman, then it's too easy to say: oh, she was talking to guys online. Or dating older men, or going out and being a bad girl. You know...'

'That shouldn't matter.'

'It shouldn't, but—hon, it's bleak, but she's Chinese and already some people might not care as much. The more the public relates to a victim the better. And some people in our community don't get as much attention when they go missing, from the media or the public or the police. If you're homeless, or a sex worker, then you can forget about...'

My face must paint a picture, because Mum trails off. The world never ceases to surprise me with how messed up it is.

Mum crawls closer to put her arm around me. 'I shouldn't say things like that to you. I'm sorry.'

'It's okay.' I rest my head against hers and sigh. 'You can't protect me from the bullshit, Mum. I'm gonna find out anyway.'

That makes her laugh a little. She drapes the mended tights over my legs.

'I should warn you, your dad wants you to transfer back to Morrison. He always overreacts.'

Even though I've been thinking a similar thing, I can't help being annoyed. 'Dad never wanted me to go to Balmoral in the first place.'

He said it was a school for the elite and he complains

every time he has to pay his half for field trips or uniforms. Mum thinks if she has those phone conversations in the laundry I won't hear them, but I do.

'Well, your dad wasn't exactly supportive of my desire to have an education either.' Mum picks up my sketchbook from the side table.

I want to ask her whether she thinks I should switch back, but the words stick in my throat.

'You know there's no reason to think that you're in real danger, don't you, Chlo? This kind of thing is so rare, even though it probably doesn't seem like that right now.'

'I know.'

And I do know. At least the rational part of me does. I wish someone would tell my body though, because I keep catching myself with my hands curled tightly, my shoulders tensed for no good reason.

I watch as Mum leafs through my carefully drawn city-scapes, the botched life drawings, my first linocut attempts that didn't turn out too badly at all. My sketchbook is more of a work of art than my actual finished pieces, even though it's messy and confused. It's my precious baby, the closest thing I have to a journal or diary.

'Have you finished your homework yet?'

Her casual tone doesn't fool me.

'I've done all of my homework, and I'm up-to-date with my reading,' I say, even though this technically isn't true. There is no such thing as being up-to-date at Balmoral—that falls into the realms of impossible. 'And I take Art, so this is homework too.'

I chose all my electives at the start of the year, under the strict eye of Mrs Benjamin. I got the distinct impression that academic scholarship recipients were expected to focus on STEM subjects, instead of pursuing anything creative, so I had to dig my heels in to get my two units of Art.

Mum kisses me on the forehead and stands up. I know she's far from being a tiger mum, but she might have finished her landscape architecture degree, might have had a completely different career, a different life, if she hadn't had babies, or had babies with a different man, or hadn't gotten divorced. I know my life is supposed to turn out differently to hers.

'I see how hard you work, hon.' Mum frowns at my mug. 'But please don't drink that crap so late in the day.'

## Natalia

**DAY 6**

Enter the dungeons and you'll find that the lockers and the doors and the rubbish bins are small, even the toilets are made for dolls. Tinytown, infantville, the basement corridor where we can observe the lowest of the low in their natural habitat, the Year Sevens and Eights.

I'm a giant of course, metres taller than the rest—I've been almost twice my usual size for six days now. Walking on stilts, walking the corridors like I have army boots on, not scuffed school shoes, stomp stomp stomping on the cack green carpet with my loyal supporters trailing behind. New headphones clamped on, shiny gold ridiculous, but what no one knows is that there's no music trickling through them. The corridor sounds muffle down to almost nothing and I move to an imaginary beat and that's how I keep fooling everyone.

Sarah is with me, and Marley too, but Ally is in sick bay with monster period pain under the care of patchouli-reeking Nurse Lee and Nurofen Plus, but only two every four hours because dependency on legal drugs is almost as serious as dependency on the fun ones.

The Year Sevens cling to their lockers like scared little baby dolls, with round faces and big eyes and squidgy mouths and spiky eyelashes. They hobbit about doing babyish things with their lunch hour, building forts with the tables, swapping worthless plastic bracelets, trying to figure out what they can afford at the tuckshop with their last $2.30.

'That's Natalia,' I see one mouth to another. 'Year Ten.'

Let them see my summer uniform hitched high, hair unbrushed for days, Sharpie tattoos on my thighs. Let them know they don't have to care about the rules despite what everyone says. Disobey, but don't get caught.

I ignore the lapping at my ankles, the still-rising tide of *if it happened to her it could happen to me*, the swishing *I need to be ready* and *what if I'm next*. Put your gumboots on because, *they haven't caught him he's still out there* and it's not going away, *how long will it be before he gets the urge again*.

I'm high and dry because I gave up at 36 hours, along with the police. Because you can choose to be hopeless, that's what I've learnt.

After six days it's almost as if she never existed at all.

I wave at Posy, this year's favourite baby doll, and Posy waves back. Even at twelve you can tell that Posy is going to grow up to rule her year level and be a mega-babe, the sort that isn't the prettiest, but is the most interesting, the most magnetic. Posy is sweet now, but she's only months away from realising her superiority and then she's gonna turn from a sugary little lollipop into a sour lemon nightmare and her parents and teachers will be disappointed because she used to be such a *nice girl*.

I turn the corner out of Tinytown right as the end-of-lunch bell rings. This next part of the dungeons smells of unwashed PE uniforms and forgotten sandwiches. The Year Eights are smack-bang in the middle of their awkward phase, labouring under their oversized backpacks like beetles.

'You are no longer cute!' I yell in celebration because I've decided that my Friday afternoon gift to myself is that I'll stop working at lunchtime. I'll spend periods five and six snipping off my split ends and planning my weekend with my phone hidden inside my inside blazer pocket because they make secret agents out of us with their nonsense rules and they make liars out of us with their lies.

I stop.

I survey the emptying dungeon with an odd metallic taste in my mouth. Something is askew, like in those puzzles I loved when I was a kid: find five things wrong with this picture.

'Where's Amanda?' I ask the closest beetle.

'Her parents took her out of school.'

'Why?' I ask, even though I already know the reason. Amanda's older sister Ruby wasn't in Biology this morning. Cowards run away, and Amanda and Ruby's parents clearly have no grasp on the statistical probability of teen abductions.

Why is everyone thinking about themselves, when they should be thinking about Yin?

'I don't know.' The Year Eight girl quails, looking away. 'I'm gonna be late for Maths. Mr Scrutton will give me detention.'

'Please,' I say. 'Scrotum is way too nice for that.' The

49

Year Eight looks confused so I have to explain. 'Mr Scrutton. Scrutton, Scrotum—remember it.'

I let her go. She'll run to her friends and report on what I've told her and they'll say Scrotum for the rest of eternity.

'What are we going to do with our spare?'

Sarah hasn't spoken in five minutes and I wouldn't be able to tell you the last time that happened, hallelujah it's a miracle. I'd almost forgotten she was there.

I flip my headphones off.

'Oh, I have detention. I got busted wagging RE this morning.' The lie slips out beautifully—the best sort of lie, the one you don't know you're going to tell until it's half-said. A good lie gives me a warm tingle. 'I said I couldn't stay after school so Mrs Preshill said I had to do it in my free period.'

Sarah pouts. 'We have a *theory*. We need to tell you.'

I should be relieved, I suppose, that Sarah is talking about something other than herself. But if she says one more thing about Yin's parents, I don't know what I'll do.

Marley nods furiously behind her. 'But we shouldn't discuss it here.'

Sarah ignores that. 'It's Mr Martell. You know, Tyrone.'

I do know. Mr Martell is the school's official photographer and he's not ancient and he's rumoured to have had sex with a handful of Year Twelves, or at least copped a handful of almost-legal Balmoral boob.

Mr Martell is supposedly hot, but his legs are bandy and he's going to go bald early, you can already tell. He's a bagel in a shop full of sliced wholemeal bread: not that exciting, especially if there are donuts available right around the corner.

'Did I tell you about the time during theatre sports when I caught him pointing his camera right at my tits? Right at them! I should probably tell the police that.'

And there it is again. The me me me-nologue. Sarah is sparking with manufactured outrage.

'Teaghan said that Rochelle saw a folder on Tyrone's laptop that was called "Sports Day Cuties",' Marley says. 'He had close-ups of all these girls' faces and was going to take them home, you know, to fantasise over.'

'Fantasise?' I say. 'Don't you mean "masturbate"? Also, you know that Teaghan lies for attention, remember?'

There's no way that Rochelle could get access to that computer. Marley blinks at me, but Sarah takes up the thread.

'We remember, Tal. But maybe Tyrone's got a pervert room at his house with photos of Balmoral students covering the walls and that's how he plans who he's going to take next. It's his special collection of favourite girls.'

'You got that idea from *Devil Creek*,' I say.

They're squashing the buzz I built up during lunch, the fuzz that crowded out the bad thoughts.

I see I'm going to have to jog their memories. 'That happened at the end of the first episode, remember? When they found that creepy shed in the bush? It was for only a split second before the credits. They'll come back to it later.'

We binged three episodes of *Devil Creek* together on Saturday night, not together as in the same room, but messaging each other from our separate houses. No one else picks up any of the clues, though.

The small country town of Devil Creek—where everyone is suspiciously buff and good looking and totally not inbred or married to their cousins—is rocked by the murder of the prettiest girl in town, Emily Blake, and of course she's the nicest person too. Only after she's dead do her secrets come out—and not just hers. Everyone in town is a suspect and the police still haven't found the murderer, and conveniently probably won't until the very last moments of season one.

Mere hours after the first season of the show dropped, Yin went missing.

I'm pretty sure they're setting it up to reveal that lovely dead ginger Emily Blake was slutting it up with both of the two hot-but-ignorant brothers, each without the other knowing, and if they're thinking that has anything to do with anything in the real world then they need to get a grip.

Yin doesn't talk to guys. Maybe she talks to them once a year when our orchestra joins our brother school's orchestra for two weeks of orgiastic rehearsals and they compare their reeds or work on their embouchures or whatever.

I feel sick all of a sudden and that's not only an expression, because bile rises up into my mouth, acid and putrid, and I have to bend at the waist to stop things going further.

I'm a terrible human being for entertaining myself with thoughts about a fake show about a fake murder while Yin was getting ripped out of her ordinary life. When I try to imagine the first moment she realised there was a strange man in her house, I can't breathe.

I pretend to be sure that she's gone for good because isn't it better to think the worst? Deep down, though, there's stubborn hope that I wish I could wipe away forever, just for some certainty.

I push it all down and straighten up, once I'm sure I won't puke.

'Hello, are you listening to anything I'm saying?' Sarah waves her hand in my face. 'Are we going to Moose Juice on the way home?'

We're the only three people left in the hallway, but pre-weekend electricity still crackles in the air; the normal kind plus extra nasty electricity because girls go missing on weekends and don't come back to school on Monday morning. I realise that I don't want to do anything this weekend but lock myself in my bedroom and stay in bed.

'Maybe,' I say.

We get the announcement at lunchtime that they've cancelled our classes for periods five and six and instead our entire year level crams into the gym and we spend the final hours of the school week trying to maim each other.

'Ladies!' hollers our new self-defence teacher, a blonde-haired, blue-eyed woman who used to be on TV and calls herself the Ninja Trainer. 'I'm going to teach you to use your natural feminine strengths to defeat attackers who are bigger! And heavier! Than you! Get into sparring pairs!'

I've read that 'In the Unlikely Event' email three times and I'm pretty sure peeing myself will not be considered a natural feminine strength.

I put up my hand. 'Why do we have to learn to defend ourselves? Maybe men should have classes about not assaulting and killing us?'

But my voice gets lost in the chaos of everyone trying to pair off for the ticklefest and I consider going over to Mrs Benjamin to ask her, but I can see that Audrey is already monopolising Benjo's attention to complain about the Ninja Trainer's name on the grounds of cultural appropriation.

A wide circle devoid of all human lifeform has opened up around me, but luckily I find Petra hiding behind the vaulting horse.

'You are the Chosen One!' I say, but instead of looking ecstatic, as she well should be, Petra looks terrified. She'll change her tune. I'm a natural actress and she's really going to benefit from fending off my believable attacks.

Chloe from my Art class has been left with no partner, so when Audrey finishes complaining to Mrs Benjamin she comes over to try and manipulate the pairings.

'Can we switch so I can go with Petra and you go with her?' Audrey asks me. Rude.

'Absolutely not,' I say. 'And she has a name, by the way; it's Chloe.'

Chloe is tall and big and broad like an Amazon, with long long hair down to her butt and square black glasses. I suspect she's good-looking under those two things, but you'd never know it. Audrey, on the other hand, looks like a movie star from the silent era. Her natural setting is a satin-sheeted boudoir where two half-naked manservants fan her with palm leaves. I'm positive Chloe can take her.

I sincerely hope she sits on Audrey's face repeatedly.

White Ninja has us doing warm-ups, then drills, then combat situations. Petra and Audrey gaze across the two-metre gap between them with yearning, although surely trying to beat up your best friend isn't great, right? They should thank me, truly.

Mrs Benjamin leans against the climbing wall and everything in her body language indicates her extremely low expectations.

I prove her completely wrong by pinning Petra against the wall before she even has a chance to yelp.

'You win, you win!' she gasps.

'Balls, Petra.' I release her and point to my eyeballs and then my groin. 'Balls and balls. I had you easily. If you don't find a way to get pissed off, you'll find yourself tied up in someone's van.'

'Well, I don't think she should be encouraging us to get angry,' Petra says. 'If we're in a dangerous situation, it's better to stay calm.'

'Switch roles!' White Ninja calls out. 'Remember, he won't want you if you're loud and strong. If he gets within striking distance, shred him.'

The gym fills with yelps and shouting and laughter. Audrey strolls over to Chloe and taps her on the shoulder.

Chloe sighs and looks at me.

I take a deep breath. 'HEY! CAN I HELP YOU? ARE YOU FOLLOWING ME, PRICK?'

Petra pushes her hands out but I'm already rushing her and then she's flat on the ground with her arms cradling her head. I crouch over her, miming all of the moves we've been shown—jabbing her in the throat, poking her eyes, play-pulling ears and hair.

'Ow!' Petra yelps loudly. 'You got my eye!'

I sit down on her chest, attack over. 'Oh, come on, it was a mistake, Petra. I slipped. I barely touched you.'

I prise Petra's hands away from her face. Her eye looks fine. Maybe it's watering a little bit. I guess her cheeks are quite red, too.

'Why are you so angry all the time, Natalia?' she asks.

If anyone sounds angry, it's her. I'm not angry. That was controlled technique right there.

'Are you okay?' Chloe comes over. White Ninja is making Audrey do punishment sit-ups for not trying hard enough.

I stand up and hold out my hand to help Petra up, but she closes her eyes and shakes her head. Sarah and Ally are laughing like I planned this; that suck Teaghan is in hysterics too. I wish she would stop trying to get back into our group.

'Suit yourself,' I say. I find my water bottle and suck on it. I won't apologise, then.

Chloe and Petra whisper to each other, and then they both go off to the change rooms. Audrey watches them go.

I don't hang out after school, despite what I've sort-of promised Sarah. Instead I throw my blazer on over my PE uniform and sprint the secret shortcut through the Junior School to get the jump on my friends and am rewarded with an almost-empty tram.

I hang off the handle, lifting my feet and spinning as if I'm still a kid. My dress hikes up, my arms ache, I scrape my school shoes along the floor and I grease off any man that dares look in my direction, even the pensioners.

Don't they know I could shred their balls right now?

The look on Chloe's face as she led Petra away sticks in my mind. For some reason I would prefer that Chloe doesn't think I'm the kind of person who pokes people in the eye deliberately. I don't know why everyone always assumes the worst of me.

The Junction races past the dirty tram windows and still I don't get off. Instead I wind up near the train station and the shopping centre.

I should be thinking about Sarah and Marley's theory about Mr Martell, but now I can't stop thinking about whether I went too hard on Petra. A restless itch sits under my skin. What do I hear all the time, from Mum, Dad, teachers? *Natalia, you always go too far.*

I buy a handful of red liquorice twists at the sell-every-thing kiosk by the station, and the old guy there says, 'You're too pretty to look so sad. Why don't you smile?'

So I smile, and while I'm smiling I drop a pack of chewing gum into my school bag, down low where he can't see it. Smile, smile, white teeth, fresh breath, smile.

'And you're way too ugly to look so happy,' I say in my sweetest voice, only I don't say it for real.

When I look down I see Yin's Year Seven school photo smiling back at me from a tabloid front page. KIDNAP VICTIM FEARS, it says. Every muscle on my face tenses.

Was he following Yin for weeks without her noticing? Is he watching us all from a distance now, checking our reactions, feeling superior? Is he someone I know?

I go into the heat of the shopping centre and trawl the shops, liquorice twist dangling from my lips. Touching candles and buddha heads and prayer flags in the hippy shop, saucepans and cupcake trays and Thermomixes in the kitchen shop, memory-foam pillows and bamboo sheets in bedbathland. I stare through the window at the blonde ladies getting their toenails painted by Thai women, until one of the customers looks uncomfortable. She has a smooth bob and could be my mum.

The next shop has dance music pulsing into every crevice and I trail my hands over the racks of clothes. Stretchy leggings with mesh panels, crop tops, yeti jumpers, my fingers stick to everything they touch.

The assistant smiles at me, and picks at her phone like a chicken pecking at the ground.

I take an armful of clothes to the change room and they're not what I'd usually wear, but I dutifully squeeze into them, zip and button and pull into place.

All of it is cheap and horrible but when I slip into a satin bomber jacket with a dragon embroidered on the back and a light sprinkle of plastic jewels, I can't help but pause. I look at myself in the mirror. Plain schoolday face, tinted-moisturiser-only face.

The jacket isn't me, but it's something Yin should want to wear half-ironically, half-defiantly, on account of it being so blingy and Oriental. She never did have any fashion sense.

I zip up the jacket and put my school dress on over the top, arranging the collar carefully. Woollen school jumper next, even my blazer.

Saunter out, put things back, pretend to look for one minute more.

'Thank you!' I call out to the shop assistant as I leave, but she doesn't even lift her head. She's swiping her phone left and right, left left left left left left HOT. I hope none of the dudes she meets is a serial killer.

The side gate is open and the back door ajar when I get home and the prophecy unfolds right before my eyes. I leave my school bag on the back step and creep through the laundry. My feet won't stop moving forwards, it's as predictable as a B-grade horror movie, until I grab the squeegee my dad uses to keep his precious windscreen pristine.

I didn't think I was worried but all of a sudden I'm close to being a complete mess.

Our cat Dylan Thomas wraps himself around my ankles and together we flow towards our doom.

Dylan Thomas: *Your squeegee will save my fluffy little tail.*

Me: *I will smash their brains out. I will.*

The cogs in my brain start turning over but my panic levels plummet when I see Liv parked in front of the open pantry doors, scooping giant wads of peanut butter out of the jar with her fingers. Making a big spoon out of her hand and ladling it in. Disgusting. I drop my weapon.

On the kitchen bench lies an unwrapped block of cheese, a jar of olives and an open packet of chocolate biscuits.

'Where do you put those calories?'

Liv jumps. She's rake thin and always has been, always will be. Even now, the only thing keeping her jeans on her bony hips is a studded belt.

'Anywhere I can, little sis.' Liv wipes crumbs from her face and sloppy kisses my cheek, and I pretend I hate it and don't want her anywhere near me. I catch a whiff of comforting menthol smoke through the peanut butter haze and stare at her head. Just when I think Liv can't choose an uglier hairstyle, there she goes, with the shaved bits and the spikes.

'I've been waiting, so bored and hungry. What's this?' She points to the photo pinned to the fridge.

'It's my abduction photo.'

She doesn't get it so I have to explain it to her like she's a child.

'It's so if I get abducted Mum and Dad don't give the police an awful photo of me that winds up on the news. That one's a good one.'

Mum keeps taking the picture down and I keep sticking it back up again because I had no idea it would bother her and it's a genuine superpower being able to irritate her this much. It's up-to-date, unlike Yin's photo. It was taken on my birthday earlier this year, and I look hot.

No one seems to be able to tell us if it's safer to look good and be noticed, or whether it's better to be forgettable and fly under the radar.

Instead of laughing, which you'd think she'd be generous enough to do, Liv's face twists into something I'm horrified to see is pity.

'I should have come much earlier, Tal. I've been flat out this week. I'm so sorry.'

I turn my face away, quicksmart. 'He doesn't take the pretty ones, don't you know? So I think I'm going to be safe.'

I don't count the moment a minute ago when I knew for a fact that I wasn't going to be safe.

'It's not about you getting kidnapped. That's clearly not going to happen, so it's not what I meant,' she says.

I pick up the biscuits. The stolen jacket under my school clothes is scratchy. Liv's duffel bag is on the floor. 'Are you staying the night?'

'I thought we could do a movie marathon.'

I'm sensing pity in everything she's saying and doing now and I won't have it. I can't let her crack me open.

'Well, that's a shame, Liv, because I'm going out tonight,' I lie. 'Dad's working late and Mum's at the Parkers' for book club. So you'll be hanging out on your own. It's going to be sad for you.'

I line all the unbroken biscuits from the packet along the bench. 'Mmmm.' I pop the first one in my trap, planning to eat them one by one until she leaves me alone.

'Stay home with me.'

'No.'

Liv gets down on her hands and knees and clutches my ankles. She looks up with her puppy-dog eyes. I can see she's got a brand new tattoo on her forearm, shiny and furious-red, plastered with greasy lotion.

'Pleeeeeaaassse, stay home. Pleeeaaasse.'

I look down at my sister and try to feel nothing. I can feel nothing about most things, but not Liv, unfortunately. A diversion is what's needed.

'Is that a hickey?'

I point to the red blotch next to the flower tattooed on her neck.

'Yes. I have several, if you want to see them.' Liv lifts her t-shirt. A black sports crop flattens her boobs.

'You're such a slut, Liv. Do you even know who gave that to you?'

Liv works at a bar in the city, and as far as I can tell, between the customers and the hornbag staff, it's a good place for finding hookups.

'That's the little underage pot calling the consenting adult kettle black, isn't it, Tal?'

I narrow my eyes, but my traitorous mouth turns up at the corners. Liv tugs on my bunched-down school socks, tugs on the invisible strings between us. She's good at reeling me in when she wants to.

'I miss you, Tal,' she says and there's no way you can doubt her sincerity. 'I want to know if you're okay.'

I play it like a soap opera, tossing my hair about, because all the world's a stage et cetera. I've been acting for my life ever since Yin was taken.

'I take pity on you, my sister. I will stay home.'

After Liv has tortured me with me one of her favourite Japanese horror movies I torture her with episode six of *Devil Creek*. Even though I'm pretty sure I hate the show, I have secretly watched two more episodes on my own, breaking a sacred promise to only watch it with my friends.

We fall quiet as the opening credits start.

A beautiful pale redhead in a nightie runs through the bush barefoot; everything around her blurred and streaky. The soundtrack is composed of ragged breathing and a pulsing drumbeat.

'Nope, no, no way, we're not doing this.' Liv tries to pause the computer and I grab her hand.

'Don't be silly, I've already watched half the season, it's fine.'

Two detectives, a man and a woman, stand by their car in the early hours of the morning, eating sausage rolls. Senior Detective Hillary Burns wears a woollen jumper, a no-non-sense parka, and has unbrushed hair and no makeup. By contrast, Senior Detective Pokerface McUptight is in an immaculate grey suit. He crumples his sausage roll packet and wipes his mouth.

'You've got sauce on your face,' he tells the woman, but she gives no fucks because all she cares about are the victims and she's crushing patriarchal standards on a daily basis.

Together they cross the car park and head up the stairs of the huge glass-and-concrete building. McUptight, real name McManus—way too close to anus—tries to wave her through the door first but Burns won't have a bar of it.

You'd think that the makers of *Devil Creek* would run out of reasons to show Emily Blake's corpse, but you would be wrong. They keep sliding her out of her drawer in the morgue to do different things to her body or pan the camera over it one more time. When they're not showing the body, the police detectives are flapping the crime scene photos of her wounded, half-naked corpse in front of every single person they interview, trying to shock them into a reaction.

This episode, the quirky forensic pathologist with purple hair is fizzed-up over something she's pulled out from underneath Emily Blake's toenails and also what she describes as 'tiny ritualised marks' she's found on the body. She says her 'intuition' tells her that the murderer is someone very close to the young woman, which is a weird thing for a scientist to say.

'I don't think Yin knew the person who took her,' I say without taking my eyes off the screen. 'I don't think it's anyone we know.'

'Me neither,' says Liv.

When the pathologist folds down the sheet covering Emily, Liv shuts the lid of the laptop completely, with a snap. 'I don't care if you can take this, I can't.'

'Don't you know it's make believe?' I ask her, but she won't be moved.

'Do you want to talk about it?' she asks, but she already knows I don't.

Liv squishes into bed with me and won't leave me alone. She makes me draw on her back with a finger, as if we're still little kids. I hold one of Mum's old orange paperbacks in my free hand, trying to read and draw at the same time. Liv's back ribs poke through her pyjama top.

'You reading that for school?' Liv throws her head backwards. You can still see the puckered scar at her hairline, from when a German shepherd bit into her ten-year-old head.

I grunt. I can read and back-scratch at the same time, no problem, but talking is too much.

Half of me is in my lamplit bedroom, but the rest of me is hanging out in the English countryside with this posh family called the Mitfords who have a bazillion daughters, each of them more bizarre than the last. Every time my finger stops, my sister twitches to remind me to keep drawing.

'Tal, you know I'm always here to help you,' Liv says, out of nowhere. She flips over to face me. 'I'm crap at keeping in touch, I know, but if you ever want to come over to my flat and hang, or just talk. You can call me any time of night, for any reason. I know what Mum and Dad are like.'

I close the book. Liv's face is currently twenty centimetres away from mine.

'I'm okay,' I tell her and I'm not lying and it's not the truth either.

No one at school has asked me how I'm doing since it happened. Mum and Dad have, but they don't count. Maybe no one remembers who I used to be, and I did work hard to make it that way. Junior School is distant enough to seem like a dream.

Liv looks younger close up, all her tattoos and piercings and spikiness blur out at the edges. We've got identical eyes, and would have the same colour hair if she didn't dye hers black.

65

'Why do you have to make yourself look so bad, Liv? You could be so pretty.'

A wheezing laugh escapes from her, that turns into a racking cough. 'Crap. I've gotta give up the smokes.'

She flips on her back and thumps herself in the chest, which actually makes it worse. 'You sound like Mum.'

'Don't you dare—' I start, and bash her with my pillow.

When I wake it takes me a few seconds to remember that I'm on the downstairs couch after Liv hogged my bed and snored too loud.

My book is steepled on my chest and something is scraping at the front door.

I sit up. The lounge is awash with moonlight from the back windows. The lawn is empty, peaceful. It sounds like a possum is trying to get into the house, but possums don't normally use doors.

I shuffle towards the front of the house and nearly walk into the corner of the hall table. There's a heavy vase on it that I could smash over someone's head. A person-shaped blob hovers behind the glass panels on the front door. The security door has been opened. A pink hand slaps against the frosted glass, fingers spread.

I hold my breath and wait. My senses are so alert I could hear a mouse's footstep. A key scrapes in the lock, the door clicks and swings open. Dad sways on the doormat. He straightens as soon as he sees me, but forgets to stop the screen door banging when he enters. You can tell how messy he is by how far his tie has wandered around his neck.

'Thought I'd lost my keys.' He holds them up, then drops them. I can smell the booze vapours from three metres away.

'Where have you been, Dad?' He pushes past me. It was only a few days ago that he and Mum had a massive fight about him coming home at all hours, every day of the week. It's always work, or mates, or work mates.

'Gary,' he mumbles.

Figures.

Big Man About Town Gary, Head of the School Board Gary, Golf Gary. Sarah's dad, Gary.

'Gary—not too good,' Dad says and continues unevenly through the house. He's not looking crash hot himself. He stopped drinking for years, but now he's back on it, and I don't know what that means.

After he's gone upstairs I do a full circuit, checking the locks on all the doors and windows.

DAY 7

The house feels empty when Liv finally leaves on Saturday afternoon. She's good at leaving spaces emptier than they were. The pantry hangs open, its contents ravaged, and there are dirty dishes piled up in the sink that no one can be bothered putting in the dishwasher.

Dad is playing golf, leaving Mum bored and desperate to interact, so I duck upstairs, saying I've got homework to do. It's not a lie, I do have homework, but I've got no intention of doing it.

I lock my bedroom door and light my candles. My phone is going off, everyone trying to get me to say what we're doing tonight. I put it on silent. The smell of liquefying wax relaxes me.

Standing on tiptoes, I can barely reach the storage shelf at the top of my wardrobe. A garbage bag of shoes I've grown out of falls first. My fingers latch onto a handle.

The green leather suitcase is a time machine.

I almost threw it out when I moved from my old bedroom to this one, but something made me keep it. I slide both clasps to the side, and the case springs open.

There's a lot of junk inside, photos and badges and broken necklaces, my old school diary and bits of paper that contain a forgotten world. Forgotten people. Notes passed in class, invitations to birthday parties.

Here's a photo of me and Yin, in matching t-shirts with our arms linked, goofy grins. Ten years old, major dorks and joined at the hip, as we had been every year of Junior School. Yin's thick black hair kicks up at the ends and I'm in the first year of braces. We're on a summer camping trip with the Mitchells; I remember Yin still wasn't sure about her new stepdad.

It hurts to see her baby face. All the breath leaves my body.

You know who I could always rely on to tell me the truth, to warn me before I went too far? Yin.

She'd tell me to stop eating cupcakes or I'd spew, she'd turn the volume down before I got in trouble, yelled at me to stop climbing that tree, told me when I needed to apologise.

I try to see something ominous in the photo, dark shadows or figures in the trees or mysterious streaks of light, something to show that things were going to go very wrong for one of these girls, but there's nothing. We might be the happiest kids in the world. Dirt smudges on our cheeks and twigs in our hair.

I dump the contents of the case onto the bed.

A photo of our graduating Grade Six class, ribbons from school athletics days, a certificate to say I'm allowed to write in ink. And then there are other things.

Plastic 'gemstones' imbued with magic powers. Silk flowers in colours that show which clan we belong to. A rubber rabbit from a farm animal set that travelled to earth from the moon. Yin's mum used to tell her stories about the moon rabbit coming down to earth so we wrote it into our stories. The exercise book we scribbled our secret language in, and the written history of our lands, our spells.

At the bottom, the greatest treasure, the worn piece of paper that we'd spent hours on. We always fought over who got to keep it at their house. I had the stronger will, even then.

A map of our home kingdom and the rival kingdoms surrounding it. Drawn lovingly in gel pens and Derwent pencils.

Wingdonia.

Oh, so childish.

I haven't seen it for years, and it's surprisingly detailed. The mountain ranges come back, the waterfalls and valleys, villages and ports. Wingdonia was shaped like a boot; it kicked the neighbouring kingdom of Plentificent off into the Aerie Ocean.

Yin had the best ideas about the geography, because of the dozens of fantasy novels she'd read, but I had the best ideas about the people, the families and the politics.

There were four clans, each with their own back story and special powers.

Have I been homesick all these years for a place that doesn't exist?

Yin and I were travelling warrior queens of the Opal clan, fairy immortals imbued with magic, but masquerading as flesh-and-blood humans. We'd built our world from scratch, painstakingly, over the years. Etching the lines deep and adding sprinkles of glitter. There'd been times when Wingdonia had seemed more real than reality.

But the kingdom crashed, war broke out and the game ended. It didn't make it through the transition to high school, and neither did our friendship.

Everything goes back into the suitcase again, except for the map, which I fold up into a small rectangle and slide into the hidden compartment in my purse, wedging it up against a condom that Liv gave me.

I go to the mirror and look at my dry eyes, trying to see beyond myself, underneath to where the ten-year-old might still live, but there's nothing there. I try to picture Yin standing behind my shoulder, but I can't conjure her.

Why did I push her away? I can't remember now.

I have a huge red pimple welling up on my chin and a few suspect bumps on my cheek, and it's typical that I had good skin all week but now I'm breaking out for the weekend.

I unscrew the jar of expensive clay mask that Mum's allergic to and paint thick lines across my face with the plastic spatula, tough battle lines like a rugby player, and then I don't stop, I paint my whole face out until it's nothing but crackly pink mud and I erase all my thoughts with it until I have a blank blank brain.

# Chloe

As soon as school ends I join the trail of girls walking across the main oval to the tram stop. The parklands adjoining the school are visible through the wire fence. Police in navy and hi-vis yellow walk up and down the U-shaped trough of the creek, sweeping across the park in rough lines. They weren't there last week, so I wonder what's happened to bring them out now.

'Let's see if any of them are hot.'

A gaggle of Year Nines peel off and plaster themselves to the fence. I slow so much that someone behind me treads on the back of my shoe.

More police, in orange overalls and waterproof waders, push through the water. One of the closest police officers—a normal navy-and-yellow—looks up and sees us staring. For a moment it seems she might come over and talk to us, but then one of her colleagues calls her away.

'I don't like it. It's scary.' A tiny Year Seven looks close to tears. One of her friends hooks her arm and comforts her.

The teacher manning the gate gets impatient.

'Come on girls! Pick up the pace!'

There are more cars than usual on the side street, a long queue from the gate almost to the highway. Some parents or drivers are paranoid enough to congregate around the gate, scrolling on their phones.

I cram on the tram with the mass of Balmoral students, my face right up against a Year Twelve's armpit. Three separate groups of Year Tens dominate the rear of the tram; talking too loud and checking their phones and oversharing. More than a few of them hold the letter we'd been given at final roll call, the one marked strictly for parents or guardians. I guess what it contains is too sensitive for an email.

Eventually, inevitably, someone cracks and rips the envelope open.

I hang onto an overhead handle and eavesdrop.

'It's an emergency parent info night.' The girl scans the letter. 'This Thursday night. That's not much notice.'

'Something must have happened.'

'What is there to say? Don't be scared even though there's a Hannibal Lecter on the loose?'

'Please don't take your daughter out of school because we need your money to build a new theatre?'

'Shit, do you think Grace's party is going to get cancelled?'

This causes a wave of panic through most of the Year Tens. Grace Chapman's sixteenth has dominated conversations this week. It's amazing how people can switch from gossiping about our teachers providing DNA samples to what they're going to wear on Friday night in one breath.

Teaghan sits behind Brooke, braiding her hair. 'Can't

they see we want to have one night where we don't have to think about anything?'

I jump off at the Junction with dozens of other Balmoral girls, feeling as if I've collected strands of everyone else's hair on my blazer and need to shower.

After acquiring my usual can of lemonade and apple scroll from the bakery, I move on to the bus stop. I could do this trip in my sleep, if I had to. It takes me forty-five minutes to get home: a tram and a bus. The first three years of high school I could walk for ten minutes and be at the entrance to Morrison High.

A handful of army-green All Saints boys are at the bus stop, along with two pensioners and a tired mum with a stroller containing a sleeping toddler. The bus is late. I haven't called Dad yet, and I haven't spoken to Liana since last week or answered any of Katie's messages.

I'd thought I could show up at school and do the work, then catch up with my real friends on the weekend. I'd make some friends at Balmoral, not close ones, and not heaps. Maybe a trio, like the one Claire, Milla and Yin formed, a loose bond with girls that are in a few of my classes. That would have been enough.

The thing is, I don't think I can reverse my decision now.

I've seen what it's like.

Balmoral girls get more homework, extra reading, extension exercises. The world is expected of us. Our teachers are available at lunch, after school and even on holidays, to go over our assignments and tests in detail. They're paid to push us hard, we have to deliver, and I'm doing things that I wouldn't be able to achieve at Morrison. I've got to pedal hard just to keep up with the pack.

I can't go back to my old school.

If Liana could see the brand-new science labs we get to use, the shiny state-of-the-art equipment, she'd be amazed, and maybe furious. Sitting the scholarship exam wasn't even my idea, it was hers.

She wanted to get into McGowan, a selective state school with a good netball team and specialist STEM program. We did practice exams together, then sat in the same massive room at the Showgrounds, along with hundreds of other hopeful teenagers vying for spots at independent schools around the state. But when the results came in, it was me that got the offers: a full scholarship to Balmoral, or a half-scholarship to Sheltower Girls Grammar.

I jam the rest of the scroll into my mouth and crumple the paper bag. Natalia and her gang are hanging out the front of the juice bar, right next to the bus stop. They must have been on the tram before mine. Apparently there's a secret shortcut through the grounds that gets you to the tram stop early, but no one's ever shown me. The boys they're with, some spoilt guys from Norton Grammar, are making a big show of flexing their muscles and pushing each other around, even while they're sucking on hot-pink takeaway cups.

Sarah has taken off her blazer and rolled her winter skirt up so it barely covers her butt. She's sitting on one boy's lap, but the rest of the girls are more interested in their phones than the Grammar boys.

Natalia stands apart from the rest, eyes on her phone, with Ally looking over her shoulder. They don't care that they're blocking the footpath, forcing shoppers to flow around them.

I pretend to read my Biology textbook while I eavesdrop.

'I can't believe she'd go out in those pants,' Ally says. 'Again. I've got chills.'

The two girls watch the screen quietly, and at one point Ally squeals.

When whatever they're watching finishes, Natalia looks up and catches my eye. I can tell that she's pissed off with Ally by the way she's angled away from her. Her eyes are hollow.

'What are you looking at?' Natalia calls out, but I know it's just a reflex. There's no fire in her words. She seems blank, empty as a lost sock, especially compared to how she was last week. She was so jumped up in self-defence class that she was lucky she didn't take Petra's eye out.

Behind her I can see the Grammar boys checking her out, and I don't blame them. Perfect tanned skin, skinny legs and boobs the exact right size, those supermodel eyes, blue-green, set far apart and a bit alien.

I hold her gaze and shrug. I can read your mind, a bit, I think. Something's wrong with you. I can tell you're wearing a mask.

Natalia eyeballs me for a few more seconds before turning back to her friends.

I check the bus timetable. I don't think the 3.50 p.m. is coming, so I decide to walk to the next bus stop. I'm hauling my second-hand Maths, International Studies and Biology textbooks home and my bag straps cut heavily into my right shoulder. Once I'm far enough up the street, I slip my backpack on properly, both straps, a proper dork.

I realised two days into my new school that no one uses the green Balmoral backpacks; they all use the green duffel bag instead. There is no way I can use anything other than this perfectly good new backpack that Mum bought, though. When I got the scholarship it felt like a free ride, but it turned out that there were plenty of extras apart from the fees. Summer uniform, winter uniform, sports uniform. Straw hat, school swimsuit, textbooks, excursions.

The air is thick with exhaust fumes at the next intersection. Cars fly by; one driver wolf whistles. I have no idea why school uniforms do this to men, they're literally an advertisement that I'm underage.

A new billboard looms above the crossroads. A pale girl in a silky cream slip lying on the ground, her sleeping face surrounded with a bright red blot of hair. Her legs cross at the ankles, her wrists turn soft side up. Her skin is dirty and scratched.

She might be selling perfume or shoes, but that can't be right.

The girl looks damaged, and sexy. Something crawls deep in my gut.

Around the fallen girl everything is dark and foreboding: the thin silhouettes of trees, a shadowy, indistinct figure hiding behind one of them. The half-seen figure is bulky and powerful; the girl so beautiful and bare. The photographer has managed the lighting perfectly, illuminating the crumpled figure of the girl and then letting patches of darkness take over.

I think of the police and rescue service workers walking methodically through the parklands next to school, and imagine them finding a discarded body in the creek. Should an assaulted girl look this sexy and glamorous? I flash back to mum saying that the community cares more about some women than others. What is wrong with people?

I squint at the text in the bottom corner.

*Who Killed Emily Blake?*

Much later that night, during the late news, I figure out what it was that Natalia and Ally were watching at the bus stop.

The police have released CCTV footage of Yin from a convenience store close to her house. They don't say what day it was taken, only that it was in the week before the attack. The footage is grainy, but you can still tell that the short girl with black hair is her.

Yin walks into the store and disappears from view. A guy in a flannel shirt and a baseball cap follows her, then stops to look at the sunglasses stand. Yin, wearing the pyjama pants Ally was griping about, comes into shot again, holding a bottle of milk. While she rummages in her pocket for money, the guy in the flannel turns to look at her. She has her back to him, so wouldn't have noticed. A few moments after Yin leaves the store, the guy in the flannel exits too.

The police are stressing that the man isn't a suspect, merely a 'person of interest' they want to talk to.

Even though Mum is at work and it's not a good idea to spook myself while she's out, I watch the footage again and again, until it plays behind my eyelids as I'm trying to go to sleep.

Close to midnight I give up on sleep and search for articles about the abduction on my phone. I find one that includes a list of other recent missing or murder cases in Melbourne. I read through the list and wonder if any of the things Mum talked about has made a difference in the way that they were investigated or reported.

An economics student from China who hasn't been seen in three months. A trans woman who was beaten to death on the way to her work as a chef. A fourteen-year-old who ran away from home with her boyfriend but has since gone missing. A Gunditjmara mother of three who was found dead next to train tracks and I don't remember there being a manhunt or media frenzy about it.

All these girls or women from different circumstances, all missing or dead. There's a burning in my chest about the unfairness of it all. It could happen to any of us.

Yesterday Ms Nouri showed us a documentary where eight famous artists spoke about their careers. They all had very different approaches to their work, but the one thing they all said was that you needed to be passionate, to make art about what you believe in, what you feel most strongly about, what you're obsessed with.

I wonder if I can turn this burning feeling into anything good, anything meaningful. It seems impossible, I'm not even a proper artist. Still, I flip open my sketchbook, find a blank page and start writing.

## DAY 11

I think they're joking when they remind us about compulsory house cross-country at morning assembly, but they're not. I'm forced to put on a musty sports bra and crumpled PE top from the bottom of my locker.

The serious runners paint house colours on their cheeks and jostle to get close to the start line. I tug on the awful purple house jersey over my PE shirt and dawdle at the rear. A biting wind whips across the grounds.

The gun goes off; the girls at the front leap forward. Their feet pound the mushy oval, throwing up chunks of mud that hit the runners behind them.

The course circles the oval, then climbs between the tennis courts. At the end of the first hill the runners have stretched out to a thin thread. I think about walking, but by the time I cross the main driveway it feels good to stretch my legs, even though it's not as much fun without Arnold by my side.

At the bottom of the hill we cut through a large pine plantation, an abandoned part of Balmoral that looks at least fifty years older than the rest. I pass a disused portable classroom and head into the thickest section of trees.

The fallen pine needles are soft to run on, swallowing up every footfall. I've left the last group of runners out of sight and the next girl is way ahead. The only sign that I'm not in the middle of a Grimm's fairytale are the yellow course flags tied around the trees.

My head flashes with images. Young girls running through the forest, red-cloaked with wicker baskets. Gold rings. Spinning wheels. Tower prisons. Maidens asleep under trees. Girls with black hair and snow-white skin, lying on the pine needles with a school blazer for a blanket. Eyes shut, but not sleeping. Taken. Not a fairytale at all.

I trip on a half-buried tree root and lose my rhythm. I pick up my pace, striving to get out of the shadowy copse.

I bolt full speed into the long, torturous climb back to the oval, where everyone has to do a final lap before collapsing across the finish line. I'm not too tired so I push my legs a little bit harder, passing the trickle of struggling runners one by one.

By the top of the hill I'm regretting everything.

Ms Hammond, one of the PE teachers, stands at the side of the oval, directing the runners onto the track. When I draw close she frowns and consults her clipboard. If I had any puff left I'd laugh at the confused look on her face. With only a few hundred metres to go I decide to stick it to the PE teachers and the man and hungry wolves in forests, and I put in a final burst of speed. I pass one staggering girl, then another.

At the top of the straight, the purple house captains jump up and down as I take two more runners. My legs are rapidly turning to jelly, but I manage to keep my dignity to the finish line. I swerve to avoid Sarah, who is doubled over ahead of me.

Mrs Wang hands me a piece of cardboard with the number 4 on it and claps my gross sweaty back. Your choice, lady. I'm going to die.

'What's this?' I gasp. Then I'm leapt on by two screaming girls in purple wigs.

I wash and change as quicky as I can after the race and rush towards the main building, trying to balance my PE bag and Art folio. There's barely time to eat my sandwich before fifth period. I want to write down the ideas I had while running, before they float away.

Fairytales. Tangled hair. Blue lips. Beauty.

'Chloe Cardell!'

Ms Hammond chases after me, sans clipboard but sporting her trademark whistle around her neck. Once she reaches me she gets straight to the point.

'I want to talk to you about joining the cross-country squad. We train three times a week, starting at 7.30 a.m.'

I shake my head straight away, but Ms Hammond either doesn't notice, or chooses to ignore it.

'Every year we go away for a training camp to Swansea, it's a lot of fun. It's not all training. We go whale watching and cook big dinners together. It would be a good way to make some friends—some more friends—'

It's clear she thinks I'm a social pariah in desperate need of help.

'I don't think so.' I'm pretty sure Sarah is on the team, and she's not the kind of friend I'm looking to make. Also, I don't see any way to add 'runner' to 'mediocre artist' and 'person who gets As in Maths'. There's nothing that Balmoral won't turn into a cut-throat competition.

'I'm pretty busy with schoolwork actually.'

'But you ran so well today, Chloe. You looked great out there, your form was perfect. With the right training you could improve astronomically.'

I force myself to be brighter and bubblier than usual, to soften any possible offence. 'Oh, thanks for asking, Ms Hammond, but I don't think I have the time for it.'

I clutch my folio tight to my chest, like armour, and hurry away.

## DAY 12

Mum does a pretty good job of parking Ron and Pearl's car, even though she's only driven it once before. The Barina hatchback is a dung beetle in a school car park full of four-wheel drives and shiny gold sedans.

We get out and put our jackets on.

'You sure?' I'm probably asking myself this question as much as I'm asking Mum. 'You never wanted to come to another school thing ever again.'

'This is different.'

Mum was short with me the whole way here, which means she's nervous. I spent the drive catching her up on the week's events at school. Mostly that there were a suspicious number of substitute teachers in rotation, but that only male teachers were missing class. Petra also told me at morning recess that she'd seen a group of four detectives after orchestra practice. And there were the police searching the creek next door, of course.

We join the stream of parents flowing through the main doors and into the Great Hall. There are a few students loitering in the foyer, mostly Year Sevens and Eights with violin and cello cases in hand.

It's petty, but I note that Mum is younger and prettier than the other mothers. She's got on her good jeans, heeled winter boots that boost her several inches, dangly gold earrings and a silky shirt. I'm the slobby giant next to her, as usual.

'You look nice,' I whisper.

'I'll try not to embarrass you, baby.' She lets her eyeballs roll and flops her tongue out. I'm not sure we should be joking, but I smile.

There are a lot of parents already in the hall as we file in, rows and rows of navy jackets and cashmere jumpers, bald spots and helmet-bobs. No students, even though the letter didn't say anything about students not being welcome.

After a brief moment of panic I notice a handful of girls sitting right at the back, in the dark corner where the spare chairs are stored.

I point in that direction and Mum continues into the centre of the hall. I feel guilty for putting her through this.

'Hi,' I nod to the small group of girls. I climb over a few rows of fold-up chairs and perch up high, to see better. I spot Mum's dead-straight black hair in the audience.

There are at least four people sitting in a row on the stage, but I'm too far away to figure out who they are. The velvet curtains are drawn behind them, there's a lectern and plain lights. I can at least recognise Mrs Christie by the puff of grey hair worn extra high. She steps up to the mike.

'Thank you for coming this evening. This has been a difficult couple of weeks for everyone in the school community...'

My attention drifts as Mrs Christie introduces the people on stage. The metal bars of the chair are already digging into my bum. I realise the majority of the girls are international students from my year, most of them boarders. Some have their homework with them, others play with their phones.

Bochen from Art class waves and comes to sit with me.

'I thought there would be police here.' She holds up her phone, with the recorder running. 'I promised my father there would be police. I told him we have security guards on all the school doors.'

Bochen is chattier than some of her friends, maybe because she's spent time in the States and is more confident with her English, maybe because that's just the way she is. If I could pick who will win the art prize, it would be her. Give Bochen a pencil and a piece of paper and she can turn out photorealistic portraits.

'It's even in the Chinese media, so everyone is scared for us,' adds Cherry, then zips it, returning to her notebook. The page fills with tiny characters written in mechanical pencil.

Despite Cherry's words, none of the international students look that worried. Maybe, like me, they feel one step removed from what's happening.

Bochen picks up a strand of my hair, and I try not to jump from her familiarity. 'Where are you from, Chloe? You're mixed, yes?'

'Mum's from Singapore. She's here tonight.' I point her out in the crowd, and Bochen rubbernecks majorly. I don't mind her curiosity.

'Chinese?' she says, after finding her.

'Yeah, I guess.' It's a bit more complicated than that, but it will do. Mum has tried more than once to explain Singaporean race politics to me but I never pay enough attention to fully get it. 'Dad's Anglo–Australian. I was born here. Like Yin.'

'You got a good nose,' Bochen says. 'Lucky.'

We're quiet, because on stage Mrs Christie is running through advice from the police. It's all very obvious and in no way resembles the advice in the chain email that I haven't bothered to forward to anyone. Mrs Christie keeps repeating that there's no reason for the 'Balmoral community' to take any greater care than the general public.

I crane my neck and wonder how Mum is going.

The Head of the School Board gets up and starts fielding questions from the parents.

'Sarah's father,' Bochen whispers.

No, he doesn't know how many calls the police hotline have taken about the case.

No, there hasn't been a ransom request.

Yes, he has seen the CCTV footage, it would be hard not to have seen it the last few days, but he has nothing more to say.

The rumbling in the audience grows.

Sarah's dad looks and talks like a bulldog politician, so it's no wonder Mrs Christie has left question time to him. Not that Mrs Christie is a pushover, but these parents are plain intimidating. They've decided that they should stand up to ask their questions, which each of them do in turn.

He has no opinion on whether this is a serial offender. That is a matter for the police.

This causes one dad to yell out, 'Do you think we're all fools?' Bochen raises her eyebrows at me and presses 'stop' on her recording.

Yes, it's true that there are similarities between Karolina and Yin's abductions, but he's no expert.

No, there is no truth to the story that school computers have been seized. Cherry clicks her tongue when he says this, so maybe the boarders have seen something the day girls haven't.

A woman in a patterned shift dress stands up. 'I would like to know what the school is doing to ensure my child's emotional and mental health?' She stabs the air with her finger every couple of words. 'I've got a little girl at home who is scared, and not sleeping. She can't get offline and she won't eat. What are you doing for her?'

Mrs Christie steps up to answer this question, trotting out the types of support services offered by the school. The questioning continues, as if this were a political debate for the federal election.

Sarah's dad can't comment on whether teachers are being interviewed. That is a matter for the police.

The police will be looking at every angle, including all employees of the school.

Yes, that will include gardeners and grounds staff. Yes, he expects that he himself will be looked at, as one would hope, if the police are doing a thorough job.

Yes, it's possible that some parents will be contacted by the police taskforce, and yes, we expect you to show them your full cooperation.

It gets so boring and repetitive that we start talking among ourselves.

'How is your major project going, Chloe?' Bochen doesn't need to mention that she's talking about Art.

'Stressing me out,' I admit. I still think my ideas from

cross-country yesterday are interesting, but I haven't had much of a chance yet to think any further. 'How about you? Have you started?'

She scoots closer, takes out her phone and scrolls. 'I'm drawing my friend Mercury. In ink, nothing complicated, but very big.' She stretches her arms out to indicate the scale of her piece. 'Here.'

I look at her screen. Bochen has drawn a light graphite map of Mercury's face, but I can already tell she's playing with perspective and distortion in interesting ways.

'It looks great,' I say. 'What are your themes going to be?'

'No idea!' Bochen says. 'Sometimes a drawing is just a drawing, you know?'

I wait until we're halfway home before I empty out my spinning brain.

'Mum?'

Mum turns her head only a fraction. She's a careful driver. The passing streetlights glance over the planes of her face.

'Will Dad's record come up? I mean, will the detectives know about that?'

She flicks the indicator on, shifts lanes to merge onto the freeway. It's a few seconds before she speaks. The freeway lights give her the pearly complexion of a sixteenth century Flemish painting. I try to mentally record the way she looks, the way the light hits her. Imagine being able to recreate that in paint or on film. She looks as young as me from where I'm sitting. I want to erase every part of Dad and be one hundred per cent like her. I don't want his nose.

'It had crossed my mind,' she admits. 'But they can't investigate every man associated with the school. How many girls are there? Two thousand? How many dads, stepdads, boyfriends could that add up to? I don't think they have the resources.'

Mum has never held anything back about Dad's past, or hers either, at least as far as I know. I know she was a wild-child in the nineties, first a grunge groupie in her teens, then a raver at university. I know about her fighting with her family and the fallout over Dad.

I know Dad was more enthusiastic about drugs than her, and that his enthusiasm led to two charges of possession. Mum has always said that as soon as she got pregnant Dad cleaned his act up, but I don't remember what it was like when I was a toddler. I'm not sure if it was that simple. But being into drugs when you were young has nothing to do with abducting teenage girls.

'Are you glad you went tonight?' I ask.

'Those parents were intense.'

I laugh. 'I know! I was terrified!'

'I guess they pay through their nose for the fees so they think they have the right. They expect so much.' She puts her indicator on. 'Are you sure you're good for tomorrow night?'

Mum had to change shifts so she could come tonight; she wouldn't normally work Friday nights.

'It's fine.'

'I can ask Pearl again.'

'Not two nights in a row,' I say. 'Me and Sam will have bonding time, it'll be good.'

'You should be out with your friends,' she murmurs, taking the exit ramp. We're almost home. 'Who was that nice-looking girl you were talking to up the back? Is she a Balmoral buddy?'

I snort at her casual tone. I know she's concerned that I haven't adjusted to Balmoral as well as I might have. In all the thinking about whether to take up the scholarship offer, I didn't think about whether I would fit in, or what it meant to trick your way into somewhere you don't belong.

'I can't comment at this point in the investigation,' I say.

Sam pokes his BBQ pork with disposable chopsticks.

'I don't think it should be this colour.' The sauce has stained the mound of rice pink around the edges. 'Chlo. Chlo. Look.'

'You chose it, so eat it and don't waste my money.'

I was supposed to cook dinner for Sam and me tonight, but the better scenario is lazy times at Meridian Shopping Centre. And this way we're not alone at home, bouncing off the walls and twitching at every innocent noise. The shopping centre is always packed on Friday nights and I've brought Mum's camera with me. I've been trying to develop the habit of seeing the boring, everyday things around me with fresh eyes, but it's not easy.

In our corner of the food court the canned music is loud; the flat screen on the wall opposite us is huge. Normally it's showing music videos or football, but at the moment the evening news is playing soundlessly. Someone accidentally showed a nipple at an awards ceremony. And that's called news.

Most of my year level will be getting ready for Grace's party right now. Bochen told me they were providing mini-buses for the boarders. Even I'd been invited. Granted, it was only because I'd been standing at the lockers next to Petra, and Grace is nice enough that she couldn't help but hand me an invite too. Apparently her parents insisted on paper invitations, to stop gatecrashers finding out about the party online and arriving in the hundreds. Good luck with that, Chapmans.

I watch Sam herd the peas from his fried rice to one side of his plate, mumbling to himself. My own lemon chicken is a suspect shade of yellow, but tastes as MSG-good as ever. Maybe we can watch a movie when we get home. I let Sam watch MA-rated movies and stay up past 9 p.m. when Mum's not around. I told him about our self-defence class and now he wants to do a Bruce Lee marathon.

I should feel like a loser for preferring to hang out with my ten-year-old brother than go to a party, but I don't.

I switch Mum's camera on and fill the viewfinder with my radioactive yellow dinner, Sam's plate lurking in the background as red, white and green blotches. Snap. I try again, turning the wheel to macro and getting up real close. Mum's camera does not cope well with low light. There's no way I'll be able to hold it steady enough.

When I look up at the flat screen again the grainy CCTV footage of Yin is playing, both bits. This morning the news sites started showing the same convenience store incident, but from a different camera. From the new angle you can see the flannel shirt guy a little bit better.

I can't look away from it, as if somehow this time the video might be different.

The newsreader comes back on, but it's impossible to know what she's saying. Maybe she's saying this is definitely the guy we're looking for. Maybe someone will call the police tonight and say they recognise him. Maybe that will lead them to a house in a far-out suburb, and we'll wake up tomorrow and find out that it's over; they've found the creep and rescued Yin. Maybe then I can stop checking doors and windows and running through my dwindling list of reasons to stay at Balmoral.

'I talked to Dad today,' says Sam, out of nowhere.

'Good for you.' I push my plate away. A layer of congealed skin has formed over the lemon sauce. 'Are you done?'

Sam skids in his slippery shoes all the way to the bargain games shop. I give him twenty minutes and twenty dollars of my own money. That kid has no idea how much I do for him.

The shopping centre is swarming: teenagers cruising each other, security cameras, security guards. Peace descends for the first time this week. I'm a bee in a swarm, a particle, part of a larger pattern. I have no separate thoughts or significant problems. I wander the corridors with Mum's camera held in front of me, looking around for colours and patterns.

The tubs of jelly cups and coconut water at the Asian grocer become abstract and psychedelic if you get close enough, the reflections in the window of the brow bar fragment the customers inside, the aisles of the discount chemist warehouse are stark and artificial. I take photos of hair-netted women speed-folding dumplings in a restaurant window and old men gathered in the Greek coffee shop with their walking sticks hooked onto the table.

I swing past to check on Sam, and see him sitting on the shop floor with rows of games fanned in front of him. I snap a photo of him through the window and he doesn't even look up. If I turn it black and white, if I tweak it to make it look pixellated and gritty, it would look exactly like a surveillance photo.

At the camera store I look at digital SLRs I'll never be able to afford, not even if I take off a hypothetical $500 won hypothetically in the non-hypothetical art prize and then add all the pocket money I can save this year. Mum's old camera is a dinosaur compared to these muscly black models. I wish I'd thought to sign out one of the school's fancy cameras for the weekend, so I could have practised with it. Brooke and Audrey take all their photos on film and use the darkroom to develop and print them, but we didn't have a darkroom at Morrison, and I don't have time to learn how to do it well enough for my project.

When I've looked at every camera in the shop, I retrace my steps to the games store to collect Sam.

The corner where he was sitting is empty now. I scan the store, looking in front of each shelf and bargain bin. Everywhere I look there are rows of browsing backs. Sam's not at the info counter, or hiding behind a cardboard cut-out display.

I go to the front counter.

'Have you seen a little kid? He's ten, about this tall?' My voice sounds normal even though my insides don't. The sales assistant stops pricing games with a sticker gun.

'Oh, hey,' he says, as if he knows me. 'Who are you looking for?'

'My brother. He's wearing a purple jumper and jeans, maybe?'

'Sorry, no. Nick, you haven't seen a kid on the loose have you?'

His work colleague shakes his head.

The assistant puts down his gun. 'Do you want some help looking for him?'

'No, no thanks.'

I exit the store and look both ways up the aisle, a frantic feeling already coming on. I look at waist level among the crowds of shoppers. No Sam.

I turn to ice. My fingers, toes, all the way to the ends of my hair, and especially my heart.

I walk to the end of one aisle, look up and down the next row of shops, then go back to the other end and robotically repeat the action.

Sam is gone.

The next obvious place to check is the large entrance to the shopping centre. To the right is the food court where we ate dinner, to the left the gates to the subway.

I consider the sliding doors to the underground platforms. I picture a man holding Sam's hand and leading him down the escalators, onto a train, and away. Forever. In my chest is a cold fist.

'Chlo? Chlo?'

I turn so quickly I get vertigo.

Sam stands five metres away, holding a plastic bag with his precious games inside. He's wearing his orange hoodie, not a purple jumper, and cargo shorts, not jeans.

'There you are!' I swoop, and in the time it takes me to reach my brother, I melt into fury. 'Where were you? I told you not to move from there. You know to stay put! It's the first rule.'

'I was looking for you! I was trying to find you!'

Sam keeps repeating these meaningless words over and over as I grab his wrist and drag him towards the doors. I'm hot all over; something flutters around my body, something has been let loose. I keep moving to disguise it.

'Chloe!' Sam pulls away until I stop. He pulls his hand free and rubs his wrist. 'You're hurting me.' His lower lip is suspiciously trembly. Then—whispering—'I couldn't find you.'

I look back at him, and he looks so confused and indignant, and little, really. A little kid. And I haven't been thinking clearly, because the guy doesn't snatch boys from shopping centres, he goes for girls in their homes.

I remember the quad last week—which already seems eons ago—and Milla repeating the police's questions: *Was she scared of anything?*

Yes. I can almost hear the thoughts of every single girl in my year level. We're all scared, of almost everything.

## Natalia

**DAY 18**

The library doors are so heavy it's no wonder that I only go in there when I'm forced to. There's a *schunk* as the doors come apart, as if I'm stepping into an airlock, shortly to be sprayed with disinfectant and handed a Hazmat suit. Our school librarians give off the very strong vibe that they would prefer students to stay out of their facility.

I shoulder in like the brave pioneer I am, keeping my head down, and I swear there's a pause in the beep-beep of the barcode scanner when I walk past the loans counter. The library smells different, a foreign country that I barely realised existed. There's a row of girls along the far wall, glued to computers, and a cushion pit full of people reading.

'What is this mystical language?' I ask the neat laminated signs taped to the end of each row of shelves. I tap the Dewey Devil number 666 and abandon the non-fiction section, prowling up the alphabet in fiction until I find my prey.

Eight identical brown spines line up next to each other on the shelf, which I guess is because we were supposed to be studying this book in English. Supposed to be, because the teachers have changed their minds: as of this morning it is off our reading list. Of course I asked why, and of course Ms Clarke was super vague. So here I am, in uncharted lands, looking for a *verboten* book.

'Hello, my forbidden fruit that tastes all the more sweet,' I whisper to the paperback as I remove it from the shelf.

*Picnic at Hanging Rock* looks boring and historical, with a pretty blonde girl on the cover in a ye olde white flowing dress.

'Hi, Natalia.' A tiny mousy voice.

Grace Chapman hovers nearby, cradling a stack of books. She always has her head in a book, usually a novel featuring a supernatural love triangle, although in a change of scenery I accidentally saw her with her head in Andrew Taylor's crotch behind the pool house last Friday night. Which is a bit weird, because it was *her* birthday party, so whose head should have been in whose lap, I ask you.

As much as I try to act normal, the fact remains that I can't meet Grace's eye. And it's not because she's caught me talking out loud to a book, or because I spotted her with Andrew, it's because of what else happened on Friday night.

Let me paint the scene:

It is the aforementioned birthday party, a massively exaggerated affair attended by almost the entire year level, including the boarders who were bussed in and kept on a huge leash made from hundreds of school ties knotted together. No one has stopped talking about it all week: who hooked up with who, who spewed on one of the family cars, who was rejected by which Grammar boy and who smoked pot in the laneway out the back.

Is it abnormal to obsess over a party while someone you know is imprisoned in a house somewhere far from home? I think we all know the answer to that question.

We, by which I mean my lady squad and I, arrived fashionably late. Despite the fairy lights and the gazebo and the waiters with bow ties and the sparkling turquoise pool, the Chapmans' backyard did not so much resemble a sophisticated soiree as a scene from a zombie film where the zombies can't decide whether to eat brains or hump each other on the dance floor. As one of the few responsible non-zombies present, it was I who went to inform the adults that the bathrooms were fresh out of toilet paper.

It was I who followed Mr Chapman upstairs to fetch the paper, and it was I who was diverted into the study so Chapman could fetch more whisky, which he'd clearly had quite a bit of already. This was sketchy but ideal because I may or may not have remembered from my Balmoral brain catalogue that Grace's dad is a detective and this may or may not have encouraged my very attendance at the soiree that evening. Do not underestimate my ability to focus on my goals.

Me: Is it true you're a detective?

Chapman: Have you girls been talking about me behind my back?

Me: (Vomits a little bit inside my own mouth but carries on.) Haha, yeah of course. You're all we talk about.

Chapman: I used to be, I'm in security consulting now. I was in the force for twenty years. The drug squad, then the homicide squad.

Me: So, do you still get access to inside information then?

Chapman: (Vagues out slightly while pouring whisky before snapping to.) You mean about the Mitchell case? You two were—

Me: Yes, of course, about Yin. Have you heard anything?

Chapman: I've heard they've sought advice from the FBI, so they're taking it very seriously. (Leans sloppily on desk.) They'll make another announcement soon, I think.

Me: What kind of announcement? Tell me.

Chapman: Be patient, it'll come. It's normal to be concerned. You're very mature for your age, aren't you Natalia? (LITERALLY X-RAYS MY TOP WITH HIS EYES.)

Me: Can we get the damn toilet paper, sir?

Or something like that. Maybe I didn't say the last bit. But think about it—Grace has to live with that slimebag every day of her life. And I didn't learn anything useful. Everyone else might be moving on, or pretending they're not still counting the days Yin has been missing, but not me. Under the surface I'm not just paddling, but kicking anything in sight.

'Great party last week, Grace.' I back away fast, clutching my book.

If I needed further proof that the library is a nightmare if you don't want to run into people, around the very next corner Art Class Chloe is practically living in the stacks, confirming several of my suspicions about her. She is kneeling on the ground, surrounded by folders and pencils and looking at several million art books.

'Please save me from an awkward situation,' I say, with maybe too much desperation. I'm too weird for my own good sometimes. Too weird for even the official weirdos. I sit near her on the floor.

Chloe looks startled and more than a little wary. I decide right here and now, looking at her geeky glasses and her high ponytail, that she's so uncool she has come out the other side as very cool.

'What awkward situation?' She cranes her head, trying to see who's nearby.

'Never mind. It's not important.'

I take a look at the scatter of books she's pulled off the shelf.

'Ms Nouri recommended these,' she says. 'I'm struggling with our self-portrait. And our main assessment too. All of it really.'

I have no reason at all to talk to her. I clutch for what we have in common. I'd better not mention accidentally blinding Petra in PE and how Chloe swept in like Mother Teresa and nursed her back to health.

'Art prize. Are you doing it?' I say.

'I don't know. No. I don't think so. Why does everyone keep asking that? Are you?'

I snort. I took Art because it's easier than taking politics or another language. I clock Chloe's list of artists, written neatly in her exercise book, and the ripped up pieces of scrap paper she's using as bookmarks, and her bulging sketchbook and the photocopies she's made. For someone who isn't entering the prize and says she's struggling, she sure is doing a lot of work.

There are people like Sarah, who think they have

something amazing to offer the world, and who do not in fact have anything to offer, and simply want to be internet famous. And then there are people like Chloe. She has plenty of interesting things to say, and yet she persists in acting like a creature lying at the bottom of a lagoon covered in mud, like a mythical mega-slug. Am I the only one who notices these things?

'You should enter,' I tell her. 'I can tell you love that class and you love Ms Nouri. God knows why, but you like that sad, hairy lady. And you're actually talented, so you should. I'd go for it myself if I wasn't completely hopeless and lazy, and I'll drop out of school if Audrey wins again.'

She looks at me with surprised hazel eyes and doesn't seem to have anything to say to that, and then my cheeks start to go pink.

'Well anyway—' I say, right at the same moment she says, 'I'll think about it?'

And then it's even more awks for sure and I juggle the paperback I took off the shelves from hand to hand and Chloe jumps in, trying to save this sinking ship.

'The real history of Hanging Rock is more interesting than that book.'

'You've read it already?'

Chloe nods but only for a split second before she realises she has done a big fat nerd tell. She read this term's English texts last holidays, in advance, I know it. Maybe she even read them all before the beginning of the year.

'All that spooky fictional stuff distracts from the actual meaning and history, which is that the rock is an important ceremonial place, and huge numbers of the traditional owners were murdered in the area by settlers or died from introduced disease or got forcibly moved to missions.'

I look doubtfully at the beautiful lily-white girl on the cover. 'That's…disturbing,' I say, and then I run out of things to add. I focus all my mental energy on the carpet beneath me, but the floor refuses to gape open and swallow me. I didn't do anything to stop that tasteless too-many-Asians conversation in art class and now I have nothing to say about our country's genocide so I'm pretty much living up to the low standard of who I'm supposed to be.

'Look up the history,' says Chloe. 'It's true.'

'I will.' I rise to my feet and I'm about to go when I turn back and say, 'Do you know why we're not studying this anymore?'

Chloe's cheeks are flushed; she blushes a lot when people speak to her. 'I guess, because it's about missing girls?'

That sort of stops me dead for a moment and then I do this jerky head nod and continue on my way, singing to myself *la la la* because it seems like the teachers actively want us to never think about Yin again and at the loans desk Mrs Berryman looks at me like I'm trying to steal *Picnic at Hanging Rock*, not borrow it.

'It's not on your English list anymore,' she says.

'I know.' I slap my library card down. 'And yet, here I am.'

I put my world-mufflers back on while she says something else, but she might as well be talking to me through a tin can and string. No, scratch that. She might as well be talking to me from a very distant planet.

The pretence of normal lasts until about two minutes into History when Mr Wright announces that a police officer is gatecrashing and before you know it, there she is in the doorway.

They've picked a young policewoman so that we can relate to her and everything, but quite frankly I'm surprised that Mrs Christie has let us be exposed to the people in blue at all. The principal has been blowing off steam about predatory journalists after several students were approached at the Junction last week, and you pretty much get the feeling she would like to turn Balmoral into a moat-circled fortress, inside of which we put equal effort into protecting our virginities and our grades.

This is how the policewoman starts:

'Hi, I'm Celeste, and I'm part of the team investigating Yin's disappearance.'

She uses Yin's name, but she doesn't say 'home invasion' or 'abduction' like they do on the news. Disappearance is a watered-down, inaccurate word and I immediately get an itch on the back of my knees.

The policewoman sits on the edge of the teacher's desk, like Nouri does, and she kicks her feet as she talks and she has her hair in a low bun and they've picked her well because with her countryish round freckled face you might trust her so much you'd be able to tell her anything.

'It must have been a really scary couple of weeks for you, so I've come in today to tell you what's going on and answer any questions you have.'

She runs over the official police line, but it's the same as what's on the TV and in the papers and what I hear when I eavesdrop on my parents' phone calls to their friends by picking up the spare phone in the entertainment room. My head starts up with the *blah blah blah* and prickly fire creeps up my legs and I have to refocus hard.

'We have forty people working on this case, and we're looking at every possible angle and taking every phone call we receive very seriously. We're working around the clock to find Yin, and we want to get her home as much as you do.'

She makes it sound like they can bring Yin home, like that's still a possibility, but that can't be true, can it? Not now. The hot prickles wrap around me and it's unbearable but I stay still in this forest of alert green-and-orange backs and watch.

What I see is that Petra sits straightest of all in the front row, with her hands resting on a piece of paper covered with writing, staring at the policewoman like she would never break eye contact in a million years, not even if the room caught on fire. This is normal for Petra, because she is literally trying to hoover the knowledge from every corner of the room, all the time, and you can't even stand near her for fear of your brain getting vacuumed. But there's an extra level of hoovering today.

We're all listening when the policewoman says, 'I know you've been told not to talk to the media, so I have to tell you that some outlets will be running reports this week on something new. The police will be confirming at a press conference very soon that we're looking for a serial offender.'

Petra jolts in her seat like she's received an electric shock, but the rest of the class are a little more confused, looking at their friends, screwing up their faces.

'What that means is that we're now certain that we're looking for someone who has done this before.'

That sets everyone whispering, wriggling, flapping. Celeste soldiers on calmly.

'In the next few days we'll be releasing a detailed profile of who we're looking for, what this person might be like. What the media will say is that this person has to be connected with your school.'

Celeste scans the room, grave but calm. A buzzing noise builds in my head, threatening to drown everything out. I shouldn't be confused at all because I remember what Ol' X-Ray-Eyes Chapman said about the FBI and this is probably what he meant. A profile.

'That connection is not confirmed. This person might be connected with Balmoral, maybe even very remotely connected, or they might have nothing to do at all with your school. We're considering a large number of cases to determine if they're linked. Are there any questions?'

Is it more likely that Yin is dead now, or less likely? Wasps are loose in the room.

Milla puts up her hand. 'Why did you let the guy on the CCTV footage go?'

'We investigated him thoroughly. He has no criminal record, a solid alibi for the night in question, and no unexplained absences.'

'What do you mean by "unexplained absences"? Is that

something we should be looking for?' Anusha forgets to raise her hand.

'It means if someone suddenly changes their routine and is out of the house a lot more, or goes on holidays or weekends away more than usual. That's all.'

I try to will someone to ask the right questions, but they don't. My earlobes get oh-so-hot so I tug on them and still the buzzing grows louder.

Bridie lifts her hand. 'Is it true that we should pee ourselves if someone attacks us? Or say we have our period?'

Our self-defence teacher had been no help on this matter. Mr Wright tries to chameleon himself into the whiteboard.

Celeste is stoic. 'If you ever feel physically threatened by anyone it's better to focus on getting away from them, or attracting attention and help.'

This isn't enough for Bridie. 'I have another one. Should we try to escape or should we not try to escape?'

Everyone knows that she's asking because of the 'In the Unlikely Event of' email.

'No one involved in the investigation thinks that this offender will strike again in the near future,' is all that Celeste will say.

Predictably, Petra's hand shoots up, shoots for the sky. She wiggles her fingers and bounces in her seat like we all used to do in Junior School before we realised how dorky that looks.

'About the profile and the other cases and the possible connection to the school,' she says in that posh debating-team voice of hers. She's holding a piece of paper in her hands as if she's prepared notes for a speech. 'What about Emma-Maree Jones? Don't you think that her abduction is important? She was on the waiting list for Balmoral.'

Celeste finally looks freaked. She whispers to Mr Wright and he hands her a whiteboard marker. He has to push her over to the smart-board side so she doesn't write on the actual wall. She writes 'PREJUDICIAL' in large letters on the board.

'We understand that you're all really worried about Yin, and you need to air your worries, but some of the information that's being shared could affect the court case when we catch the perpetrator.'

Petra's arm goes ballistic again but Celeste ignores it.

'We've already had to shut down the "Find Yin Mitchell" page and a few others that have cropped up. It's not because we don't want you to be informed, it's because we're trying to protect the investigation, and Yin and her family.'

'I know what prejudicial means,' Petra calls out again in a desperate voice. 'My father is a barrister. But you haven't answered my question.'

Before I know what's happening my arm shoots up, pushing through the hot prickling and the buzzing. I look up at it in surprise, as if it's not attached to my body. Celeste looks relieved to take my question instead of answering Petra's.

The words tumble out hard and fast like marbles.

'Firstly, is it true that most kidnap victims are dead within the first twenty-four hours of being taken?'

The room gasps and grows restless. Petra turns in her seat

with her mouth hanging open. I realise that what I really, really want is to smash everything in here: the mood, the hope, the furniture.

'Secondly, why are you saying "the person" and "the perpetrator" when really what you mean is "the man"? It's a guy we're looking for, everyone knows that it's men that do this sort of thing, and they're likely to keep going until they're caught. You only have to look at the statistics.'

My voice is loud and powerful. Everyone turns to look at me.

Mr Wright looks plenty red in the face. He actually gets a hankie out of his pocket and wipes his forehead. I've probably offended him in his sensitive man parts.

Petra speaks again. 'There are a few cases where married couples have killed together...' Her voice trails off when she sees the way I look at her.

I realise that sometime in the last minute I've stood up. 'Just tell us, is she still alive, or not?'

Celeste looks genuinely stricken. 'I'm so sorry, I know how difficult this is, but we don't know. We're trying to remain hopeful.' She walks around the room, handing out her business card to each of us, along with an understanding look. 'You can contact me about anything. I realise it's a lot to ask, but if you could keep what we've discussed today within your school friends and family, that would help us a lot.'

Mr Wright claps his hands, probably keen to put a stop to all the emotion. 'Thank you, officer.' He escorts her to the door.

The class erupts, and for once Mr Wright doesn't try to contain it. When the sound dies down slightly he raises his hands.

'Girls, can I remind you that Miss Starcke and Mr O'Connor are available to speak to if you're worried about this.'

No one listens to him.

While everyone is deep in conversation I zip over to Petra's desk and grab her sheet of paper. Audrey is telling her how amazing her questions were and Petra is lapping it up as she always does.

'I need to go to the bathroom,' I tell Mr Wright and he can't stop me.

Celeste the policewoman is still visible at the end of the corridor but I'm only interested in Petra's piece of paper. I slump against the lockers to read it.

6 years ago—Lisa Wu—10 years old—abduction, 2 hours, returned safely, no connection to Balmoral?

5 years ago—Emma-Maree Jones—12 years old—attempted abduction, on waiting list for Balmoral

3 years ago—Karolina Bauer—14 years old—abduction, 20 hours, returned safely, exchange student at Balmoral

2 weeks ago—Yin Mitchell—16 years old—abduction, Balmoral student, still not returned

The list is so clinical, so unexpected.

I look at the words 'returned safely' next to Lisa Wu and Karolina Bauer's names. Why is it different with Yin? Two weeks have passed, which is so much more than twenty hours, so why hasn't she been released?

The bell must have rung because the corridor floods with girls. A pair of shiny shoes come into my line of vision. Petra stands with her hand out, a tight expression on her face.

'Where did you get this from?' I ask.

'It's mostly from the *Cold Crimes* website.' She swallows. Her voice is barely audible above the clamour of locker doors slamming and people stampeding their way to the next class. 'There are a lot of people interested in the case and they post and share information in online forums. I've been doing my own research. It's been obvious from the start that it's a serial offender, but it's very significant that the police are making it official now.'

'*Cold Crimes.*' I file the name away. I hadn't thought to look at any forums. 'What are you, a girl detective?'

'It's wrong to assume we can't do anything. Last year there was a group of high school reporters who interviewed their new principal and exposed her as a fraud. It turned out her resume was completely fabricated. So.' Petra waits but I don't respond. 'Can I please have it back now?'

My head is busy, full, exploding. 'No. I'm keeping it.'

Petra opens her mouth to argue but then closes it, perhaps remembering self-defence class. Instead of leaving though, she lingers.

'What?'

'Yin lent me her physics notes.' Petra swallows hard. 'You know, before she disappeared. Now I don't know what to do with them…do you think I should give them to a teacher? Or her parents?'

'Can't you hang onto them?'

But I can tell from Petra's face that she doesn't want something belonging to a maybe-dead girl in her possession.

'It seems wrong to throw them out.' Pause. 'She was so generous to loan them to me. Especially because we were—I mean, we are—neck-and-neck, grades-wise.'

I can picture Petra harassing the Mitchells or the police with this. 'Give them to me if it's bothering you so much.'

'No, no, I'll use them. We've got a test coming up.' Petra has blushed from her toes to her scalp. 'She was better than me. Nicer. And a better clarinet player too. Perfect tone.'

She's being strange and I don't like it. The vibrating restarts in my body, from the feet up.

'Are you done?' It comes out harsher than I mean it to.

Petra backs away incrementally, then turns properly. Audrey is waiting for her by the water bubbler, a snarky look on her face. I wiggle my fingers at her and smile wide and fake, because it drives Audrey wild with jealousy whenever Petra gets chummy with anyone who isn't a boarder and who she can't keep her big green eyes on.

'Don't worry—I'm not stealing your wife!' I yell.

Somehow I've come down with a cold on the way home from school. My skin is on fire and my head aches so I put on my favourite soft-as-marshmallow pyjamas and light all of my candles all at once and can't put down *Picnic at Hanging Rock* once I've started.

It's the turn of the century and a party of girls and teachers from a ritzy private boarding school go on an excursion to Hanging Rock, which the traditional and rightful owners call Ngannelong because after what Chloe said I'm not going to be totally ignorant, and after lunch when everyone is sated and languid four of the schoolgirls walk off on their own.

Even though the language is outdated and there are descriptions that go on for half a page and the author is totally obsessed with 'bosoms', the school and the teachers in the book aren't that different to Balmoral, not really. And from the moment the group of young girls go off on their own, my skin starts to tingle.

I can see them, in their long white dresses, pale and hopeless and weak, the opposite of angry modern girls. The massive Rock looms, wild and covered with trees, full of dark crevasses and winding tracks that lead nowhere. These floppy, flower-petal girls are no match for it, I can feel it already.

Something bad is going to happen to them.

Dylan Thomas slides under the covers with me, leaving only the tip of his tail poking out. I let the bad feelings I've been keeping at bay seep into bed with me too, a familiar pressing, hovering grey cloud.

Serial offender. Connected with the school. Detailed profile. Returned safely.

I breathe in the grey cloud and it's a relief to give into the fog for once. Dylan Thomas presses into my side and rumbles like a tiny tiger.

✦

The messages start at 9 p.m., while everyone is watching the late news. The police have held the predicted press conference and the profile has been released.

I click the link that Marley has sent us. 'HUNT FOR DOCTOR CALM', says the headline.

Doctor Calm is the name the media have invented for Yin's abductor, a fancy villain name for a monster who can't be stopped. I try to read the report, take it all in, but my head swims.

Sarah follows up quickly with the video of the press conference. I put my headphones on and the quilt over my head.

Senior Detective Zambesi, the head of the newly-named Operation Panopticon, speaks as cameras flash around him and microphones cluster. He has a craggy, Hollywood-handsome face and the reporters love him.

'As you're aware, Karolina Bauer attended the same school as Yin Mitchell for a period of one year as an exchange student. We can now confirm that an earlier case, that of Emma-Maree Jones, also has connections to the school. That young girl had her name on a waiting list to attend the school when she reached Year Seven.'

Petra was right.

One of the reporters asks a question, but it's hard to hear what she's saying.

'I can't comment on any other cases,' replies Zambesi.

'How many abductions or assaults do you think Doctor Calm may be responsible for?' another reporter asks.

'That's your name, not mine.' Zambesi's mouth tightens

with annoyance. The reporters clamour for attention but he holds up his hand.

'Our main objective today is to tell you what we know about this man. He is between the ages of thirty and fifty, with medium skin tone. He is of average height, or tall with a slight stoop, and of average build. He is highly educated and well spoken. He may be in a prominent or respected position in the community, and it's possible he has a job in which he travels frequently. Friends or family will know him to be a gentle and reserved person, and would be shocked to learn he is capable of violence.'

'Make no mistake, we are looking for an extremely dangerous criminal. His methods are thorough and he may have some knowledge of police procedure. We are looking for an unusually intelligent individual who will not stop until he is caught.'

He calls an end to the press conference, even though the reporters are still wetting their jocks and yelling out questions.

I sit on my bed and let it sink in. I wasn't expecting them to describe someone so completely bland. Beige beige unusually intelligent beige. A forgettable man with an unforgettable name.

I shut the computer. I try hard not to be sick.

It's pointless even thinking about any of this police stuff. What can we do with the profile anyway? They don't want us to discuss the case online. The teachers won't tell us anything, and our parents don't seem to know. Would they even listen to us if we went to them with information? I picture telling a teacher or police officer about Mr Chapman staring at my tits and emitting sleazy vibes and even I can acknowledge how tenuous it sounds.

The *Hanging Rock* cover girl stares at me from my bedside table, ethereal, blonde and disappeared. Miranda. She acted strange right before she went missing.

I saw Yin in the hallway on the Friday before she was taken. Normally we ignore each other—so studiously, so completely I'm surprised no one notices—but this time we stood and looked at each other, eye to eye, for a few seconds. It was odd. Had she been trying to tell me something? Did she have a premonition that something was about to go wrong?

If Yin had been trying to send me a message that day, I didn't receive it. Sarah came up behind me and leapt on my shoulders, and we both turned away slowly, Yin and I, like ships trying not to collide.

Ally stands on Marley's bed and reads from a phone.

'Number one: reach ten thousand followers. Number two: make out with someone famous. Number three: take Luca Henning-Smith to the formal. Number four: win Regatta.'

As per usual we are getting ready at Marley's house because her parents are the slackest and her room hangs right off the back of the warehouse, almost like she has her own apartment.

We're not being quiet enough, because Ally gets pissy, or as pissy as Ally gets, which is not very. 'Shh, you guys! Listen.'

'You're not going to do any of those things,' I say from my position at the mirror. Ally has a floppy headband on that definitely has to come off before we leave the house. Her legs are still covered in bruises from self-defence class. Ally has tissue-paper skin, she's as delicate as the princess lying on the pea.

Even though I'm here in the room with my friends, my mind keeps wandering back to Wednesday in the library and wondering what Chloe thinks of me. Few people can make me that off-kilter.

Why did I even go up to her in the first place? She likes it at the bottom of her lagoon and I came along and disturbed her moss, her leaf litter, her driftwood, her algae.

'Tal, are you even listening?' Ally puts her hands on her hips. 'It's not my list, it's Sarah's.'

On cue, Sarah yells, 'Someone proper famous! I want

you to know that. Not D-list famous. And I've got to get this done this year, or by the end of summer, at the latest.'

Both have started early on the vodka, way too early in my humble opinion.

Ally loses steam and slumps to her knees, burying her face in the covers. 'We shouldn't have to make bucket lists at our age. It's depressing.'

She pauses then adds, because Marley has been on anti depressants all year, 'Sorry Marls, I didn't mean that.'

'No probs.' Nothing much touches Marley. She keeps scrolling on her iPad. In between scrolls she grabs a Tim Tam from an open pack. Ally and Sarah ignore the biscuits, because they're in a yearlong competition to see who can eat the least.

'If you want to try pot, I think I know someone who can get some,' Marley offers.

I feign surprise. 'Your parents make you pay?'

'Ha ha.' Marley throws a Tim Tam at my head, and misses.

Marley's parents are rock-and-roll royalty without actually being musicians. They own practically this whole factory block—the warehouse, the rehearsal rooms and the recording studios—and for all we know maybe they do deal pot on the side.

I smooth on more BB cream to cover the red marks on my chin. Too much of my brain is taken up with wondering why the media is calling him Doctor Calm. It's a messed-up name—it makes me think of surgery masks and bright lights and big syringes.

'Why've you got so much eyeliner on? You look like that goth from Art.' Sarah tries to hand me the vodka bottle but I wave it away.

Marley's makeup is spread all over the vanity. Her mum buys the expensive stuff, the kind that comes with toiletry bags full of free gifts. Usually Sarah is in charge of eyes, because she's got the steadiest hand, but she's already too smashed. Her lipstick is wonky, but I don't plan on pointing that out to her.

Sarah pushes Ally's feet away from her. 'When are you going to change those?'

'They're my good-luck socks,' Ally protests. 'I can't take them off, they could be the only thing keeping me alive.'

'Well, just so you know, you're killing me with the smell.'

My makeup inspiration for the evening is: Teen Crystal Warrior Queen. I've used about five different types of highlighter to achieve the Opal clan's updated look. 'I don't expect you to understand,' I say mildly. It's embarassing to go around looking the same as your friends anyway. I leave the zip on my stolen satin jacket at half-mast to maximise my boobs. Nice.

'Have you seen this Report Card thing? People rate their teachers. Balmoral's on it, there are twenty-three teachers listed.' Marley reads from the screen. 'Mrs Wang, Ms Baker, Ms Nouri...*Ms Nouri needs to get some waxing strips immediately*—ha! *Interesting fashion sense because she dresses like a medieval peasant.* That's accurate. Mr Purdy, Mr Scrutton.'

'Read about Purdy.' I had him last year and it's fair to say we had a major personality clash.

'*Mr Purdy blocks every website on the internet when we're in the labs, plus he's moody*—oh, that's an old comment, he's been at the school forever. Hang on. *Mr Purdy is creepy, he sits with his legs wide open to show off his family jewels*.'

'More.' Sarah is agog. She feeds off the comments section.

Marley continues. '*At first I really liked having him as my teacher but then he started creeping me out…people like him because he's slack and tells us what's on the test but sometimes he says inappropriate things*. Um, then there's: *This one time when he was handing back my exam he deliberately brushed my hand and I'd bet anything that he's Doctor Calm*.'

Sarah is enraged by this.

'What? Noooo! It's Tyrone, the hot serial killer photographer. Gimme that.'

She grabs the iPad. 'I'm making an entry for him. *Tyrone Martell is the school photographer and he's a sex manic and perv and if anyone should be the main suspect of being Doctor Calm, it's him. If you search his house you'll find photos of the students with the most developed breasts*. There. You should all put comments too.'

'Maniac,' contributes Ally, 'Not manic.'

'He doesn't fit the police profile.' I'm gripping the mascara wand so hard it might snap. 'No one we know does.'

'Is Mrs Mancini on there?' Ally asks. 'She promised that we could watch a movie on the last day of term, then she wouldn't let us and I complained, and she goes, "Don't put lies in my mouth, Allison."'

Marley swings her fancy Bao Bao bag. 'Tal, shouldn't we get going soon? Mark and Ben and the others said they'd meet us there.'

For a second I can't take how immature it all is, and then I imagine the girls from *Picnic at Hanging Rock* superimposed over my friends, imagine that they're excited about a wholesome picnic in the bush rather than getting groped by Grammar boys at Shelter.

The illusion doesn't even hold for a second. Sarah is splotchy from booze, Marley's under the impression that she's wearing pants when in fact she's not, and Ally looks like an adorable little girl. I hug her. She smells of Marc Jacobs Daisy and fierce liquor and arranges her thin arms around my neck like a toy monkey.

I whisper in her ear. 'I saw you sniff Marley's pillow. Pervert.'

Ally squeals and pushes me away. 'Taaalll! I did not!'

She's traffic-light red, burning up with guilt, even though I made the whole thing up. I'm full of a bursting mean, poking feeling. I want someone to ask me about Yin so I can tell them to shut their faces. I've been waiting for someone to finally inevitably actually be brave enough to say something to me about her out loud.

'We'll go to the park for a bit,' I announce, 'then Shelter.'

They don't dispute the schedule, they never do.


'I'm cold,' complains Ally. 'And bored.'

Her whining is irritating, even though I agree with her assessment. There's fog hanging low on the grass, and clouds billow from our mouths.

Sarah is flat-out on the merry-go-round, kicking at the ground to spin herself around and checking her phone at the same time. 'What are we still doing here?'

'No one gets there that early.' I sit at the top of the slide and can't imagine why I was ever scared of sliding down it.

'I hope tonight's better than Grace's,' says Ally.

'That won't be hard,' Sarah says, even though all the pics she posted of Grace's party online made it look like she was having the time of her life.

The park perches at the top of Bleecker's Hill, and the whole city is visible as a glowing strip along the horizon. I still haven't had a drink, but no one has noticed. I'm tilted sideways as it is, a couple of degrees off, followed around by shadows and reflections.

Mum and Dad didn't want me 'prowling the streets' tonight so I lied and said that Marley's parents were dropping us off and picking us up too. We're too many to attack, but someone could easily be watching us, waiting for a sheep to drift from the pack. All our parents made us switch on location services and Find My Phone before we were allowed out, like a thin slice of electronics can protect anyone from anything.

Marley totters back from the nearby bushes, trying to straighten her tights. Her bracelets shine in the dark.

'I remembered something I have to tell you,' she says. 'Mum gave me a Zen book. It says that an individual life is a wave in the ocean. The wave rises up and exists, and then it disappears back into the ocean. The wave is gone, but the ocean continues.'

'That's amazing.' Ally looks at me. She's sitting on a wobbly seat shaped like a chicken. 'Don't you think?'

I turn my eyes to the darkest corners of the park and say nothing because that is the dippiest thing I've ever heard. Who wants to be a fucking *wave* when you could be the ocean?

I examine the line of trees at the edges of the oval, the bit where the ground dips steeply, and the barely lit football club building near the car park. There are houses not too far away, but the eucalypts and ti-trees form a thick barricade around the reserve. Every few minutes there's the faint growl of a car driving along the crescent.

A memory crawls out of the shadows, as thin and insubstantial as a ghost. When I open my mouth, steam clouds spill out, and words too.

'When I was eleven we went camping in a national park,' I say, 'and got lost out in the trees. I went for a walk and stomped around until I couldn't recognise anything. When I realised, I tried to go back the way I'd come, but the campsite wasn't there. I walked around and around in circles until all the trees and tracks looked exactly the same.'

Yin had been there as well, of course, but I don't say that. After two hours of walking we'd both started to cry, tears and snot and dust mixing on our faces. It got dark early, and it wasn't until the first stars were visible that we'd heard Mr Mitchell cooee in the distance.

I erase Yin from my story, snipping her out neatly. It's not difficult to do; I've been doing it ever since we started high school, when I realised that she wasn't going to keep up. Even in the first weeks of Year Seven I could tell which girls I should make friends with, which older girls I should emulate.

Yin couldn't be part of the project, and so I cast her off. She went quietly, that was always her problem. You have to fight in life to get what you deserve. She should have fought harder.

Shelter is only just beginning to fill up when we arrive. If we'd got here at nine, like Sarah wanted to, we'd have been dweebs sitting around on the couches, waiting for things to get started. It's not rocket science, but I'm the only one who seems to understand these things.

I hang in the shadows near the pool table while Sarah and Ally talk to Bill and Ben the Private-School Chinos Men. Sarah and Ally both acted more sober than they actually are for the bouncers, and now they're pretending to be drunker than they actually are for the boys. Thanks to my impeccable planning skills, the boys were excited to see them arrive, rather than the other way around. Sarah is leaning up against Bill/Ben's shoulder, faux-laughing. He flicks his floppy blonde angel curls, looking like he keeps Rohypnol in his pocket.

I already need to pee, but I don't want to go through 'the carwash'—the narrow corridor to the bathrooms where boys congregate on either side and try to grab parts of your body.

Shelter is almost over, let's be honest. There are some kids who look barely thirteen and we're definitely the oldest ones here. If you turned on the lights and turned off the smoke machine and the music, all you'd have is a bunch of loser teenagers sitting around drinking coke.

Liv has offered to get me a fake ID so I can go to real

clubs. But when I think about hauling everyone around town with me, pantless and tipsy and way-too-excited, it exhausts me. Maybe all my friendships are dissolving right before my eyes, maybe the group is too hard to keep together, maybe I can't be bothered anymore.

The dance floor is aquatic, with purple-tinged arms waving in the air like seaweed. I keep my eyes on Marley in the middle, happily drowning, and I smile a little. The girl can dance, I'll give her that much.

In *Picnic at Hanging Rock* you never find out exactly what happens to the girls, but there are hints. That's probably why it was on the English list in the first place, so the teachers could wring the joy out of it with endless theories.

I don't need to theorise; I know what happened to those girls.

They followed vixeny Miranda through a crack in the rock, through an almost-invisible tear in the fabric of the universe.

I imagine the cracks that might exist in our daily lives, in ordinary places. Secret doors at school, jagged edges of air that don't match up at the train station. Fractures leading to another world. Where do they go, those girls that accidentally fall through a gap in the universe? What's on the other side?

I blink. The lasers sweep across the dance floor and I can't see Marley. It takes me a few seconds to locate her again. My heart keeps beating.

There's a boy standing at the edges of the dance floor, watching me. He's tall, with a shaved head.

His friends orbit around him in a way that suggests he's the male version of me. You can tell they're not private school boys, because they don't look like their mothers have dressed them.

I pull the V of my bomber jacket down until it sits in a better place.

Their tall leader pushes off the wall and saunters towards me. I do the same and meet him in the middle.

In unspoken agreement, we make our way to the multi-storey car park next door.

The car park is open at the sides, the concrete floors and pillars recycling the cold, whipping it down ramps and slaloming it through rows of parked cars. I'm forced to zip up my jacket.

His name is Marcel and he goes to a performing arts high school I've never heard of. When I tell him about Balmoral, he shrugs. He stops next to the fire escape door and I get a chance to look at him properly. He's beautiful, I'll admit it, with perfect skin and huge eyes.

Now that we're here, who's going to make the first move? Things are a small step away from getting awkward.

'So, um, what year are you in?' Marcel says eventually.

'Ten,' I answer. 'How about you?'

He dips his head, smiles. When he raises his eyes again, he looks defiant. 'Year Nine.'

I can't keep the shock out of my voice. 'How old are you?' He towers over me.

'Fifteen.'

'I'm sixteen.' I shake my head. If this gets out, I'll never live it down.

Marcel smiles. 'Well…I like older women?'

I smile back.

He reaches out and traces a finger around the outside curve of my breast, making me draw breath. 'You're really hot,' he says.

He stoops and kisses my collarbone, then lower, pushing my tits up with both hands. He moves back up to my neck, the space below my ear lobes, then finally, my mouth. His lips and tongue are hot and wet, he kisses like he has plenty of experience. When he pushes me through the doorway and into the stairwell, I relax and let him. My back rests against the cold concrete wall.

Marcel presses his whole body against mine, and finally all the thoughts and visions from these last few weeks melt away. The ghosts creep back into the dark corners.

Marcel has a stubbly scalp and ridges of muscle on his arms. Skin on skin and soft mouths and I don't see flashing blue lights and think about how I gave up on Yin long before she disappeared and maybe now I'm going to pay for it. We steam up the whole stairwell. We're both out of breath when Marcel finally pulls away.

'You know,' he says, a newly sheepish and innocent expression filling his face. 'I've never had a blowjob.'

I stare back. The lone light bulb in the corner casts distorting shadows over his gorgeous face. He's batting his eyelashes with the best of them, namely me. I know his game. I tilt my chin and the corners of his mouth twitch.

'Liar!' I say. 'You big fat liar.'

He smiles with full brilliance, dazzling teeth in the darkness. 'It was worth a try, wasn't it?'

'Here's a deal,' I say, once I've made up my mind. 'I'll use my hands.'

I close the front door so gently it makes almost no sound. The lights are on in the back half of the house. I shuck off my coat, kick off my shoes and pad to the kitchen, where I spit my chewy in the bin and fill a glass of water.

It's not until I turn towards my bedroom that I see Mum sitting very still at the dining table. I almost drop my glass.

'Mum! What are you doing up?'

As long as I message her at a decent hour and promise to taxi home, she doesn't wait up. There's a bottle of wine and a glass on the table, and a stack of books. Mum is barefaced, her hair frizzy. Sometimes she looks so washed-out and saggy I have to promise myself I'll never let things get that bad.

'I couldn't sleep, hon.' She rubs her eyes. 'I haven't been sleeping in general.'

'What are you looking at?'

She shows me.

An old photo album, open on somebody's birthday party. Yin is right up in the camera, face painted, grinning with one tooth missing. A slap in the face.

'I had no idea you kept these.'

It never occurred to me that Yin would be on Mum's mind too. She sinks underneath me when I put my hand on her shoulder. I can see the weekend paper peeking out from underneath the photo albums, Yin's photo on the front yet again.

I don't want to step too close with my night-out grottiness, the debauchery behind my minty breath, the details of what I'd done with Marcel lurking in my eyes. It's not often I wish I could be Mum and Dad's little girl again, but perhaps tonight is one of those times.

The wine bottle is empty though, so I'm probably safe.

'What did you used to say?' I point at a photo of Yin and I with our heads together, my hair shockingly white-blonde, hers as black as it comes.

'Double the cute, that's what I used to say,' says Mum. 'You had the Polish hair. Mine was the same colour at that age.'

The remaining photos show us in a whirl of colour and activity as the party games heat up—musical chairs, giant's treasure, pass-the-parcel. In the background is Mum, blurry, and Yin's mum, right off to the side. Pages of half-forgotten dreams.

'Were you friends with Chunjuan back then?'

I can't remember our mums together, but they must have spent time in the same places, while Yin and I played. They must have talked on the phone and dropped us off at each other's houses.

'I suppose so…I found her hard to figure out though. Her work was so demanding and she was so serious. We would only talk about you kids, nothing else. I got along with Stephen—Mr Mitchell—better. Once he was on the scene.'

I'd forgotten how much time I used to spend at the Mitchells' house. Chunjuan fed me and made up a blow-up bed for me on Yin's floor and left out a clean towel and face washer for me when I stayed over and washed my knees when I scraped them and patiently watched the silly plays Yin and I performed using our dolls.

'I can't stop thinking about her trapped in that bathroom,' Mum says. 'What she's going through.'

I've hardly thought about Chunjuan at all these last two weeks. Sometimes, I'm scum.

'Is Dad home?'

Mum nods and turns to look me up and down and I am definitely not her little girl anymore.

'What are you wearing?' She tsks, so she can't be that tired. 'Oh Tal, it's like feminism never happened.'

'Technically speaking, I have the right to wear whatever I want,' I say in an oratory style, because this is well-worn territory with us, 'even though some of my choices could be seen as perpetuating objectification.'

'You do listen.' She sounds surprised.

'I listen to everything you say, Mummy dearest. But I still don't think it's my job to take care of other people's outdated attitudes. Or their lack of control.'

'I know.' Her arms and legs are dangling, the chair barely holding her. 'I don't disagree. But it's different when it's your daughter. As soon as you turned fourteen and men started looking at you—'

That makes me laugh, one sharp, loud, 'Ha!'

'What?'

'Oh, Ma. Try eleven. There were pervs looking at me in Junior School.'

I lean in to kiss her shocked cheek, she grabs my wrist. 'Sweetheart, how are you doing? Really.'

I don't like that 'really'.

'Fine.' I try to wrestle my arm free.

'It's good to talk. Don't you want to talk about it?'

'No.' I decide to be straightforward for once. 'I *really* don't.'

I pretend not to see the flash of hurt across her face.

'I'm always here,' she says and then she unlocks the handcuffs and my wrist is free and I ignore the invisible pull of her, which could destroy my composure so easily, and I slip away.

Even though I'm exhausted, sleep won't come. Little strips of street light show through my blinds.

Helicopters drone overhead, tracing circles over our suburb. There have been helicopters over our area more often recently. Every time I hear them I imagine a masked intruder running through backyards, climbing fences and darting down alleyways.

I watch the plain white ceiling of my bedroom, trying to imagine the inside of my head being as bland and empty as plaster. It doesn't really work.

When we were not-so-little, just before high school, Yin and I believed that we were linked psychically. Or perhaps I believed, and Yin went along with the idea to be supportive.

For years we'd communicated in fragments of our made-up language, and the summer before Year Seven we decided we could also talk with our eyes. We'd sit at the dining table and stare at each other, having long 'conversations', breaking into laughter only when someone asked why we were acting so strange.

And what did I do with that connection? Took a big pair of scissors and severed it, right across the middle, because it didn't suit me anymore, because I knew Yin wouldn't be cool or popular in high school, or stand out in the way that I wanted to.

But even after we stopped hanging out, I'd sometimes catch her eye across the assembly hall or netball court, and wonder if we were still talking without talking. Sometimes she would look sad, I could see it in her eyes.

I empty my head to match the ceiling, and wait to hear Yin's voice, calling out as if she was on a really bad phone line.

No voice comes.

*It's been three weeks since you were taken*, I say to her, silently. *I haven't known what to think, how to act, what to do. I can't figure out if there's any hope and how much I've lost.*

*Sorry*, I say, *sorry sorry. Can you forgive me?*

Radio silence. Yin isn't sending out signals to me anymore. But why should she?

# Chloe

**DAY 28**

Katie offers me a cigarette, and I take it even though I don't really smoke anymore. Maybe it will warm me up, because the bonfire isn't exactly blazing. We huddle around the struggling flames in Brandon's backyard, instead of retreating sensibly into the shelter of the house.

'I never see you anymore.' Katie and I pass a can of beer back and forth between us. It's quite the juggle with the smokes and the can.

I flip my hood up, stamp my feet. 'You wouldn't believe the homework they give us. I can barely keep up.'

'I got homework too, you know. Doesn't mean I'm gonna do it though.'

I give Katie a quick one-armed hug. She's a bag of bones wrapped in an oversized cardigan.

In theory I should be able to go to Balmoral and still see my Morrison friends on the weekends, but in practice it hasn't worked out that way, I'm not sure why. I haven't hung out with the whole group since Easter. It's not really homework getting in the way, that much I know.

On the other side of the fire, Katie's boyfriend Tim threads marshmallows onto sticks. Brandon's mum is framed perfectly in the kitchen window, dish brush in hand. Brandon pokes the fire with a broken cricket bat and looks confused about the lack of heat, even though we always have the same problem at the start of every spring.

It's a scene frozen in time from last year, the actors transported and arranged in almost identical positions. Nothing has changed with my friends, but maybe something has changed with me.

I've been trying all night, but nothing can hide the fact that I'm bored, and cold.

Brandon shoots me a slow, snaky look over his half-gallon man-cauldron. I think it's meant to be seductive, but I can't be sure. I turn to Katie.

'Things still good with Tim?'

'Yeah, guess so.' Katie stubs out her cigarette on the sole of her boots, flicks it into the non-fire. 'It's been eighteen months, so we're an old married couple, don't you know.'

She's joking, of course, but I wouldn't be surprised if that's the way it ends up, and for some reason that scares me, even though I like Tim.

Compared to Liana or me, Katie doesn't really want much—she doesn't want to travel, doesn't want to study after school. She likes to keep things simple. She's been made a supervisor at her cinema job, and they've promised to make her a manager as soon as she turns eighteen, so she'll be able to make real money and buy the car she's been saving for.

'You look happy,' I say, and she does. Old Katie used to be much pricklier than this.

'I see Brandon hasn't forgotten you.' Katie gives me a pointed look.

I'm saved by hot breath in my ear; Liana collars me from behind and smooshes her cheek against mine.

'Who can blame him, she's such a babe.'

I slap at her head blindly and she wriggles away, not wanting her look to get ruined. Liana's face is perfect as usual, her tan skin glowing, brows immaculate, eyeliner swooping in thick wings, highlighter making her cheekbones zing.

'Although, so far this year he's dated Teresa Vi Nguyen and Kristy Au, and made out with Glydel from Year Eleven,' she continues, 'so his yellow fever is real.'

'Real and deep,' Katie says to the bonfire.

'Yuck.' It grosses me out, but I don't want to think about it. 'You have to teach me how to do that braid.' I tug on Liana's hair. She's wearing the same Fuzzy Peach perfume that she's had since Year Seven.

'Hate to break it to you Chlo, but that's not all her real hair.' Katie pops another can.

Liana refuses to rise to the bait. Her hair has been down to her bum since she was eight. We have a pact to keep our hair long until we're eighteen. 'When are you coming back to Morrison, seriously?'

'I don't think I am.'

'Aren't you scared of Doctor Calm, though? I swear, Chlo, I'm worried about you, all the time.'

'They haven't proved he's connected to the school.' I take

the beer off Katie and drink until my smoky throat recovers.

Katie snorts. 'Yeah, he's connected! How clueless do they think we are?'

'It's wrong, that's what it is!' Liana's volume ramps up. 'They've got loads of money and they should be protecting you more. I can't believe there aren't security guards! If someone was snatching girls from my school, I'd get *armed* guards.'

'Won't matter,' says Katie. 'Because it'll turn out to be one of your teachers, of course. The one you least suspect.'

There had been a lot of gossip going around about various teachers, but the police profile seemed to have put an end to it. It said that the offender might travel with his job, and would definitely be away from home or work regularly. That couldn't be any of our teachers.

After the profile came out I thought it only had to be a matter of time before someone came forward, but nothing has happened. It's gotten awfully quiet around the school this week, and in the media too. We've had exams, and everyone has been studying.

'Listen,' Katie says, 'I heard that they've got new DNA evidence from an older case, and that they're getting things together for an arrest. Have you heard about that? Tim's cousin is in the police force.'

'I don't know.' I give the can to her.

'If you get taken…' Katie sips. 'The thing you're supposed to do is breathe in real deep when you're tied up, and then when you breathe out—bam! The ropes are loose.'

'Did you get that email too?' I can't believe it's travelled so far.

'We want you back!' The fire has finally caught, and orange light flickers across Liana's face. 'I always imagined we'd graduate together.'

I let her hug me. I imagined the same thing too, and that we could go to the same uni as well, even though Liana has been settled on Biomedical Science for ages and I have less of a clue than ever.

Katie wanders off to find more firewood. I'm left alone with Liana, so now's my chance.

'Hey, L, I was hoping you might be able to help me with an art project.'

'Yeah?' She looks interested so I plunge on. It's not like Liana hasn't posed for me in the past.

'I've decided to do a portrait for my final art project this year, and I need a model.'

'You want to paint me again?'

'No, I've been concentrating on photography recently.'

She screws up her face.

'I need to do something different,' I say quickly. 'Mix things up. I've already got enough sketches and paintings in my folio. Let me show you.'

I pull up some Bill Henson images on my phone, the ones that look like teenagers have had a wild night out, and Liana scrolls.

'Nope nope nope,' she says. 'They've hardly got any clothes on! You want me to flash this butt around in public? On a car bonnet?' She scrolls. 'Mum'd have a heart attack and they *will* throw me out of the church choir.'

'It's more the light and the mood. You don't have to

show any skin at all, if you don't want.'

In my folio I've pasted Henson images alongside Vermeer paintings as examples of the light and mood I'm trying to capture, as well as all sorts of other things that have caught my eye. Advertisements featuring sleeping or reclining women, exposed and abstracted parts of women's bodies, fairytale illustrations from falling-apart anthologies, newspaper snippets about missing women. I have no idea yet if any of it fits together.

'I thought we could go out to the netball courts at sunset?' There are rickety bleachers at the courts behind Meridian. If Liana sat right at the top, her hair might fly around in the wind, maybe the streetlights and the sky might combine to make something good.

Liana hands my phone back. 'Sorry babe, you know I'm way too self-conscious.'

'It's okay.' I half-knew she would say no. It would have been a nice excuse to spend more time with her.

'Why don't you stick to your drawings? They're so good.' Liana squeezes my arm. 'I've still got every single one you've given me.'

I stare at the rising flames.

I know Katie and Liana say they miss me, but no one has asked me about anything but the kidnapping. And while they've filled me in on the Morrison news, they don't seem that interested in what's going on in my life. I could tell them how I'm avoiding Dad's calls or that Arnold got in a fight with Ron and Pearl's cat or that I think Mum has a crush on someone at work but I can't figure out who.

'Shit!' Tim hops around the circle swearing. Dirty grey smoke plumes off his shoe. Brandon picks up the esky full of ice and instead of tipping it on Tim's foot, tips it over his head. Tim swears even more and starts swinging furiously at Brandon.

Liana immediately rushes towards them, getting the situation under control like she always does. In the kitchen window Mrs Barrie moves like an automaton, between bench and sink. She doesn't notice the chaos outside. I realise that I can't go back to Morrison, and I don't want to.

It's impossible not to be affected by the shiny, revving Balmoral girls who plan to climb confidently to the top, to be engineers and lawyers and surgeons and diplomats. They know they can be anything they want to be. Being around them has made me think differently about my own life, and what I expect from myself.

I remind myself about the outrageous levels of privilege my new classmates have, the money and opportunities thrown at them every day, not to mention that, despite their advantages, they seem overwhelmed half the time with eating disorders and anxiety and expectations, but I still feel like a traitor.

Katie couldn't care less about Tim's smoking foot. She rattles the empty beer can at me. 'You little cow. You drank it all.'

Mum is surprised when I get home. She puts down the fat crime novel she's been reading and pushes her empty chocolate wrapper between the couch cushions.

'I thought I was going to have to wait up until at least midnight worrying about you.'

'I'm tired.'

And hungry. I go to the kitchenette and grab a bag of rice crackers.

'How's everyone?' Mum yawns.

It's nice to see her relaxing for a change, on the couch in her sloppy tracky daks and old Nirvana t shirt. She's taken the next week off for annual leave and already has a stack of library books waiting for her.

'Fine.' I can barely talk around a massive crunchy mouthful of cracker. I check out her library haul on the bench as I chew.

Every crime novel has the same cover. Dark backgrounds with bold all-caps titles in white, blue or yellow. A surprising amount of them have dead girls or about-to-be-dead girls on the front cover. The blurbs speak of unhappy wives who drink so much they can't tell if they've seen a murder or not, women whose pasts have come back to haunt them, and promising young girls who'll never get to realise their dreams. The titles tell us how lost, how alone, how trapped all these lovely girls and women are.

Even though the photos are supposed to show some-thing raw and horrible, they're actually incredibly polished and posed and digitally altered. I look closely at *Blood Sisters*, which has the best cover. It fits right in with all the reference images I've been collecting for my project.

'Are you planning to elaborate on that?' Mum asks.

'Not right now, no.' I hold up *Blood Sisters*. 'Can I borrow this for a few days?'

I sit on my bed with my earbuds in, listening to music and flicking through the photos I took at Brandon's tonight. Selfies of Katie, Liana and I with our faces squished together. Was being at Morrison High the main thing we had in common? Is that all it takes to end friendships, a change of habit or routine? I thought we were stronger than that.

A hot whoosh of air rises through the vents in the floor and I realise that Sam has sneakily turned the heating on even though I tell him all the time we can't afford to turn it on every night.

When I go to the control panel in the dark hallway to turn it off, something shifts in the very corner of my vision, in the shadows.

My heart leaps for a brief moment, before I realise it's Sam, shuffling slowly out of his bedroom. A white smudge in the dark corridor, arms dangling by his sides. His eyes are open but he doesn't see anything.

I catch up to him in the middle of the living room, swaying uncertainly.

'Back to bed, Sam.' I take him by the shoulders and try to steer him gently back towards his room.

'I saw him,' he mumbles. 'Hiding…'

'You're sleepwalking, buddy. Come on.'

I walk him back to his room and tuck his covers around him after he lies down. I switch his old nightlight on, still plugged in at the socket, and stars made of light oscillate around the room.

The sleepwalking started just over a week ago, around

the time the media started calling Yin's abductor Doctor Calm. The name has invaded Sam's brain, we don't know how, because we've made sure he doesn't watch the news. They've probably been talking about it at school.

We keep finding Sam in random locations around the house, asleep and confused. He's fine during the day, but at night he roams.

I return to my room and check the latest news reports— my sick new ritual before going to sleep each night.

After four weeks most of the information is old. The only new thing is a sketch of a house that police say could be Doctor Calm's, made from evidence given by Karolina Bauer.

It's disconcerting how ordinary the house looks.

The bedroom has a double bed, two bedside tables, matching lamps with yellow lampshades. Striped drapes, tan carpet. A door to an ensuite bathroom.

White and tan tiles. Shower over the bath, half-screen door. Sink and vanity, wall radiator. Small frosted window up high, too high and too small to climb through.

It could be anyone's house.

Maybe there was a time when I thought the police had a chance of finding Yin, but if this is the best they've got— this, an identikit of someone in a balaclava and a pretty vague profile of an imaginary man—then there is no chance at all.

I lurk outside the art rooms like a super-creep. My folio is tagged with pink notes. The last week has been a frenzy of sketching, finding visual references and trying to make my ideas gel. I feel like Arnold when he's got the scent of something at the park and can't let it be.

All my other homework has fallen by the wayside. I can only hope my concept makes sense, and that I can get Bochen excited enough about my project to help.

I can't believe I've finally settled on an idea I like.

'What are you doing?'

Natalia pops up at my left elbow, chewing gum and staring with those uncanny blue-green eyes of hers. She's finally joined the herd and switched to winter uniform. I want to throw back a childish 'none of your business', but I don't.

'I'm waiting for someone.'

'You're always so cryptic, Cardell.' She peers around the art room door, assessing the small group of girls inside. 'Curiouser and curiouser. Who are you waiting for?'

I can see that she's not going to let me be. I'm pretty sure Natalia is similar to Katie. If you resist her too much she'll go out of her way to cause you trouble, but if you give her just enough info to satisfy her, then she's more likely to let it drop.

'I need a model for my art project. Someone with a certain look.'

'One of them? Which one?'

'Bochen.'

'Why? She's so strange looking.'

Bochen has long, straight black hair like Liana. I want the picture to be dark, mostly black and white with small accents of red. Snow White colours. Snow White is supposed to have dark hair and pale skin, and Bochen ticks both of those boxes.

'She's got an interesting face.' And you've got no imagination, I want to add. Bochen belongs in an elegant woodcut from the nineteenth century.

'Her mouth is so small I don't even know how she can eat.'

'Why do you have to always say stuff like that?'

Natalia's mouth falls slack. 'Uh, because it's true?'

'Plenty of things are true, it doesn't mean you have to say them. You do have a choice.'

Natalia's face is blank, like she really doesn't understand what I'm saying. And she wonders why people call her names behind her back.

'She'll never do it,' she says.

An exasperated huff escapes me.

'I know she won't,' Natalia insists. 'Show me what you need and I'll suggest someone.'

Natalia snatches my folio out of my hands before I even realise what she's doing. She slouches against the wall—she makes even our spinsterish winter uniform look like a deliberate fashion look—and flicks through my jumble of ideas.

I've added some crime novel covers and sketched out how I want the photo to look: a maybe-sleeping girl in a forest, or somewhere else, I haven't decided yet. She could be asleep, or unconscious, or even dead. There's an air of something supernatural, or slightly magical, about her. I might use fairy lights to create that atmosphere, or maybe even paint colours over the photo, like I did for my self portrait. I want the viewer to be confused about whether they're looking at a fairytale or a crime scene.

I can't read Natalia's face at all as she turns the pages. 'Can I have it back, please?'

'This is kind of twisted, Cardell.'

I hold my hand out for my folio but Natalia hoists it above her head.

'Come and get it.' She dances backwards.

'You do realise that I'm a foot taller than you, don't you?' I try to grab it but she jumps away. 'I can take you easily.'

I grab again and Natalia shrieks like a child having a really amazing fun time and somehow my folio ends up spilling its guts all over the floor. I crouch down and try to stuff the pages in. Natalia tries to join me but I give her such a dirty look she steps back.

'What's going on?' Bochen stands in the doorway of the art room. 'Are you two spying on us?'

'No,' I say, at exactly the same time Natalia says, 'Yes. Yes, we are.'

Bochen laughs. 'Now I don't know what I think.'

'Chloe has something to ask you, Bochen.'

If I could make Natalia spontaneously combust using the power of my furious mind, I would. But there's no way of avoiding it now.

'I need help with my project.' My voice squeaks and I swear Natalia smirks. I swallow and continue. 'I need to take photos of someone and I think you'd be perfect for it.'

The smooth, casual things I'd planned to say to Bochen to persuade her to pose for me have fallen out of my brain.

'So, would you do it? It'd be one afternoon of your time. They're not close-ups. You'd be…lying down…'

My cheeks are flaming. Bochen looks surprised, pushes her glasses back up her nose.

'Oh, not me, Chloe. You need a pretty girl, maybe Cherry. You should ask her. She likes to show off.'

I don't need a show-off. That's the last thing I need.

'You're pretty too.' I don't know who I'll ask if she doesn't do it.

'Sorry, Chloe!' Bochen gives me a big smile but I can tell she's trying to escape. 'You're so talented! You're going to beat my ass at this prize!'

'It's not for—' I dribble out, but she's gone. The heat from my cheeks spreads up my face and heads for my tear ducts.

'Bochen is failing maths and her parents are threatening to bring her back home if her grades don't improve.'

I turn my head away from Natalia and blink fast. 'Why are you telling me this? No, actually, why are you still here?'

'She doesn't have time to help you, she's cramming. It's nothing personal.'

'I'm not taking it personally!' I say, too loudly. I stomp down the corridor. I feel foolish for not knowing the first thing about Bochen's life, despite our friendly conversations, when apparently Natalia knows everything about her. She even tried to warn me, which only makes me feel worse.

'Your folio is really good.' Natalia follows me. 'You've done a lot of work.'

'Doing a lot of work doesn't matter if your ideas are shit.'

'Who said your ideas are shit?'

'Shouldn't you find your minions? Or are you coming to the tuckshop with me?'

She ignores my questions. 'Turn to that page with the crime books.'

I hold my defiled folio tighter. 'I know the one you mean.'

*Dead Girl Walking. When She Left. The Wife You Knew.*

'They remind me of that TV show, *Devil Creek*? Do you know it? My *minions* love it.'

I'm quiet but listening. I slow down.

'*Devil Creek* is totally dead girl porn. A bit like some of those covers. We should watch it together some time.'

I let that weird invitation slide. But the name, *Devil Creek*, sounds familiar.

'What about me?' says Natalia. 'I'll be your model if you ask nicely.'

'No.'

'Why?'

Too posey, I think, too obvious. I think of the dark and delicate and subtle things I want to express and Natalia is not any of them. I jangle my tuckshop money in my skirt pocket as we walk. 'Why do you want to help me?'

We stop and I stare at her innocent angel face, which hides the personality of a demon. I try to figure out if she's making fun of me.

'It's not about *helping*.' Said as if it's a dirty word. 'You're going to do this thing, it's going to win the art prize, and I'll be part of it. I'll bask in your glory, or whatever.'

'I'm not doing this for the prize.'

'What? This is going to be good, I can tell already. You should go for gold.'

We're on a collision course with Sarah and Marley, linking arms near the stairwell down to the tuckshop. Ally is practising some seriously filthy dance moves on the banister. She looks like obscure European royalty but she doesn't always act that way.

Natalia fixes her supernatural eyes on me.

'I don't know if you've got the right look.' I bite my lip. Who am I kidding? My vision for the photo keeps dissolving every time I try to grab onto it.

I try to look at Natalia objectively, and mentally adjust what I've been picturing.

'You look otherworldly enough…but too dangerous for what I've got in mind. It's supposed to look like a fairytale gone wrong. You're more of a mean pixie type, or the old sort of fairy. The kind who tangles mortals in wishes and promises, and tricks them into eating fairy food so they can't return to the human world.'

This alone should be nerdy and insulting enough for permanent excommunication, but instead something flashes inside Natalia, an extra spark of interest. Up until now I could have sworn she was playing with me.

'All of those girls come from in-between places.' She points at my folio. 'Dead and alive. Heaven and hell. Or some other place and the real world.'

'Yes, that's it,' I say with shock in my voice. That's better than I could have described it. Maybe that's what I'm aiming for.

'Give me your phone, Cardell.'

She calls herself on my phone, while still keeping a close eye on her friends.

'You know what makes me sick?' she says. 'Everyone skating along the surface and not talking about what's really happening.'

She's lost me. 'I need to think about it more. I'll let you know.'

She hands me my phone. 'Well, when you decide yes, I'll be waiting.'

'Right,' I nod. 'Okay.'

She joins her friends and they pour like oil through the corridor in the way that they do.

## DAY 34

Mum beckons for me to join her in the lounge room. The six o'clock news is just starting, and the anchorwoman is saying something about Yin.

My heart stops. 'Did they find her?'

'I don't think so.'

I sit close to Mum on the couch, my heart beating again.

Yin's parents appear on screen, looking a little stunned. They've both aged in the last five weeks. You can tell from the camera flashes and the clusters of microphones that the press conference is jammed full.

This time it isn't Mr Mitchell that speaks. Yin's mum reads from a sheet of paper held in shaking hands. The faintest trace of an accent runs through her words.

'Yin was born on this day sixteen years ago. She was my first child and I was so happy to meet her. She was a perfect baby with a full head of black hair.'

Mrs Mitchell starts hiccup-crying. Her husband's arm sneaks around her shoulders.

'Oh, man.' Mum grabs my hand and starts kneading it.

Mrs Mitchell swallows, continues.

'Dad, Mum, Nelson and Albert wish you a happy birthday, Yin. Wherever you are. Tonight we pray that you will return to us soon. To the man who has my daughter, please be kind to her on this special day. I think you are a good man who can do the right thing. To the public—thank you for your kind words and thoughts. We announce that we are offering a reward of one hundred thousand Australian dollars for information leading to the return of our daughter.

Please, we are begging you, if you know anything that might help the investigation, please contact the police. You can be anonymous. Help us find Yin.'

A reporter shouts a question, but a woman in a suit steps in and takes over the microphone. The footage cuts out and the newsreader takes over.

'Police have released an updated photo of Yin Mitchell, which may be closer to her current appearance.'

The photo they show is more recent, maybe even this year's school photo.

'Again, if any member of the public believes they have any information related to Yin's disappearance, they are urged to contact the hotline number below.'

A tear slides down Mum's cheek. She wipes it away, pretends it wasn't there in the first place. 'Albert and Nelson? Those kids will be getting hell at school with those names.'

I give her a rueful smile as my phone vibrates in my pocket.

It's an unknown number.

'Hello?'

'Are you watching it?'

I can't tell who it is. The person on the other end gets impatient. 'It's Natalia. From school. Are you watching the news?'

'Yeah. Yeah, I am.' I get up and go to my bedroom. 'Did you know it was her birthday?'

'Yes. Yes, I did.' Silence and uneven breathing.

I flop down on my bed. 'A hundred thousand is a lot of money.'

More breathing, then, 'The reward shouldn't be for her return, it should be for information that puts that sicko away for life.'

'She could still be alive.'

All of a sudden I'm afraid the reward will work. It's been more than a month. What if it's not about Yin's safe return, but about finding her body? Maybe it's better not knowing. I look at my neglected picture wall and everything on it seems so old, from a million years ago. Irrelevant.

There's dead silence for so long I wonder if I've messed up.

After way too long, Natalia speaks. 'So, do you want me to do the photo shoot with you, or not? I don't do nudes though.'

'Well that's a relief.'

She snorts in a humourless way. 'Okay, so when do you want to do it?'

My brain spins, trying to figure out how soon I can be ready, or even if I want to be ready. I'm still not a hundred per cent sure this isn't an elaborate plan to make fun of me.

'How about the first week of holidays?'

That will give me time to plan the lighting and find a location and see what equipment I can borrow from school, and then time to edit the photo and paint on it and anything else I decide to do afterwards. If I'm lucky.

'Nup, can't do. We're at the beach house that week. What about the second week?'

It seems as if everyone at Balmoral is going somewhere for the September holidays. The end of the holidays will be way too late.

'That doesn't give me enough time to finish it. How about the first weekend after we go on break? Sunday?'

'You mean next Sunday?'

She's right. How did the term get away from me so badly? 'There's a lot to organise...'

'God, Cardell, settle down. You're a massive geek, I'm sure you can pull this off.'

It's difficult to know what to say to such a double-edged insult-compliment.

'I don't know. I've still got two exams left this week to study for. Let's forget about it.'

'*Please.*' She sounds desperate, although I can't imagine why. I'm the one that's going to have a half-arsed Art project, and probably not be able to finish my homework for any other subjects as well.

Natalia sounds calmer though when she speaks again. 'Don't overthink it. I'm free on Sunday arvo, so pick a place, get some props or whatever and we'll do it. I'll sort out what I'm wearing and what I'll look like. No stress.'

I'm quiet for a good few seconds. 'Okay?' I say, eventually.

'You can do it,' she says. 'At least you're doing something.' And then she hangs up.

## DAY 35

I wait until the next morning to call Dad.

'Chloe, everything okay?' is how he answers my call. He's out of breath; he always seems to be out of breath when he answers his phone.

'Yeah, nothing's wrong. Just called to chat.'

This is not the truth. I've been sitting in my room for the last hour, looking at all the tests and due dates scribbled in my school diary.

'Oh, good, good.'

There's a pause. My hope is that he can get me out of this Art project mess, because he does actually have some skills in this area, from the olden days when he used to help put on underground raves and events.

'How's school?'

'A bit better now, I guess.' I haven't spoken to him since the week Yin disappeared, but I know Mum has probably been giving him updates.

'Any news on the police front?'

'Not really. There were rumours today that they're interviewing teachers again. And some people's dads as well. And bus drivers, that sort of thing.'

'I should hope so.'

'I guess. There's a reward now, so...'

I don't even believe the rumours that police are interviewing students' fathers. People will say anything when they're feeling desperate.

'Listen, Chlo, I've been thinking. You know how Jarrod is an expert at Dim Mak? It's a self-defence technique using pressure points. You can temporarily paralyse someone with one finger. Anyway, he's offered to teach you, if you want.'

I rub my face. I haven't gone to Dad's house much in the eighteen months since he's been back from Western Australia, it's too far away. And I'm pretty sure I don't want to voluntarily spend time with Dad's housemate who wears Thai fisherman pants 24/7. Or experience that much power in one finger, for that matter.

'Uh, no. I mean, thank you. That's really nice of him to offer. But we're doing self-defence in PE.'

'The offer's there, Chlo. Or we can look into something else.'

'Maybe.' I take a deep breath. He's taken me way off track. 'Hey, so I'm calling because I need your help with something. It's kind of short notice.'

'Of course, yes! What do you need?'

I try to ignore how eager he sounds, practically panting like Arnold. I tell him about my project, as best I can, without getting into it too deep.

'So, we need a location,' he sums up, 'and you need help picking up the equipment from school and driving it there and back?'

'Yeah. And we'll probably need to pick my friend up. Sorry. It's a lot of work. I can't ask Mum, with her roster and everything.'

'It's no problem, love. I've already got a place in mind. I'll make a few calls and get back to you.'

'Thanks Dad.' I feel hypocritical but I remind myself that he probably owes me this. I'm allowed to ask him for things.

'Let me take care of it, Chlo. Is little Sammy there?'

'Nah, he's at soccer practice.'

'Oh, right. I should watch one of his matches, shouldn't I?'

'Yeah, he'd like that.'

'Speak soon,' he says, and we hang up.

After I speak to Dad I do my homework. Not all of it, because at this time of year it's like a bottomless pit of things that should have been done a week ago. Balmoral runs on pressure, like a big steam train you can't get off once you're on. Every teacher thinks their subject is the most important, and they get annoyed if you haven't paid enough attention to their set tasks. They've got no idea how much it adds up to across six subjects.

The house is quiet, with Mum and Sam both at soccer. I do my maths exercises and then make grilled cheese on toast with so much French mustard my tongue burns.

Natalia has sent me a link to the TV show she mentioned, *Devil Creek*. I realise that the billboard I saw on the way home from school just after Yin was taken was for the same show.

The opening credits roll: a girl runs barefoot through the bush at night, her legs and arms painfully scratched, the soundtrack built from driving drums and panic.

I decide I don't really love it halfway through the first episode. Detective McManus is experienced and professional, but distracted by his messy divorce. His work partner Detective Burns is dedicated and cares too much, but keeps pissing off witnesses with her blunt manner. The people of Devil

Creek all have secret lives, but nothing ties together, at least not yet. Everyone is white and every time it seems like the plot might go somewhere, they cut to a confusing dream sequence.

But Emily Blake, the victim, the town's prettiest girl with the sordid secrets—she gives me chills. The music builds to something sinister when they find her body.

Her nightie is ripped low on her chest and a fly hovers around her face.

The camera zooms in on her pale lips, which are as cracked as the mud she's lying on. A strand of hair snakes its way into the corner of her mouth, searching for a way in. There are droplets of blood along the actress's forehead, as pretty as rubies, and her staring eyes wear the reflection of blue sky and clouds above.

Every time they show the autopsy photo, or show Emily Blake when she was alive, or give us her blueish body on a mortuary gurney, I can see the resemblance to Natalia, I see every fallen body on the cover of a crime novel, and I can't help thinking that everyone wants their teenage girls ruined.

# Natalia

**DAY 36**

A police car fills our driveway, and when I take a survey of what other gargantuan shifts have taken place in the universe, I see the Baillieus' front curtains twitch across the road.

Welcome to the show, everyone.

I pull my headphones off, look through the police car window to see a black leather void inside, with extra screens, extra gadgets. First the Mitchells on TV, and now this. I let myself in the front door instead of the back.

Mum is a treble clef silhouette in the distance, leaning against the kitchen counter. She's supposed to be visiting Nan at the retirement home today. It usually takes her most of the day to drive down to the peninsula and back.

'You're home early,' Mum says.

'What's going on?'

The question sends her slumping even further against the counter. She looks unexpectedly beautiful in this moment, pale and tense, beige and blonde, surrounded by the marble countertop and gleaming kitchen appliances.

'It's nothing.'

Faith emerges from the laundry holding her jacket and bag, heading for the back door fast. She's scared of anyone in uniform, and who would blame her when she's already survived a civil war in her home country. She has a nursing degree but works as a cleaner for several families on our street. Mum raises her hand goodbye.

A strange man walks across the picture window behind Mum, looks up at the garage eaves and makes a mark on a notepad. He disappears around the side of the house.

'Is our house being searched?' My mind leaps to my bedroom immediately, completing a detailed inventory of my drawers and closet.

'Not exactly. I don't know.' My mum, the lawyer, doesn't know. She worries away at a cuticle. 'Your father is upstairs talking to the police. It's…routine.'

I stare. When my voice comes out again, it's high and not really my own. 'It doesn't sound routine. This is because I used to be close to Yin, isn't it?'

A shower of illusions crash around me. That I can stay at a distance from the abduction, that the police won't drag us into it anyway.

'I don't think so, love.'

'Then it's about Dad? Do they suspect him?'

'Darling…'

Every word costs Mum energy she doesn't have. She's about to say more, but Dad clomps down the staircase that leads to their bedroom. He looks grey and ashamed when he sees me, the way he should look all the times he comes home drunk.

He's followed down the stairs by a rumpled, friendly looking guy in a suit.

'This is my daughter, Natalia,' Dad says. 'Natalia, this is Detective Barbero. We're helping him with his enquiries.'

'Are you going to interrogate me as well?' I ask.

Detective Barbero looks like someone's unfit dad, not a person who chases criminals for a living. I haven't seen him around school or on the TV either. He's got nothing on the handsome head guy who gets interviewed on the news.

'No one is getting interrogated, Natalia. We've got everything we need at this stage, and your parents have my number.'

It's odd to be so irrelevant when I know Yin better than anyone else. Or I used to. Maybe someone should talk to me.

The detective gestures to his colleague in the backyard. After weeks of doing nothing, I wonder what other waves of activity are spreading across the city, stirred up by Friday's reward announcement or rising up of their own accord. Why now?

'We'll be in touch if we need anything else.'

Detective Barbero is barely out the door before Dad deflates, the wind and puff and strength ripped out of him. He staggers to the couch.

'Get me a Scotch, Tal,' he says, and I do, making it the way he likes it, neat with a dash of water.

His hand trembles when I hand it to him; the whisky ripples like a miniature earthquake has rocked our house. He's not my lion dad, the king of the dinner party, master of the golf course. He shrinks inside his clothes, and even though he sometimes gets like this, how unfamiliar he seems.

'They asked the strangest questions.' He presses himself into the couch, closes his eyes and sips.

'Like what?'

'Give your dad a moment,' Mum says. 'We'll talk later.'

I give her my most cutting look, because I know with them that later never happens, and I'm not supposed to notice that.

Mum is heading to work early so I let her drive me to school, even if it means getting there thirty minutes before I want to. She stops the car at the student gate and leans forward, looking at the great green expanse I have to walk across to get to the main doors. It's a misty morning, so the empty grounds look spookier than usual, and we're the only car on the street.

'By the way,' she says. 'The police have asked me to run a few things by you. Some information about the offender.'

She could not have picked worse timing. 'Is this a secret from Dad?'

'I don't want to distract you before school, Natalia. We can talk tonight. I just wanted to flag it.'

'Why bring it up at all, Mum? Tell me. I won't be able to concentrate now, and I've got my French exam today.'

She's so annoying.

'I don't want you worrying. I hate that you have to be involved in this.'

'I *am* worried! The police ransacked our house yesterday. How can I not worry?'

Mum sighs like I'm the one being irrational. She reaches behind my seat for her handbag. 'The kidnapper uses unusual words or phrases. You know, endearments or pet names.'

'Like what?'

Mum pulls a slip of paper from her handbag and gives it to me. It's been ripped off from the notepad she keeps on the kitchen bench to write shopping lists and communicate with Faith.

I read the list. *Sweetpea. Honeypie. Sleepover party.*

Bile rises in my throat. 'Gross. If a grown man called me any of these I would know for sure that he's a certified paedophile.'

'The detectives want to know if you've ever heard someone use these words, a teacher who might have left the school, or a substitute teacher. Or any of your sports coaches.'

'Why didn't they ask me directly?' I try to hand the note back, willing my hands to stop shaking, but Mum pushes it towards me.

'Keep it. I don't want you obsessing over it, but if you hear anything even remotely similar, obviously tell me or your dad.'

'And run a mile.' I tuck the note into the pocket of my school bag. She doesn't smile, of course she doesn't.

This basically reminds me of the million questions I have like, why offer a reward now? Does this mean they've shifted to looking for Yin dead rather than alive? They're acting awfully like we should be scared of someone very close to us. I think of all the rumours that are trickling through our year level, rumours that are scabs we can't stop picking at, like that Doctor Calm takes baths with his victims and pretends that a rubber duck is talking in a tiny duck voice, that he likes to sing them to sleep with lullabies, that he puts on our school uniform and pretends to be a Balmoral girl.

I start to wonder if it's better if she's dead.

After I get out I see Mum arrange her makeup bag carefully on the seat so she can do her face on the freeway.

The supernatural mist soup sweeps me through to

reception, where I swipe my attendance card, nodding at part-time receptionist Susan, who is one of the saddest people any of us have ever seen. Whenever we study a tragic story in English, I think of Susan.

Our usual nook, the triangle of couches next to the window that overlooks the quad like an observation deck, is depressing without my girls in it, besides which it's littered with empty chip packets and none of the corridor lights are on yet. I reverse along the corridor and try not to look at the morbid shrine that's formed around Yin's locker. Polaroids and origami cranes and silk flowers gathering dust, and even a handwritten Bible verse that has to have come from that happy-clapper Lisbeth.

Surely they'll clear this up over the holidays, they can't let it bleed into next term.

When I inch closer my feet knock into a pile of paper held together with a plastic clip in the shape of a frog. I bend down to see equations and symbols—Petra obviously couldn't hack the heat and dumped Yin's borrowed physics notes here.

I straighten up and I'm surprised to see Yin's locker door is open a crack. She's got a sticker of a sparkly clarinet on it so it's easy to find and the darkness inside pulls my attention—come closer come closer come closer—like a black hole or a portal.

The silence in the abandoned school building is total.

I flick the door open.

A short stack of textbooks. A lone scrunchie. A neatly folded school scarf. An orange box of clarinet reeds. One picture of Yin, Claire and Milla stuck to the inside of the door.

The locker is too empty, too tidy. Yin has had a lifelong stationery addiction, so where are the sticky notes and the cute notepads and the patterned washi tape and the glitter gel pens? Where are the tablets she takes for hay fever? If the police searched her locker, why wouldn't they have given the rest of her things straight to the Mitchells? And what did they take as evidence?

I put my head close to the square dark hole, reaching to touch the cold back wall. The wall gives way, something catches my hand, tugs my arm, dragging me along a cramped metal tunnel, no bigger than an air duct. I'm squeezed in a tube, tighter than a water slide, darker and more sinister. Gravity pulls me through time and space, down down, through to another place, the other place, the other side.

I step away, breathing hard.

I look around at the cack-green carpet, pocked with old chewing gum. The lemon-vomit walls, the dusty windows high up. The row of gunmetal grey lockers. Everything ordinary, nothing changed.

The library is the only warm bright spot in the early-morning school. Mrs Lithgow lifts her head and smiles when I enter and I think about if she only knew about the overdue copy of *Picnic at Hanging Rock* in my bag that I have no intention of returning.

The other librarians gather in the inner sanctum of the back office, plunging coffee and loading croissants into their mouths and talking about the wild orgies they participated in on the weekend.

A group of international students are already hitting the books and a poor Year Nine waif is curled up, asleep, in a beanbag.

I try to focus on the art shelves, because when I called her on Friday Chloe sounded stressed, and if she needs all the help she can get, then I need all the distraction in the world right now. If I can find a book about that Bill Henson guy she's always banging on about, then maybe we'll have something to talk about in fourth-period Art today.

When I think about Emily Blake and dead girls in general and sweetpea honeypie sleepover parties and Mrs Christie's pursed-up face and everything that has been swept under the school carpet, a red tide of rage threatens to engulf me.

I blink it away and think about the open locker and how I could get a bag and scoop everything inside into it, I could collect and preserve those small leftover bits of Yin and take them to Chunjuan and Stephen to compensate for the fact that I didn't send a card, I didn't send a text, my family didn't make food and bring it to them.

I give up on art and round the corner and see Petra at a carrel with her human security blanket Audrey. They both still think I poked Petra in the eye deliberately, so I reverse before I'm seen. I collect a pancake stack of magazines and install myself in the new cushion pit that smells of dry-cleaning and Old Collegian donations, realising too late that the opposite curve of the pit is occupied by Claire and Milla, hunched over an iPad. They're engrossed and don't see me, so I pick up a magazine and start to flick through it.

'Go back further.'

I strain to hear Claire. Milla's finger swipes at the screen and my ears rotate like satellite dishes.

'I'm sure I saw it around here,' Claire says.

'That's when they went away at Easter…Oh! Is that it?'

Claire grabs the iPad right out of Milla's hands and reads from the screen.

'*If you could see me now you would know I'm not your little girl no more.*'

'What does it mean?'

My mind surges. The words sound familiar but I can't place them. I can see why Claire and Milla are caught on this one thing, because it's not the way Yin speaks at all.

'The day before she's complaining about her Geography assignment.' Milla again. 'Later that day, that's in rehearsal, see? You can see the back of Petra's head, and that's Sunita.'

I'm still friends with Yin, but I hide her updates. I don't think they'd show anyway, we never interact anymore and we're probably completely algorithmed out of each other's lives.

'What were we doing in April?'

Claire forgets to keep her voice down. Mrs Lithgow's head swivels in our direction. And then I get it.

'It's a song lyric,' I say.

Claire and Milla realise—finally—that I'm in the pit with them.

'*If you could see me you would know, I'm not, not, not your little girl no more*—it's a song by Lana Dreams.'

They look more confused than ever, as if I'm taking the piss out of them, as if I'm trying to cause trouble rather than solve the biggest problem they have right now.

'Look it up if you don't believe me.'

Claire taps doubtfully and then turns to Milla.

'Does Yin even like Lana Dreams?' I hear her whisper. 'It still doesn't explain why she would write that.'

I forget for a moment that I'm dealing with orchestra nerds. 'That song was everywhere over summer. Didn't you hear it?'

Everything I say seems to beat Claire down further into her seat.

'I guess so, yeah, of course.' Milla sounds anything but certain. She seems on the verge of saying more, but then the curtains go down, the impenetrable wall goes up, and both girls curl back in on themselves, shutting me out.

'Have either of you heard anything?' The words pop out of my mouth and keep tumbling, tumbling, boinging about the cushion pit, sounding desperate. 'From the police or the Mitchells? Did the police come to your house again?'

'No.' Milla's response is mumbled and Claire looks away like she's trying to pretend I'm not there.

They must hate me.

Yin must have talked about me, complained. They probably heard all the worst stories about me.

And who has been crying the most these past five weeks, who wrote tributes and poems and laid flowers, who missed out on days of school they were so upset, who kept looking at their phones like a miracle could happen, who had gaping space left in their weekends—well, not me.

I get up and leave the pit.

It's pouring with rain by lunch so everyone crams into any space they can find on level three, but not our spot, obviously. I sit on the floor and watch the babydoll Sevens in the quad below, squealing their way through puddles of water.

I play a game where every time I blink, one of the girls vanishes. Even I'm spooked when a fork of lightning cracks the sky above the quad. Claire and Milla think I'm a witch, and maybe I am, or maybe some of my lost Wingdonian powers are slowly returning.

Sarah and Ally buzz in the background, talking along to a Learn Italian app, trying to nail the filthiest phrases before the art and design tour to Tuscany and obsessing over how many pairs of shoes they can fit in their suitcases.

Normally I'd roll my eyes at Marley and she'd do it too and that would make their intensity bearable, but Marley's not here today even though she's sitting right next to me. She doodles in her diary, sucks on the ends of her hair and looks as miserable as the weather. Around us the rest of the year level festers, eating lunch, watching videos, catching up on assignments. The windows fog up on the inside and there's no escape from the smell of wet jumpers and perfume and old sneakers.

My phone chirps. Since our phone call on Friday I have been bombarding Chloe with visual inspiration. This time I sent her a photo of the movie version of Miranda from *Picnic at Hanging Rock*, one where she's wearing her long white dress and looking out from between two rocks.

*Almost, but too pretty*, I read.

When I look down the corridor I can see Chloe's broad back at her locker. As always, she has her hair in that tragic ponytail, and she's stuck talking to Petra now, which is her bad luck.

We could have said hi to each other, of course, at any point during the day, but we haven't yet. It's not a secret telepathic language, but it's good enough. I've kept my foul mood held close to my chest all day, through English, French and a double period of Art where I worked on my brilliant concept of scratching out the eyes and mouths of women on vintage knitting patterns. I'm alone in my head, cut off from everyone. I used to enjoy the aloneness of my head, but today it's not so good.

'Who you writing to?' asks Sarah. Ally hangs off the couch, her hair cascading.

'Marcel,' I lie, locking my phone. 'He won't leave me alone, it's starting to get embarrassing.'

'While you're on your phone, can you please like the pic I posted this morning?' Sarah holds up her phone to show me which one she means. 'I'm sick of your lack of support.'

'Make Marley do it,' I say, but when I look across at Marley again she's silent-crying and there's an expression of such pure despair on her face that my heart falls out of my chest and bleeds all over the floor.

'What's going on, Marls?' I scoot closer.

'Don't,' she mouths, but it's too late because we have

extra-sensory tear perception and gather in a knot around her.

'The police came to my house yesterday.'

We have to lean in to hear her. Pleasure and horror mixes on Sarah's face. 'Why didn't you message us?' she says.

This is the moment I could tell everyone about my dad, but my skin is tight, a membrane hardens around me, a cocoon to keep everything contained.

'They asked both my parents questions, but they asked my dad the most. And they searched the house and even the rehearsal studios.'

'What questions?'

'They wanted to know what sort of pyjamas I wear. They wanted to see my dad's pyjamas too.' Marley's eyes slide about. 'They asked what size my dad's feet were, and what kind of slippers he wore. Why would they ask about that?'

I'm silent. My parents didn't mention pyjamas or slippers. I consider sharing Mum's list of serial-killer pet names with them, but I quickly shelve the idea. There would be no quicker way to spread the information like wildfire and maybe that's not what the police intended. I wish someone could be witness to exactly how much I understand the consequences of my actions right now.

Sarah's brow is furrowed. 'Think carefully now, Marley. Like, really carefully. Try to forget that it's even your dad, and ask yourself: is there any chance he could be Doctor Calm?'

It's all I can do not to slap her. 'Sarah—seriously? Of course he's not!'

'Oh yeah, well, do you know that he videos his victims?' Sarah stares at me defiantly. 'Dad's position means he gets told this stuff.'

Sarah has to turn everything into an *I'm Special* moment, but I bet most of the parents know about it and not only Gary-Head-of-the-School-Board.

Marley looks up at the ceiling as the tears flow, like a penitent in one of the religious paintings hanging in the Great Hall. I put my arm around her and whisper in her ear, furious and sure.

'Listen to me, Marls. Your dad is not Doctor Calm. The police are desperate, and they're probably interviewing anyone they can think of. In fact, I overheard one of the Year Eights earlier saying their dad was interviewed as well.'

'Really?' Marley is instantly hopeful and my skin starts to breathe again. I squash the thought that it would be better if it was Marley's dad, because that means it isn't mine and he won't be going to jail for life and we won't have to sell the family house and be completely ostracised from society.

'It's nothing, I'm sure of it. It's less than nothing. Your dad is your dad. Everything's fine.' I'm out of breath. I might have been stabbing the ground with my finger. Sarah and Ally are looking at me strangely. 'Don't let anyone see you lose control,' I say, to Marley, to the others, to myself. 'I have to pee now.'

But I don't. I walk around the corner and then I quickly double back, hiding myself behind a group of younger girls trying to sell chocolate bars to the Year Tens because of our reputation for emotional eating.

The corridors are an unpleasant, desperate end-of-lunch-hour whirl, a dizzying blend of colours and voices, a frozen yoghurt gone way too far with flavours and popping candy and too much syrup.

Chloe and Petra are both still near their lockers, even though they aren't talking anymore.

'Miss Cardell.' I give Chloe a formal nod and she raises her eyebrows. 'Have you found a place yet for this weekend?'

She frowns. 'Not quite.'

'I'll wait to hear from you, then,' I say and I'm a girl made of concrete, a veritable feelings bunker, so I cut my losses and turn away.

## DAY 39

Liv's hair sticks up in points, her eyes are pillow-puffy. I swing my school bag and gym bag onto the bench and sit down.

'You just woke up.'

Liv massages the hollows of her cheeks, as if that can revive her. 'Nah babe, I've been awake for hours.'

'Liar.'

Liv is almost entirely nocturnal, possibly even a vampire.

I take off my school jumper, remove my tie, muss up my hair. As if I want to be in a hipster cafe in my dirty old man's dream of a school uniform. Liv almost always makes me come to her. I wouldn't take that from a friend, but she's been lording it over me since I was a baby, so what hope do I have?

'What's in the bag?'

She's better than a beagle at sniffing things out.

'PE stuff.'

'Doesn't sound like it.'

'Alright, Sherlock. Stuff for an art project, then.' Both of these answers could be true, but neither are.

Liv orders coffees for us and smiles too long at the waitress. When our coffees come, she smiles again, in case the waitress missed it the first time. The waitress is petite and olive-skinned and has a Spanish accent, so exactly Liv's type.

'Wow.' I stir two heaped sugars into my coffee, destroying the heart poured into the foam. 'Did you notice how big that waitress's nostrils are? I couldn't stop looking at them. You could fit this whole biscotti up there.'

I can see doubt on Liv's face as she regards the foxy little waitress, which means my work here is done. Even with the sugar this coffee tastes gross.

'So, what's the drama, Tal?'

I pull an innocent face.

'You only message me when you're upset.'

'I don't,' I say, but I do and I have.

Even though the cafe is overheated and too noisy, even though the guy next to us deserves a punch in his face for his hipster glasses and porn moustache, it's nice to see my sister across the table. To call her and know she will come running. Or allow me to go running to her.

She stares me out. We have the same eyes but her gaze lasts longer and I yield.

'The police came to our house and interviewed Dad. At the house. Which they also searched.'

'When?' Liv is surprised enough to grab my arm. Venue stamps line the inside of her wrist.

'Sunday.' I pull free.

'What did they want to know?'

'Where he was on certain dates and certain times. They asked about his habits, I don't know what else. Bear in mind that he wouldn't tell me this himself, I had to pester Mum to tell me.'

I leave out Marley's stuff about pyjamas and slippers, and all the other rumours that have been floating around school this week.

'They asked Mum if he has any catchphrases and sayings, or funny nicknames for us. And then they asked her to run a list of creepy words by me.'

'That's disturbing.' Liv's fingers rip a napkin to shreds. 'What were they?'

'Like, I don't know, honey-bunnies and slumber parties.'

'Yuck.' Liv pulls a face. 'That is warped. I'm so sorry.'

I picture a sister-wall forming around us, keeping all the unwanted armies out. I already feel better.

'Other people's dads have been questioned as well. You know Marley?'

'Marley with the muso parents? That doesn't surprise me. Well, that makes me feel a bit better, then, that they're doing other parents as well.' Liv stops worrying away at her napkin. 'Maybe it's something to do with Dad's indecent exposure thing.'

I spray biscotti crumbs for kilometres. 'What?'

Porn moustache glances sharply at us. I lower my voice but not before greasing him off. Go sit in the library if you want quiet, loser.

'They never told you? It was at some interstate conference Dad went to, with the whole firm. Everyone got trashed, and Dad agreed to do this ridiculous dare. You know how competitive he gets. He had to streak naked up and down the street, and then dance in the hotel fountain. Police came by, Dad got mouthy, refused to cover up or get out of the fountain, and he was arrested. Our father is, officially speaking, a pervert.'

'Eww.' I try to banish the mental image of Dad frolicking naked in a public water feature. It's bad enough when he wears his cycling lycra. And it's so typical that Mum would tell Liv and not me. 'Was this part of his breakdown?'

'I don't remember, Tal, I don't think so. He only got a warning but I bet it's on his record. That would be enough to make the police visit. I wouldn't worry, it sounds like they're just ticking the boxes.'

'Yeah, I know, you're right,' I say, but my coffee's lukewarm and I feel sick. The last thing I need is to start worrying about Dad, but he's been working long hours and drinking a lot and I don't want him to go off the rails. He had a rough patch when I was around ten, but I was too young to understand it. I don't even know what really happened, and no one in our family ever mentions it. Is it only my family that never talks about anything important or real?

'I saw in the paper,' Liv says. 'The reward.'

The tabloids keep running Chunjuan's statement, laying it out like a sappy handwritten letter, decorated with cheesy love hearts. Anyone who knows her knows she's not the love-heart type.

'Have you seen them since it happened?' asks Liv.

'No,' I admit, avoiding her eyes.

'I don't think the Mitchells have a hundred grand,' Liv says.

We're both quiet for a few moments, listening to the hiss of the milk steamer, the clank of saucers.

'You know, I used to be jealous of you and Yin, the friendship you had.' Liv swishes the coffee around in her cup.

'You've always had heaps of friends.'

'Yeah, I've always had a group to hang with, but I never had a best friend. One person you always go to, the person who knows everything about you. You two were really lucky to have that.'

'Well, I really screwed that one up, didn't I?' I try not to sound too cut up. I look at the gig posters on the wall and I can still hear the scorn in Claire and Milla's voices.

'I don't think so. People change and grow apart.' Liv is sincere, for once. 'It doesn't take away what you had for so many years. That still counts, that was real.'

I can't reply, but I give Liv a little smile to let her know I appreciate what she's said, even though it's not true. She doesn't know how hard I pushed Yin away.

'What do you have planned for the holidays?' asks Liv, after a quiet moment.

'I don't know. Sarah and Ally are going on this school trip to Italy, Marley's going to Thailand. Mum said something about the beach house.'

'Do you want to come and stay with me for a few days? You should try and stay busy.'

'I am going to be busy!' I reply far too quickly. 'I'm helping a friend with an art project. Like a feminist statement thing.'

'That sounds cool.'

Liv shifts in her seat and I wonder if she's already getting impatient about the next thing in her day even while she's pretending she has all the time in the world for me. It's impossible to pin her down for too long. I can't stay with her, she's only got a studio apartment and we'll get on each other's nerves.

'Why did you move out of home so young, Liv?'

She baulks. 'What made you think about that?'

'I don't know. It always seemed like a big secret.'

'There's no secret. And I was with Aunt Helen, not on my own.'

'Was it Dad? Was that why you couldn't live at home?'

'No! God, Tal. Do not let this police stuff get in your head.' Liv rakes her choppy hair. 'I was unhappy. Suffocated. I had to leave so I could grow up properly.'

That makes me snort.

'You still haven't grown up properly,' I say.

When I arrive home the only person around is Faith. Mum thinks I haven't noticed that she's asked Faith to come late and leave late when she and Dad work overtime.

I grab a packet of biscuits and some juice, and shut my bedroom door so the noise of the vacuum is a distant hum.

My PE bag fits behind my shoes at the bottom of my wardrobe. No one saw me empty Yin's locker because it was a charmed action. The reason I know is that almost as soon as I'd shut the locker and zipped my bag, who walked around the corner but Petra, voted by me the most likely person in the entire year level to dob? Instead of busting me, she merely walked on by, and the whole thing was ordained by the universe. Even Liv couldn't crack me.

The coat hangers are spaced evenly along the rail. My ugg boots, my spare school shoes, my wedges, white trainers are lined up neatly, as neatly as if someone had used a ruler. It's the first time I've looked in my wardrobe properly since the police visited, and things are not the way I left them.

My parents didn't tell me the police were in my room.

I remember what Marley said about the slippers and pyjamas. I try to stop my brain right there but it slides on, fast. I mostly don't wear slippers, just really fluffy socks, and my pyjamas are under my pillow, as usual.

I try to make sense of something that makes no sense.

I take my glass and plate downstairs and put them in the dishwasher. Faith is still clunking around in the front rooms so I race to the study and power up Dad's computer. I've tried plenty of times to break his email password and failed, but I can still access his calendar.

I click to the week Yin disappeared. The grid is chock full of appointments but they're all work things. I bring up his internet history, but there's hardly anything on there, as if it's been cleared recently.

My skin tingles with the thrill of snooping, but there's also a new and sickly undercurrent. Doubting my parents has never bothered me before.

The funny feeling propels me out of the study. I bump into Faith starting on the skirting board, and she points at my schoolbag, hockey stick and blazer sprawling across the hallway.

'Nutella, you're killing me,' she says with her hands on her hips, a favourite joke of ours.

I smile sweetly like nothing is going on and of course I move my stuff because Faith's trying to do her job, not like Mum who is plain old petty about clutter. I pile everything on the side table.

Faith isn't done yet though.

'Your friend is still missing,' she says.

'Yes.' We stand still and look at each other. Faith has only worked for us for three years, so not long enough to remember Yin, but she must have seen and heard a lot around here in the last month.

'I'm sorry,' she says and I nod and then skid away in my socks, galloping up the back stairs to my parents' bedroom. I know Faith never found out what happened to everyone in her family during the war. I wonder how she copes.

Wardrobe and drawer inspection.

The only moderately interesting thing is the impressive cache of prescription and supplement bottles in the bathroom cabinet. Mum's are all hormone-related and Dad's are all mood stabilisers. I read the fine print on those ones and they're years out of date. So Dad probably doesn't take them anymore. I don't know if that worries me more, or less.

And finally, there is something. Not a secret exposé of a serial killer, but something useful nonetheless.

A long, see-through white dress on Mum's side of the wardrobe, simple enough to be a nightie or a slip, but not really either of those things. It has expensive written all over it.

I sincerely hope it's not a kinky sex thing, because retch, and I must have it. I jam it under my jumper. There's no way Chloe can say I look like an evil pixie in something so virginal.

## DAY 42

The day of the photo shoot arrives and I'm more organised than I've been for anything else this year. I wait at the designated tram stop like a total dick with my bag of costumes and the beginnings of an over-the-top hairstyle and a million layers of clothing, wondering why I bossed Chloe into using me in the first place.

I scroll on my phone while I wait and see that Sarah has already posted pics of her and Ally in Heathrow airport wearing matching outfits, en route to Italy. I don't see the huge green vintage car until Chloe yells out the window. I cross the road, swimming in deep regret. I have set myself up for an afternoon of pure awkward.

Chloe's dad turns down the stereo as I get in and Chloe introduces us. I'm supposed to call him Jeremy. I see a set of piercing eyes in the rear-view mirror. He has his window rolled down, like we're not in the middle of a cold snap, and blue tattoos on his forearms. He's surprisingly pale and freckly compared to Chloe, you'd never guess they were father and daughter.

'Right,' he says, once we've pulled out into the Sunday traffic. 'It's time to discuss some ground rules with you girls.'

It's a relief to hear some classic dad-speak.

'I've cleared this with my immediate manager, but not the big boss, does that make sense?'

A layer of physical power hangs around Jeremy and an inappropriate bubble of laughter rises in my throat, something that happens when people are too serious around me. It makes school speech night and exams hell.

I grip my bag tighter and pay a whole lot of attention to the green-and-brown leather seat, the shiny chrome trim, Jeremy's massively pointy shirt collar. When I look up, Chloe is watching me out of the side of her eyes. Out of school she wears jeans and a black hoodie.

'We've got an hour, an hour fifteen max. You go in, do your thing, leave everything as you found it.'

'Yes, Dad. You've already said this a million times.'

'I'm sticking my neck out for you, Chlo-Chlo. I want to make sure we're on the same page.'

'Yes, Jeremy!' I sing out. 'We are most definitely on the same page.'

Jeremy gives me a look in the rear-view mirror that makes me wish I'd kept my mouth shut. He pumps the clutch and spins the steering wheel like a race-car driver. I wonder if the police have interviewed him too. When I glance at Chloe I can see it was worth it. Her mouth twists sideways and I know she's having the inappropriate laughing problem too.

'I'm trusting you girls.'

'Oui, Papa.' Chloe starts singing under her breath, leaning forward to turn the stereo up. Someone is mid-guitar solo, shredding hard. Her dad starts tapping his fingers on the steering wheel, bobbing his head. Chloe copies him, shrugging her shoulders and bobbing her head. She turns around to smile at me with mock enthusiasm on her face. '*Yeah!*' She clicks her fingers and points. '*Yeah, man!*'

I look out the window but a half-laugh escapes me. If we drive fast enough, we'll drive ourselves right into a time warp and pop out in the seventies.

'Your dad's cool,' I admit, after we pull into the scariest place I've ever seen. It's at the end of a nothing road with no one around for kilometres. A padlocked gate, cold wind whistling around large abandoned buildings that look like old factories or warehouses. Jeremy's Valiant is the only car in the patchy gravel car park. I couldn't even tell you what suburb we're in.

'I don't think I'd go that far, but he's okay,' says Chloe. 'Actually he owes me this, because he's not around much.'

'Sounds like my dad.' I realise too late that Chloe means her father doesn't live with them at all. To cover up, I kick a beer can lying in the dust and squint at the empty desolate horizon. Real smooth Natalia, you're such a nice girl from a nice nuclear family.

Jeremy saunters back from smoking a rollie cigarette and looking up into a gum tree.

'What did you have there, Dad?' Chloe asks.

'That'd be the Yellow-Breasted Warbling Tooter,' Jeremy replies, and a pleased look passes between them. Those two freaks don't even smile when they crack jokes.

Jeremy helps us drag Chloe's stuff out of the boot and it's when they're side by side that I can finally see that they're related. They look like the type to go camping and chop wood and fix cars with their bare hands. I can barely lift some of the bags, but Jeremy hoists them as if they're nothing.

'What is this place?' I ask. After relaxing—sort of— during the drive, my nerves rise again, a bird trapped in my chest beating its wings faster and faster.

'It's an industrial park used by craftspeople and small businesses,' Jeremy answers with a black canvas bag balanced on each shoulder. 'I work in the furniture workshop on the other side.'

We drag the whole heap of junk into a low brick building and dump it inside a reception area. Chloe waves her dad away.

'This way.'

I follow Chloe into a darker section of the building, where my eyes are slow to adjust. I lose track of my own feet as we shuffle further into the gloom. Chloe pops a door, a big metal thing with rubber seals that suck and pull apart. She flicks a switch and fluorescent lights blink into existence. I look inside with her. It smells unusual.

'Here?'

'Yep. Amazing that the power's still on, isn't it?'

We step through and the heavy door clunks shut behind us, only making me jump about a kilometre high. There are tiles on the walls and a concrete floor and the dot-dot-dash of the fluoro lights glare above.

'What is this?'

'A meat locker.'

'A whatsy?' A chill races through me, above and beyond the chill already in the air.

'You know, a really big fridge. They could have kept meat here, or maybe it was cheese or veggies. Who knows.'

Chloe's voice echoes slightly. She lays down the bags she's been carrying.

Rows and rows of ghostly pig corpses fill my mind, sides

of cow, dead flesh laid out and waiting to be eaten. It's airless in here, cloying. Something rises up inside me.

'Are you alright? You don't get claustrophobic, do you?' Chloe looks concerned.

'No, I'm fine.' I pull on the door handle with the least amount of urgency possible, but I do a bad job of it. Eventually I figure out I have to pull the lever towards me. Air whooshes into the box, the locker, whatever. I stick my head into the gap, breathe in.

'You and Jeremy aren't Australia's first daddy-daughter serial killing team, are you?'

I try to joke but she sees straight through me.

'We'll try and be in here as little as possible. Let me show you where to get dressed.' She herds me out, using the same voice you would on a doddery old person or a cat cowering under a car. 'It's going to take me a while to set up.'

A crow caws somewhere nearby as I let myself back into the meat locker. Now that my eyes can cope I see that it's just a freestanding metal box in a bigger warehouse space, nothing more sinister than that.

We'd discussed how I was supposed to look in the shot, but I'd kind of run with my ideas a bit. I tried to keep my mind on Chloe's folio and all the visual references she'd collected, I really thought carefully about it.

Chloe stops what she's doing to look, a set of leads in her hands, gaffer tape bangles around her wrists. I stand, one bare numb foot on top of the other, horribly, unfamiliarly awkward.

'It's good,' she says after a few seconds.

'Really?'

A cold draft blows up the see-through white dress I pinched from Mum's wardrobe. I've got my floral bathers on underneath, and I've blanked out my face with white powder, blending blue eye shadow here and there for that half-dead look. Most of my effort has gone into my hair, which I'd started at home, tangling and plaiting bits of it up, pinning it into place. On top is the crown that took me a week to make. It's a crown fit for a travelling Opal warrior queen, made from twigs and feathers and plastic magical stones from my secret suitcase. A relic from Wingdonia, a re-creation of the fantasy.

No one but me needs to know what it means, not even Chloe.

'Nah, it's better than good, you look great. I'm nearly done.'

Chloe seems different here, out of school. More grown up, more herself. She finishes taping the cords down and checks all the connections.

One corner of the room has been turned into a set. There are two of those umbrella flash things, a crumpled sheet on the ground, fairy lights taped up, battery packs and cords hidden away to the side. The lights bring out the mottled patterns and stains on the concrete. I can see the ideas from her folio coming together.

'How do you know so much about this?'

'I don't really. I read a lot of Wikihows.' Her long black hair hangs over her shoulder as she checks the spidery tripod and camera for stability. 'All of this belongs to school. If we break anything, we're screwed.'

She straightens. 'Right. Can you lie here? I put a little cross on the spot, see that masking tape?'

I lie down slowly, arranging my nightie around me. The cold of the concrete floor shocks my skin.

*You wanted dark, Natalia*, I tell myself, *you wanted real, so lie down already.*

Chloe takes some test pics, murmuring to herself. She rearranges my feet and arms and holds a little white-balance meter near my face.

'I have no idea if I'm doing this right,' she says.

With my eyes closed, the clicking of the SLR sounds like insects chirping.

'I don't know what the hell you've got on your head,' says Click-Click-Chloe, 'but it works.'

Damp seeps into my muscles and joints and I let it. I wanted everyone to stop lying to themselves and each other and look at what's really happening, to all of us.

*I'm dead*, I tell myself. *My heart has stopped, my blood is sludge, the electricity in my brain is gone.*

When you're dead everything stops, the activity in your cells creaks to a halt. Your brain powers down, the sparks that leap from neuron to neuron cease, all your thoughts and memories and what you think of as your personality is gone because your brain machine has stopped. You don't have a soul, because what you thought of as your soul was just electricity in your brain. You only exist while the machine thinks you do.

Afterwards, where do you go? What happens to all these thoughts?

I start to shiver, the smallest possible tremors all over.

'Are you cold? Can you handle a few more minutes?'

Chloe speaks to me from a thousand kilometres away. I manage to lift my head.

'How does it look?' My mouth barely moves.

'It's hard to tell on the display, it's so small. I want to try one more thing, if you can hack it?'

She leans over me and shakes a ziplock bag full of feathers. 'It needs more colour. I'm trying to do this black, white and red thing.'

The scarlet feathers drift over my goose-bumped arms like light-falling snow. I close my eyes and hear the camera beep and click.

But too soon the shivering, the leaf-fluttering shakes return. I shake from head to toe, I couldn't stop it if I tried, I'm a girl possessed.

Maybe this was what happened to Yin, or is still happening now: the cold, the bare skin, the helplessness. When we were little girls we would go everywhere holding hands, take baths together, sleep in the same bed. How could she be going through this alone? How did we end up so far apart?

'Only a few more,' Chloe murmurs.

I retreat further into my own head which is bare and calm, as empty as the meat locker. When the tears come, they're silent. They come without announcement. Plain salt water, trickling down my nose and running over my cheeks.

I think I have it in check but then the stream flows stronger, the water rises and threatens to flood. I have to push against it. Enough. Let out just enough.

'Sorry,' I say with my eyes still shut. The shivers take over my body, becoming bigger and bigger, like I'm having a fit. The more I tense my muscles the more they misbehave, my body has a mind of its own.

Chloe's feet shuffle on the concrete. I will my body to stop convulsing, ashamed for her to see me like this, but her hand comes down on my shoulder, heavy and reassuring and warm and she keeps it there, squatting by my side until the tremors have run through me and away.

If my mother were truly psychic about my bad behaviour as she claims to be then she would be able to sense that Chloe and I are currently eating our body weight in trans-fat-laden French fries and gluten-soaked burger buns and almost one inch of definitely non-organic meat slathered in corn-syrup-laced ketchup. Jeremy has gone to the enormous alcohol-barn across the road and left us to feed the empty hole that artistic genius has created inside of us. I might officially be a muse.

The restaurant is super-heated and I'm wearing every bit of clothing I brought and some of Chloe's as well, but I still can't stop the shaking that springs from somewhere in the middle of my body.

Chloe pulls the patty out of her burger and eats it first, and then eats the salad and then eats the soggy bun and it's a really gross way to eat. I try not to look at what she's doing but the upside is that she doesn't mention how shaky I am,

191

and we pretend like nothing out of the ordinary happened. I like that about her.

'I want to eat these fries for the rest of my life.' I demonstrate by putting five in my mouth at once. 'What else are you doing for the hols?'

'Pretty sure it's going to be nothing but homework and this project,' Chloe replies. 'Dad's letting me use the spare room at his house.'

'Will you send me updates?'

Chloe's phone beeps. She checks it with one hand.

'Is that your secret lover?'

'Ha! Nice try.' She puts her pillaged burger down and wipes her fingers. 'Actually, it's my friend Katie. She's worried that she's pregnant. I have to go over to hers and watch her pee on a stick tonight.'

Her face doesn't even change expression as she says this. If one of my group got preggers, you'd better believe there'd be an instant world summit. The disturbing image of Sarah, Ally, Marley and I wearing those dorky baby carriers on our fronts flashes at me, uninvited. It's horrific.

Chloe laughs at my appalled face. 'It's a false alarm. She's on the pill, but she's a stress-head. Sometimes I think she wants it to be true, because then she wouldn't have to finish school.' Chloe finally lets one half of her burger bun rest in peace. 'What would you do if you got pregnant?'

The question takes me by surprise so much I answer truthfully. 'Well, I think I'd have to have sex for that to be an issue.'

'What do you—oh. Oh, right.' Chloe looks embarrassed.

She suddenly pays enormous attention to her thickshake.

'Yes,' I confirm. 'You may say it out loud. I am the sluttiest-looking virgin in town.'

'No! I wasn't thinking that.' Chloe has flushed adorably red.

'I'm joking,' I say. 'It's not a precious gift I'm saving. My sister says I shouldn't be so heteronormative and that I've done enough stuff with enough people to consider myself not a virgin. I've done everything but *it*—what about you?'

'Everything but? Nah, I'm not into that butt stuff.'

It takes me a moment to catch her drift, and then I can see she's barely holding herself together.

'Filthy harlot!'

I throw fries at her and she grows hysterical. Finally, someone with their head as much in the gutter as me.

'TELL ME, LITTLE CHLO-CHLO.'

Eventually she relents.

'Okay, okay. I did it a few times, and I shouldn't have. This guy Brandon at my old school really liked me, and I knew I wanted to. I wasn't in love with him or anything. I thought it would be a good opportunity to…get it out of the way? That sounds awful, doesn't it?'

'No, I get it.'

'Afterwards I didn't know why I'd been in such a rush to do it. And I also figured out way too late that he's got a thing for Asian girls. I felt…like I should have realised.'

'Haven't you heard? We're teenagers. Apparently we're supposed to be impulsive one hundred per cent of the time.'

We smile at each other and it's this completely calm

moment. My smile wavers when I realise this might be the first time I've felt genuinely happy since Yin was taken.

I'm a monster.

There were so many times today when I was going to tell Chloe about my history with Yin, how close we used to be. And I knew if I did Chloe wouldn't make a big deal out of it, she would take it in, like she does with everything, like a sponge that soaks up everything you've spilled. But I still didn't say anything.

'Chloe,' I whisper, leaning forwards, shaking off the guilts. 'There's this old lady right behind you, and she's been listening to *every word we've said.*'

Her mouth makes a perfect shocked circle, and she's trying to see over her shoulder, and then Jeremy knocks really loudly on the window with his car keys and scares the living daylights out of both of us.


When I get home I go straight to the kitchen and pour myself a glass of juice. I finish it and pour another. I have a very specific orange juice thirst that will never be quenched.

I think of all the boys and the couple of girls that I've had not-sex with and it calms me to run through the list, picturing faces and names and parties and places. I don't think about cold concrete against my skin and uncontrollable shivers.

I start looking in the cupboards for a packet of those fun-size chocolate bars that Mum hides for when she's menopausal, and my plan is to eat them one after the other in the bath while the world goes away, at least for a little while.

'Keep it down,' a voice says. 'Your dad's upstairs with one of his migraines.'

Mum is on the couch, in the dark, doing nothing that I can see, which is something that she's been doing more and more of lately. I kick off my heavy boots and sit with her. I offer her the bag of chocolate bars. She takes one but doesn't open it.

Last time Dad had migraines he had to take three weeks off work. When he's not all the way on, he's usually all the way off.

'Did you have fun with your friend?'

'She's not my friend.'

I feel terrible a split-second after saying that out loud. Embarrassing crying aside, I had more fun with Chloe today than I have had with anyone for a while.

'Well, did you have fun with your not-friend?'

'Yes I did. And you're right, she is my friend.' I polish off a bar in two bites and start on another. I should have asked Chloe if she needed help over the school holidays, if there's anything else I could do. I should have made that much more clear when she and Jeremy dropped me off.

'You look pretty with your hair like that,' Mum says.

I touch my head, feeling the pointy crown atop my skull, which is where it's been the whole time we drove home and ate Maccas. I'd forgotten I was wearing it. Yin and I never told our parents, never told any grown-ups, about Wingdonia. I might have mentioned it to Liv, but that's it.

'How come Dad's not well?'

Mum sighs. 'This has been hard on him. The police coming here really upset him. Not that he'll say so out loud.

We found out that the McIlwraiths had their house searched too.'

My chewing halts. Sarah didn't say a word.

'God, this whole thing. It's not healthy for you girls, is it?' Mum rubs her temples as if she's also brewing a headache. 'Every man you know is a potential suspect. How are you going to grow up to like them?'

'I like them just fine,' I say, without even knowing if it's true. Maybe it is. Marcel keeps messaging me, even though I've hardly been encouraging. I might have spoken too eagerly, because Mum's eyebrows are now saying: *don't like them too much.*

'Are you sure you're all right though, love?' Mum reaches out and strokes my arm. 'Do you want to speak to anyone about all this?'

I brush her aside. I don't want her to start on one of her 'you'll feel better if you talk about it and you know you can tell me anything, anything at all' spiels.

'Should I go upstairs and see if Dad needs anything?'

'I think he wants to be on his own,' says Mum, and I'm relieved.

## DAY 43

Something bizarre happens as I'm standing on the Mitchells' doorstep. I shrink, like Alice after drinking from the bottle, and then I'm twelve years old and my hair is long and snarled and my boobs have just come in. I'm allowed to spend all afternoon and evening at Yin's house and all I want to do is watch dance tutorials on YouTube. All Yin wants to do is read, hold her guinea pigs and tell me about orchestra camp, boring boring. There's smoke in the air from the bushfires and we are already splitting apart without really knowing it yet, the way tectonic plates move away from each other minutely, breaking up continents.

The door opens a crack, Chunjuan looks through and the spell is broken.

I'm still drained from the photo shoot yesterday and the tote bag full of Yin's things is a burden and my head spins from the time travel.

If I was scared that Chunjuan wouldn't want to see me, I needn't have been. Welcome marks her face.

'No one there?' Her eyes dart over the garden.

I remember that they've been at the centre of a media circus for six weeks now and you'd think they'd lock their front gate, but they don't. They've always been hit and miss with it, that's the bit no one ever mentions in any of the TV reports about their supposed fortress, and also that the video intercom has never been wired in.

Chunjuan ushers me in and she doesn't hug me, she grips my arm in that way she's always had and leans her head into mine. The smell in here, the rose-scented cleaning spray and something pungent simmering on the stove, makes my head spin through layers of time again and I have to breathe to bring myself fully into the here and now.

'Ice tea, juice, Ovalteen, Pepsi?' Chunjuan says when we are installed in the kitchen.

'Ovalteen?' I didn't know you could still get it. Chunjuan moves to make it. I let my bag slump to the floor. There are bits of dried grass on it, from where I hid it on the banks of the oval during classes.

I looked through the stuff from Yin's locker properly at home, finally, and what do you know, there was nothing to worry about, nothing too sinister or heartbreaking and no reason to avoid it. I held her things and I couldn't tell if she was still the Yin I knew.

The kitchen is the same but different and Chunjuan's face is the same but different. She pops the microwave door to heat the milk.

The walls are a different colour since I was here last, peach instead of tan. Every appliance is stainless steel and new, but the scrolls on the wall are old and the photos in the frames are too. There's a picture of Chunjuan and Stephen on a cruise ship, studio portraits of Albert and Nelson, and Yin's old school photo, the one they used in the first news reports. Maybe the police are holding on to this year's photo now. I look away quickly.

'You should have come earlier.' Chunjuan places a mug in front of me and a plate of biscuits too.

'I know.' I burn my mouth on the hot drink and sneak a close look at her. Her jeans and cardigan flap loosely, her face is a hundred years awake. She doesn't look like she hates me for being alive and well and sitting in her house instead of Yin.

'How are your parents?'

'Good.'

'Your mum sent me flowers. Chrysanthemum. Very nice.'

'I have to give—' I start, but Chunjuan gets in first.

'It's good you are here, Natalia. The school wants to hold a memorial service for Yin before the end of the year.'

'What?'

'They say it will help everyone cope with their exams.'

'That's bullshit.' It slips out of my mouth before I can stop it and Chunjuan gives me a disappointed look. 'Sorry, but—it's too soon. It's not right.'

The police haven't given up, at least I don't think they have, so why should we? I don't know what to believe anymore.

'I understand why they want to do it. Maybe it's good to close it off. To finish the year properly.'

'No. It's way too soon!'

Memorials are for remembering dead people, which is a way of saying that you plan to forget them really soon. The school acts like they want us to talk about our feelings, but really what they want is for us to pretend we're only having nice pastel weepy emotions and concentrate on getting the kind of marks that will get us into law or medicine.

'We're not giving up. I will never give up.' Chunjuan places a hand on her chest. 'I still feel in my heart that she must be alive. I would know if she was gone. But it makes sense to do something to help you girls cope.'

Chunjuan reaches across the bench and catches my hand. She's got proper surgeon's hands, small and pale with long thin fingers, sinew underneath. I wonder if she's still working or if Yin's disappearance has cracked normal life apart completely. I can't imagine her operating on people's brains in the state she's in.

I really, really want to believe that Yin is still alive and I'm afraid I don't, but that doesn't mean I want a church service.

'Will you say something nice at the memorial? You know her best.'

It's Chunjuan asking, with her cold hands and lined face, haunting her too-big clothes and I nod yes, even though I'm not the one who knows Yin best anymore.

The house is too quiet. 'Where are Al and Nelly?'

'Science camp. Yin was supposed to be skiing with Milla's family this week.' Chunjuan says it in a matter-of-fact way, and it shouldn't shock me, but the thought of Yin going away with someone else's family for the holidays makes my head spin with jealousy.

We talk, or I talk, because Chunjuan wants to hear inconsequential stories about Mum and Dad and Liv and some of the other girls at school, the ones that went to Junior School with Yin and I, and the whole time the television is on, muted, in the background with a cooking show.

When I leave I promise to visit again and soon, I promise that I won't be a stranger and that's when Chunjuan latches onto me like I'm a lifebuoy and she cries like she did during the first press conferences, crying like a child who's fallen over and grazed their knees.

I hate being hugged but I let her lean into me, and I remember Chloe's calm presence yesterday, and how much it helped, so I press my hands into Chunjuan's skinny spine and I try to be solid around her until she cries herself out.

After she draws herself together, she gives me a plastic bag full of tights and hair ties, saying she bought them for Yin and never got to give them to her.

'Please be very careful, Natalia. Take care and watch and protect your family,' she says.

I can't tell her about the bag of Yin's things, so I leave it sagging on the kitchen floor and hope it won't shock her too much when she finds it later that night.

# Chloe

**DAY 44**

'It's bigger than I thought it would be.'

Mum pulls in slowly at the kerb and we get out of Ron and Pearl's car. The sky is pink and birds are wheeling overhead.

Dad and Jarrod's house sits on a big block of grassy land, shedding layers of paint and roof tiles like an animal sloughing off its old skin. They bought the house from an elderly Maltese couple and there are fruit trees everywhere and a passionfruit vine over the carport.

'More of a dump, don't you mean?' I pull Mum's suitcase behind me, the one she bought to go back to Singapore for her dad's funeral. I hand Mum a roll of paper that's almost as tall as her and try not to worry about making her drive me here.

The suitcase bucks wildly on the uneven front path.

When Dad answers the door I note that he has brushed his hair and ironed his shirt.

'Come through, come through.'

He has the good sense not to give Mum the guided tour, but I notice her head swivelling, taking in every possible detail. I hope she's not imagining the alternate future where she and Dad stay together and they can afford a falling-apart house to have all their arguments in.

We pass the spare room that Dad has set aside for when Sam and I stay over, which we never do, and which is where I assumed I would be working on my project.

Dad leads us through the kitchen and out the back door, past the Hills hoist, to the decrepit chipboard shed near the compost heap. He opens the door and gestures like a fancy butler for me to step inside. I raise my eyebrows, because I'm pretty sure this is Jarrod's reiki room, and you couldn't pay me to spend time in it.

Nestled inside the shed is the perfect art studio.

The walls are freshly painted white. The floorboards are bare and already paint-spattered, with a threadbare Persian rug at one end. The windows have been washed and cleared of vines, letting in the natural light. There's an easel and a card table. A beanbag and a milk crate with a water jug on it.

Dad flicks the switch near the door and the overhead light comes on.

'We got the power fixed,' he says. His expression is expectant, but my face has stiffened like a plaster cast and I turn away.

It could almost be a proper studio for a proper artist.

It's too good for me. I don't deserve it.

Dad starts bustling around the room. 'You can stick things to the wall…I've got to find the old trestle table some-where in the garage…I found the easel in hard rubbish, which was a stroke of luck.'

Mum leans the roll of paper against the wall. Her arm snakes around my shoulders. 'It's perfect, Jez,' she says. 'This is very thoughtful.'

She looks at me, and I'm embarrassed to feel my eyes well.

'Let's have a cuppa while Chloe unpacks some of her supplies.'

'Don't we have to get back?' I push my glasses up and wipe my eyes. Mum's shift starts at eight and she has to have dinner before she leaves.

'We've still got time,' she says and they exit.

I'm left alone in the terrifying white space with my own shaky potential.

I slowly unpack my suitcase—watercolour paints, brushes, masking tape, glue—and run through what I have left to do: pick the image, edit it, get it printed, perfect my hand tinting, and then tackle the final piece. And make sure the entire process is documented in my folio. Every decision and theme and symbol has to be justified and explained. Ms Nouri is big on that.

I've looked through all the photos I took on Saturday, my laptop whirring furiously as it tried to cope with the file sizes, and a lot of the pics are darker and gloomier than I'd planned. I didn't get the lighting quite right and Natalia has disappeared into the background. I wish I could find time to do the photography elective next term; I would love to get better at this.

What amazes me is how calm Natalia looks in most of the frames, when in reality she was shaking all over, about to break apart.

At first I thought it was just the cold, but then I realised it was more than that. It looked like shock, like sadness, like everything bad hitting her all at once. Something was wrong with her, something more than the stress that we're all feeling. I don't know her well enough to guess what it could have been, though.

All I could do was crouch next to her and let her know I was there. Maybe I should have asked her what it was about. In the end, we packed up and went to lunch, as if nothing had happened.

I zip up the empty suitcase and check my phone. We need to get moving. I turn off the light and carefully shut the door.

The librarian hands me the stack of books and my knees buckle under their unexpected weight. Somehow I manage to also grab onto the pencils he offers. Pens are forbidden in the State Library Heritage Collections Reading Room, as if they're used to people forgetting they're handling rare items and doodling in the margins.

I pick a table next to the wall, right at the back. I'm the youngest person in here by far. To my right a polished woman in hijab pores over a folder full of handwritten letters, in front of me a man with silver hair examines a map with a magnifying glass.

There's a clock high up on the wall, above the check-in desk. My print won't be ready to pick up for another two hours.

The photo lab assistant was patient while I decided on paper, explaining the pros and cons of each, and the price per centimetre. I didn't realise I'd have to pay a rush fee, but I agreed, because I have to spend next week tinting and finalising my piece. I was already too embarrassed by how little I knew about the process.

I could fill the time proofreading the International Studies essay that I rushed through yesterday, but instead I've got three hard-to-find Bill Henson monographs in front of me, the sort of thing you would definitely never find at the Morrison Heights public library, and that you can't even find at Balmoral.

When I crack the first book open, the one that covers Henson's earlier work, I'm flooded with excitement.

The paper is thick and glossy, the images shadowy, deep, inviting.

I turn pages through hazy ballet classes, haughty school-girls in straw hats, a lone house in the woods, downturned faces in the street, a little girl wearing her mother's pearls, an erect nipple, ruined buildings, dilapidated glamour, petrol stations, burning houses, city lights.

My mind settles into the same flowing hum as it does when I jog. I move onto the next book, and the next.

Beautiful dishevelled young people. Bare skin, sexy angles, tangled limbs, wet mouths, drunken abandon, muddy smears, floating. They look like adults one moment and teenagers the next. Ecstatic in one shot, miserable in others. Troubled or hedonistic, it's hard to tell.

I'd be happy if I could take one photo that matters, and here are hundreds.

The realisation that I could work at this for fifty years and never achieve anything half as good as these images thumps me in the chest. If you want to feel confident about what you're doing, don't look at great art.

I stretch my arms up and out, realising that I've been hunched over the books for quite some time. The man in front of me has been replaced by a professor-type in a knitted vest.

The woman to my right is taking careful photos of each letter and envelope, openly, so it must be allowed.

I flick back through the monographs, trying to find the images that have struck me the most, lining up my phone to capture them. I photograph the schoolgirls in hats and the little girl in pearls. The house in the woods. When I land on the city street scene with a solitary Asian face in a white crowd, something dawns on me.

Almost everyone is white.

I turn to my favourite sequence of pictures, the sullen, naughty teens. They look gorgeous and highbred, despite their degradation. Blue veins and pale skin. Tawny hair and red lips. They could be Natalia and some Grammar boys, so easily. They definitely couldn't be me.

I check again, racing through page after page, finding a world that is overwhelmingly Western and white. This is not what the streets of my town look like.

I wonder why I've never noticed this about Henson's photographs before. Does it make me like the photos any less? How could I like something that ignores my existence? It's still on my mind as I hand the books back to the librarian at the desk and sign out in the visitor book.

'Are you interested in contemporary photography?' the librarian asks. I'm so lost in thought I'm slow to answer.

'Yeah, I guess. I mean, I'm trying to learn about it. There are so many different styles.'

'You should speak to my colleague, Chris. They know everything there is to know about our photographic collections. Do you want me to see if they're around?'

'I don't want to bother—'

The librarian waves my protests aside. He makes a quick call then sends me out to the main room, to the info desk. Chris has short purple hair and a septum piercing.

'So, what exactly are you looking for?' they say.

'I don't know…' I'm positive Chris would rather deal with weighty academic requests than vague curiosity from a teenager. 'We've been introduced to some photographers at school, but they're all the famous ones. I guess…I want to see photos of someone who looks like me,' I say. 'Or a lot of different types of people, actually.'

Chris claps their hands. 'This is the best enquiry I've had all day. Come.'

They march me to the Arts Reading Room and load me up with books from the photography section.

'I'll give you too many options, then you're more likely to find something that resonates.'

Chris helps me lug the books to a table and then leaves me alone. I want to thank them for taking me seriously, but the words get stuck and they're gone before I can say it.

The array of art books is mind boggling. Most are related to exhibitions that have happened all over the world, so it's like taking a round-the-world trip in an hour.

A book about masquerade and self-portraiture and constructing different selves. A catalogue from the Lagos Photo Festival. Collections of found photographs from India. A coffee-table book about female Chinese artists. Gender performance in photography.

Some photos are posed and almost look like movie stills, some are so casual they seem like accidents. I think my photo of Natalia falls somewhere between the two, and I wish I'd thought more intentionally about that before taking it.

I spend some time on a monograph of Tracey Moffatt's work. I've seen her photographs before, but only one or two at a time. And there's something different about seeing the image on a page, running my fingers over the coloured paper, more alive and tangible than looking at photos on a screen. Her photos are carefully staged and full of symbolism.

I pause at one of her most famous images: Moffatt dressed in a cheongsam, looking expectant and wistful in front of a falling-down shack. There's a brassy blonde woman in the doorway, a sweaty guy drinking inside, a pair of blurry kids and a young Chinese man in a traditional conical hat outside. The landscape is red and hot and dusty, and obviously fake.

I wonder about where the Chinese elements fit in with Moffatt's Aboriginal heritage, but I don't know enough about her to figure it out. She's saying something important, though, it radiates off the page. The photo uses stereotypes and stock characters, but the effect is mysterious and the colours glow and Moffatt looks in control of the whole thing.

I turn next to the book about Chinese female artists, called *Half the Sky*. Brave women who worked in private without acclaim, who made large-scale ink works, who shocked everyone by shooting their own artwork with real bullets at an exhibition opening.

The introductory essay explains that the title is based on the Mao Zedong quote: Women hold up half the sky.

I'd read in the paper that morning how many calls the police hotline had received about Yin's disappearance—apparently hundreds of calls from people all over, and not just about Yin but about dozens of other missing women too. Shouldn't we be doing more to find them? Caring more that they've disappeared?

I know the longer Yin's gone, the more we should worry for her, but I've noticed that the pure fear of the first weeks has melted away. The more time that passes, the easier it becomes to forget.

If women hold up half the sky, then why are we so disposable?

I've lost count of how many hours I've stared at my photo. I have it clipped to the easel, set up near the window, where the light is strongest. It's still a shock to see something I created blown up so big. Even the mere size of it makes it seem more like proper art.

Natalia sprawls on the mottled concrete, red feathers sprinkled around her body, looking like a littered petal or a lost princess, or a dreaming virgin or a bad girl getting what she deserves. All of these contradictory things that somehow get heaped on young women.

The print turned out shadowier than I expected, but the colours are everything I wanted, even though I'd originally wanted a subject with dark hair.

A bird walks across the corrugated tin roof overhead, its spindly feet amplified into sharp clangs. I pick up my brush.

After practising on countless throwaway photos, I've finally plucked up the courage to paint the real thing. I've coloured Natalia's cheeks and given her exposed limbs the barest hint of pale blue. So far, no mistakes. I can't afford to get another print, so whatever happens, I'm stuck with it.

My phone rattles on the card table but I ignore it. Natalia has already messaged me a billion times since the shoot, demanding to see updates.

My next step will be to create a rainbow aura around the ceiling and edges of the picture, as if something otherworldly might be at play.

I walk back to the reference pics I have taped to the shed walls, looking closely at my eighteenth-century geisha, the photo that gave me the idea to hand colour my image.

Underneath her heavy costume and makeup the girl is probably very young. I imagine letting her hair down, wiping her face, putting her in a Balmoral uniform instead.

Who arranged for this photo to be taken? Was it her family, or her employer, or a tourist? Did she want to pose, or was it for someone else? Does it make a difference?

I scrawl the words that come to me—*someone's watching*—on a piece of paper and set it aside.

Even though I haven't finished colouring my photograph yet, I can tell already that something is missing. The image is too similar to the *Devil Creek* billboard, too much like the crime novel covers. There's not enough comment in the artwork yet, not enough of my opinions.

The air is stifling in here; a headache crouches at the edge of my vision.

*Someone's watching*—who? The world, the newspapers, Doctor Calm, the police, TV viewers, book readers. And me.

It's possible that the thing missing from my photo is me. Or someone like me—a teenage schoolgirl watching the scene. Watching the scene of her death, her falling, the depiction of her demise. Showing that we see it, but that's not who we are. But I don't know how to make that happen. I don't have the time or money to take the photo again.

My phone vibrates.

I scoop it up, and my drink bottle too, and go outside.

The garden is another world. There are bees and butter-flies buzzing about and I can smell the tomato plants. The gentle sun feels good on my face. I stretch my limbs, waking up my muscles.

It's not a bad day, after all. Maybe spring is almost here. It's been nice to be away from the rumours and the endless cycle of news and no-news.

I read my messages—Natalia has gotten huffy to the point where she's asking for Dad's address, saying she'll come over, Liana wants Katie and I to watch her netball grand final on the weekend, Mum needs help resetting our modem.

I go in the back door, through the sunroom, past the laundry and into the kitchen, all three rooms looking like they were tacked onto the house as an afterthought and might fall off one day. Dad is at work and Jarrod is banging drums in the bush with a group of men, so I have the place to myself.

I try to picture Natalia inside my dad's house, but it's impossible.

It would look like a slum to her, to any of the Balmoral girls, probably, instead of a major life achievement.

I fill my bottle at the kitchen sink and then drink it almost in one continuous hit.

Nestled among the bills and recipes tacked onto the fridge is the invitation to our school art exhibition opening. It's in the first week of term, after our artworks have been up for a few days, to give students time to vote on their favourite.

I'm terrified about Dad coming with me to Balmoral, what he'll say and think about the groomed school grounds, the epic buildings, the august portraits on the wall. Even worse, I'm worried how he'll act around Ms Nouri and the other parents, what random topics he'll raise or, worst of all, what will happen if he decides to talk politics with them.

I can't figure out if it's going to be the worst or greatest night of my life.

I return to the garden, squint into the light. I need to add myself into the photo somehow. Maybe I should get Dad to take some photos of me in my Balmoral uniform, then print them out and make a collage, cutting and pasting to construct a frame.

More work, in short.

Because no one's around, I allow myself a little growl that turns into a satisfying anguished groan. This project is taking over my life.

'Who's that?' Mum asks, when my phone lights up.

'Natalia. Again.'

'You two seem to get along well.'

'Hnnh,' I say, even though she is sort of right. I read Natalia's message and then stow my phone. 'She's desperate to see how the photo is going. Like, *desperate*.'

Natalia does this thing where she doesn't type out a full message and send it like normal people do, she types out single thoughts or phrases, and then sends them separately, making my phone go off like a machine gun.

'How *is* it going?'

'Don't ask.'

I wrap the roti in foil, ready to reheat in the oven. Rendang spice fills our entire flat. Sam's having a sleepover at his friend Louis's house and we don't have to cater to his kid tummy, so Mum is making this thing hot. I cough from the fumes and move further away, to the other side of the bench.

'I think I need to have a break from it. I'm going to stay home tomorrow and do some practice English responses instead.'

I kick my foot up onto the stool, leaning forward to stretch my hamstring. Ouch. Even a jog with Arnold couldn't clear my head. It's like someone is blowing up a balloon inside my brain. It's pressing outwards and I can't deflate it.

'Sounds good.' Mum tips a tin of coconut milk into the pan and stirs. 'This will need to simmer for at least an hour. Want to watch an episode of something?'

Once we settle on the couch with a pot of oolong tea I say, 'Ma, if you promise not to tell me off, can I tell you something?'

She makes that face that means she's steeling herself about the demonic sex cult I've joined.

'You know Dad was out all today? Well, I kind of had a snoop around his garage.'

'Oh, Chloe.' Mum uses her disappointed voice.

'I was looking for an extra drop sheet! And then I had...a look around.'

'What were you looking for?'

'I don't know. Like, rope or girl's clothing or something?'

An embarrassed laugh escapes. I felt completely justified while I was poking through Dad's boxes and tools, but switched to guilt immediately afterwards.

'It's just that people at school won't stop talking about everyone's dads getting interviewed by the police!'

'Hon, it's fine. It makes perfect sense.' Mum pats my leg. 'All those rumours are enough to make you do something you wouldn't normally do.'

'Well, it wasn't worth it, because all I found was a major stash of eighties Playboy magazines. And a whole box of Psychedelic Noodle CDs.'

Mum erupts. She actually cries, she's laughing so hard. Psychedelic Noodle consisted of Dad and Jarrod and a few other friends in bucket hats and furry rave pants twiddling knobs and playing out-of-tune guitars. The whole thing was over by the time I was born, thankfully.

'Oh my god. How could I forget Psychedelic Noodle? I shouldn't laugh.' She leans over and kisses my forehead. 'I'm sorry, baby. This whole thing is so bleak.'

I put a cushion on my head, hoping it will soak up my shame. I wonder what this term is going to be like, if people will still be gossiping about teachers and parents and conspiracy theories. Or will they have moved on to obsessing about exams and the Year Ten formal and subject choices for next year?

'You know,' Mum ruminates, 'your dad's a pretty decent guy, even if he has been a dick in the past.'

'*Mum.*'

There is nothing more horrific than hearing that word come out of your mother's mouth, especially while she's wearing the ridiculous cat-ear headband from last Christmas. For a second she looks like a friend, not a parent, a giddy teenager. Someone who was once so in love with Dad she defied her entire family to move to Australia to be with him.

'You remember I'm having dinner with the girls tomorrow night?' she says.

I try not to smirk at the fact that Mum calls her forty-something friends 'the girls'.

'You got anything on?'

'No.' I let out a giant sigh. 'Natalia invited me to this exhibition opening, you know, friends of hers, but I don't think I'll go…'

'You should go!' Mum sits up straighter. 'You've barely been out all holidays.'

'I saw Liana the other day.'

'One time. You need to balance relaxation and work.'

'Can't you just be normal and tell me to stay home and study?'

'Ha! Normal, as if.' Mum pours the tea. 'I used to be married to the lead singer of Psychedelic Noodle. How could I be normal?'

## DAY 54

When Natalia shows up she's wearing a black linen jumpsuit and strappy sandals and statement earrings and I understand straight away, and far too late, that my jeans and trainers aren't going to cut it.

We don't hug or kiss hello, but she does give me an overly friendly punch on my arm. Meeting up during school holidays feels like an amplification of our friendship that I'm not sure either of us are prepared for.

'You ready?' she greets me. 'Let's walk.'

'Where are we going again?' For someone half a foot shorter than me she sure can walk fast. Natalia is the kind of person who walks in a straight line down the road and forces everyone to swerve around her. All she would say in her texts was that she was going to take me to 'a proper art opening, not a dweeby Balmoral thing'.

We pass a vintage clothes shop, several cafes, an art supplies store, a pilates studio, and still she doesn't answer me. She's been pestering me every day with multiple messages and now she has nothing at all to say. Go figure.

'There.' Natalia points at the crowd blocking the footpath, standing dangerously close to bikes and traffic, beers in their hands, cigarettes to their lips, hands on their phones.

I'm not at ease in this part of town, it's the kind of street that people dress up just to walk down and be seen. Natalia, on the other hand, seems completely at home; she dives into the scrum, pausing only to check that I'm following her through the clogged doorway into a narrow corridor lined with framed pictures and up an even narrower flight of stairs. The name of the gallery—Park ARC—is stencilled on the white wall.

There are people everywhere, pushed close into each other, standing on every possible flat surface. Yelling, laughing, taking selfies, dancing, drinking, screeching, hugging.

'Who do you know in this exhibition?' I grab onto the back of Natalia's jumpsuit so I don't lose her.

'Not me, my sister!' she yells back. 'Some of her friends are in it.'

We reach the main room and the situation is no better. The gallery itself is even more crowded, if that's possible. Natalia wiggles expertly into any possible crack between bodies until we reach a trestle table holding drinks. My bulky backpack—holding a change of clothes and toiletries to take to Dad's house—is almost torn from my back.

'Two beers,' she says to a surly guy in a fisherman beanie. He points at the handwritten $3 sign and she hands over a note. He doesn't ask us for ID.

'That's Liv, over there!' Natalia points but I have no way of singling her sister out. I can't see anyone that looks like her. Two girls push us away from the drinks table. One of them manages to give me a split-second once-over (verdict: not impressed) before lunging for more booze. We ricochet into the centre of the room.

Across the topography of heads I can see that there's art on the walls, even hanging from the ceilings, but no one seems to be paying any attention to it. Instead they're people-watching, checking each other out, making sure everyone knows they're having a great time, or else playing at being mysterious and poetic. No one looks over twenty-five, but no one looks as young as us either. There are designer mullets, shaved heads, big beards, round glasses. Overalls spattered with paint, clever tattoos, ripped mesh.

Natalia's face shines. You can almost see her feeding off the crush and the heat and the noise. Her eyes flick back and forth and I can't quite put my finger on it, but she's acting a little off. But maybe this is what she's like out of school, at night, at a party. 'What a bunch of freaks. Come on!'

She drags me over to her sister, who is in the far corner with a group of friends. 'Chloe, this is my dear darling sister, Olivia.'

Natalia hugs her big sister. Olivia is ridiculously good-looking, of course, but also looks very different to Natalia—she's bony and pale, with spiky black hair. 'Liv, this is Chloe, the artist I was telling you about.'

I glare at Natalia and she pokes her tongue out.

'I'm not a real artist,' I say apologetically.

'Well, neither am I.' Olivia smiles at me. 'I couldn't explain any of this crap to you. How do you know my little sister?'

'School.'

'Ah, commiserations, my friend.' Olivia holds up her bottle to clink against mine. If you look beyond the differences she has the same aqua eyes as Natalia, and the same level of charisma. That direct look that makes you feel like you have all of her attention. 'I also survived that hellhole.'

She turns to Natalia. 'Listen Tal, I have one request of

you this evening. Don't be a dork, okay, and don't drink too much.'

'That's two requests.' Natalia does her private-school princess smile but Olivia manages to stare her into submission. There's a first. The girl next to Olivia leans forward and kisses Natalia on the cheek and they start talking.

I'm left hanging, not sure if I should look at the art or try to introduce myself to someone. I settle for a combination of looking soulfully into the distance and smiling vaguely in the direction of Olivia's intimidating friends. I take a long swig of beer.

The short, quiet guy next to me asks, 'What medium do you work in?'

'What?' I lean down to hear him better. He's also dressed like an off-duty fisherman and I don't know how he can stand to wear a beanie in this sauna. A hot flush starts to creep over my cheeks and I know I need to slow down on the beer or my face will start to look like a tomato.

'Your art…what medium?'

It takes me a few seconds to figure out what he means.

'Oh. Photography, I guess. What's, uh, your medium?'

'These are all my pieces.' He gestures around us; his fingers are covered in tiny tattooed symbols. We're in a corner of small ceramic objects: arranged on shelves and hanging up on fine wire above our heads. I look closer.

'What are—oh.'

Each shape is a vulva. We're surrounded by pottery vulvas. Some with jagged teeth, some leaking red, others with thin sausages of clay balanced in them.

Olivia's friend looks at me, waiting for my response.

'They're very powerful?' I say, and that seems to satisfy him. Someone pushes past us, squishing our bodies close together. I can feel heat from the vulva artist's front and a stranger's drink trickling down my shoulder.

'Have you shown your work anywhere?' He lifts his drink to his mouth. Maybe I'm imagining it, but it seems like he presses even closer. His head is right at my chest level.

'No. I'm still learning.' I definitely don't imagine the way his gaze slides away. He scans the room over my shoulder, looking for someone better to talk to. Natalia has been drawn even further into Olivia's group of friends. It looks like she's telling them the funniest story they've ever heard.

'You know, at high school.' I say it loudly enough to be heard over the din.

The vulva artist steps slightly away from me, appraising my underage body afresh.

'Take my advice,' he says, without checking that I want any, 'work hard on your folio. You could even take a few years after school to develop your practice, then apply for VCA. It usually takes a few attempts to get accepted, but you want to start your career on the right foot. Of course, I was accepted straight from high school, but that's quite rare—'

'Thanks, but I'm not sure I even want to do it as a career.' I stop his flow. I don't think Mum intended me to take an academic scholarship just so I could bunk off and be an artist.

The vulva artist smiles tightly, no teeth. He looks disapproving—a disapproving, creepy uncle who is only a few years older than me and might touch me on the butt. 'Well. I guess art is not for everyone.'

'I guess it's not.'

The conversation falters. We both look away and I realise anew how cacophonous, how teeming, the room is. It's the very opposite of the dignified and calm NGV.

'Congratulations on your vaginas,' I say and walk away.

I spend a few minutes trying to tunnel my way over to Natalia, who seems to have completely forgotten that she was the one who invited me to this thing, but give up after taking several elbows to my ribs.

Instead I do something radical. I look at the art.

I shut out everything around me. If I did ever decide to study art—as if I would ever do a course so guaranteed to leave me poor—this would be the kind of company I would be in.

In one corner is a pile of dirty rags, a stack of sticks and an old TV playing a video of a guy smearing mud on his face. It doesn't do much for me.

The next artist is devoted to painting highways and concrete flyovers.

There's a set of guns and other weapons made using a 3D printer.

I've almost circled the gallery when I find something that interests me, in one of the smaller rooms leading off the main one.

It's a collection of photos—studio portraits of the South Sudanese artist and her family and friends, posed on sets in a formal style. The subjects wear a combination of traditional dress, retro work uniforms, modern streetwear, beaded necklaces, head wraps, sunglasses and white trainers. Bright print fabric covers every surface, punctuated by bunches of flowers in vases.

I find myself lingering on one photo, of two girls who are posed so closely they must be sisters or best friends. They look close but individual; they look like they have each other's back. I look closer—I think the artist has started with a monochrome photo and coloured it digitally, to create the very effect I've been chasing.

The room is full of the artist's vision and personality. Pattern and colour everywhere. Confidence. The labels on the wall list the artist's first name, Adut, the titles of the works, and nothing more.

My heart thumps in my chest, my fingers tingle. My eyes open to possibility. It's the same feeling I got in the pine forest during cross-country, so I recognise it now. I take photos on my phone so I can carry the feeling home with me.

I can't even imagine creating such a series that hangs together so well.

When I return to the main room it's an abomination, a brawl of posing people. The inspiration and tingles drip away.

I try to move and somehow find myself near the door to the outside world. I am carried down the breakneck stairs and out onto the street.

The outside air hits my relieved lungs. It's good to be away from hot, sweaty bodies.

I sit on the front ledge of the pizza shop next door, finally get my backpack off my shoulders, and watch cars and bikes and trams slide by. Why would Natalia act so desperate to see me all holidays and then not look out for me at all?

My annoyance grows.

Vulva artist was a tool.

Smoke from a nearby group hits me in the face so I move even further up the ledge, closer to where a girl sits with a can of lemonade.

She glances at me. 'Intense in there, right?'

I nod.

'Way too intense,' she repeats.

We fall quiet. Metres away from us, in front of a back-drop of passing cars, a soap opera plays out.

A skinny girl in platform boots starts berating this guy, poking him in the chest. A friend of the upset girl grabs her around the waist and tries to haul her away, but she's only half her size.

The girl sitting next to me gives me such an exaggerated and comical look that I laugh. She holds out a packet of gum and I take a piece. The taste of cheap beer lingers in my mouth.

'I've got to warn you, this flavour's not for everyone. It's cinnamon.' She holds out her hand for me to shake. 'I'm Adut.'

'Chloe.' Then realisation hits me. 'Wait. Is that you up there? Are those your photos?'

She confirms it.

'I don't believe it. I *love* your photos. They're the only thing I really liked.' With some effort I force my mouth shut, before I truly embarrass myself.

'Shhh, the other artists might hear you.'

Adut looks pleased. When I look closer, I do recognise

her from the photos, but her hair is shaved in an undercut now, with two tight bleached braids on top.

'It's hell standing around listening to people talk about your art,' she says. 'That's why I'm out here.'

'I'd be so nervous,' I say. 'I noticed you didn't put up an artist statement like the others did.'

She smiles. 'I have to describe my work so much at art school, I get tired of it. I want my work to speak for itself.'

'What do you say though, when people ask you what your art is about?'

Adut thinks for only a moment. 'I say it's about decolonisation and identity and migration and recognising the traditional owners of this land.'

'That's amazing,' I say foolishly, but how does a person get to the point where they can say so succinctly and without apology what they are doing? 'Do you go to VCA?'

'That place? Full of private school wankers. I'm at RMIT, doing my masters. There's a better range of students, different sorts of people, and the lecturers are good. Working artists, you know?'

I don't know, but I nod.

'How about you, Chloe?'

I blush. 'I like making art. I'm working on something photographic at the moment.'

I show her some pics saved on my phone and Adut asks questions and I explain it as best I can, even though I don't have ideas as sophisticated or as important as hers. She listens carefully as I explain my doubts and my confusion, nodding and laughing and telling me her own stories.

'I doubt myself almost every day,' she says. 'But I remind myself that being a young woman who wants to take pictures of other young women and queer folk and people of colour is enough. Putting my own representation, my own images forward, that's powerful in itself.'

'I never thought of it like that.'

'It's hard being at the start of practising something creative, knowing you've still got a long way to go. Especially if you have big ideas. Can you email me one of those?'

Adut gives me her email address and I send her a pic. My phone is still making the swooshing send sound when a man in a loud tie-dye t-shirt rockets out of the gallery stairwell. When he spots Adut he raises his hands high—*WHY?*—and pretends to reel her in on an invisible line.

'Oh, they finally noticed I'm hiding,' she says. 'Good luck, Chloe. Thanks for the chat.'

Adut gives me a quick hug and then she's gone.

I wait on the ledge for the motivation to go back upstairs and find Natalia, but I'm distracted by thoughts of different places to study and being a beginner artist and how to be myself until my chewing gum has gone tough and gross. I spit it out and realise I need to pee. I can't remember any toilets in the gallery, so I go to the 7-Eleven at the intersection, and when I come out I turn left, instead of back towards the gallery.

I don't know what happens, but my feet take me up the street until I reach the tram stop. I'm on a tram, heading for the train station before I even realise that I've left the opening and I'm not going back.

## Natalia

**DAY 55**

The world glows green when I wake up, still surrounded by pillowy softness. I might have been asleep for a thousand years and even though I try to blink away the fuzziness, still my eyelids won't stay open.

'You talk in your sleep, did you know that?' Yin's voice, close to me.

I smile without opening my eyes.

Her mat is close enough that our sleeping bags brush together with a whisper. The morning sun creeps through the thin tent walls, our secret grotto, our private place, two girls sitting inside a cave made of curled leaves and petals.

'I've been waiting for you,' says Yin. Her voice is older, sadder. 'Nat. I've been waiting so long.'

I wake with a lurch, wake with Yin's voice right in my ear. My heart beats a sickening pitter–patter and her voice keeps reverberating in my head.

My sheets are tangled, I'm sticky with sweat. I can tell from the grey light seeping around the edges of my bedroom curtains that I've woken way too early. Liv and Naomi dropped me off late last night, after post-exhibition pizza and gelato, and I stayed up even later watching videos in bed.

You're awake, I tell myself, you're awake in your room and it's now and not then and Yin is not whispering in your ear and she's not even here anymore. So why did her voice sound so real?

I throw off my doona and sit up, hoping to shock myself into wakefulness, into reality. You can make up your mind what to feel but then your traitorous brain will lift the gate and let the monsters in while you sleep.

I dig my nails into my arm until I am back in my body, back with it.

I can't have dreams like this, I can't.

I don't mean to eavesdrop, but when I pad out to the landing with my hair mussed up, still in my disgusting sweaty pyjamas, desperate for juice and toast and coffee and daylight and normalness, I can hear Mum's voice and something about it is so instantly secretive that I know to creep.

I skip the squeaky stairs, I'm silent as a mouse as I crouch at the bottom, Mum only metres away in the kitchen. I sit my butt down.

'…working from home today,' she says.

Her soft tone means it's a personal call; she has an entirely different voice that she uses for work.

'I'm a little worried about her…keep an eye on things… uh huh, uh huh…'

I wish for a rubbery extendable neck that could wrap

around the corner like a periscope. Worried about who? Me? Liv? Grandma?

'Have you heard much from Allison?'

Aha. She's talking to Ally's mum.

'I still remember my first time in Italy,' Mum says. 'The food. The *men*!'

I roll my eyes. Get a grip, horny old lady.

'I think it's been hard for her, with all her friends out of town. We were supposed to go down to the beach house, but work took over…'

I grip the carpet beneath me. She's talking about me, behind my back, to Ally's mum.

'It's more than that though. She's erratic, moody…I don't know. She's not being herself and she won't talk to me at all…'

There's silence as Ally's mum weighs in on my craziness, my inability to be myself.

'There's my therapist,' says Mum, 'I did wonder…'

I've heard enough. I walk back upstairs, not bothering to be nearly as careful this time. Fury rises up in me. I go to my bathroom, splash my face with cold water, splash it into my mouth too and spit it out, but a scream still wells up.

I shut my bedroom door.

How many of her friends has she been calling to talk about my moods? Sarah's mum too? The whole neighbourhood?

I grab my pillow and scream into it, dig my fingers in and gouge just like we learnt to do in self-defence class.

After pummelling my fingers I sit very still on the edge of my bed until my boiling blood subsides. I scroll on my phone, looking at photos of the traitors Sarah and Ally in Florence, posing sluttily in front of the Uffizi, attending a paper marbling workshop—of all the things they would not be interested in. Sarah's main motivation for going on the trip is to lose her virginity to an Italian guy because apparently that's the fanciest cherry-popping a girl can have. Those two don't even care about art, not like Chloe, who would actually appreciate seeing everything they're taking for granted.

Chloe.

She plain disappeared last night, *poof!* into thin air, sending me a message saying she had a headache and was on a train home, but then didn't reply to any of my messages after that.

I asked her if she talked to anyone interesting, I asked her if she'd hooked up with Genital Gerard, I asked her if she liked the art, I asked her if she thought my sister was nice.

I send her another message now: *Good morning are you completely inspired now?*

Because that was the whole point, to inspire her. So that she could meet proper real-life young artists and talk about paint and balsa wood or whatever things they go ga-ga about and make connections and then have her first exhibition and live happily ever after and always remember that I was the first person to believe in her vision the end.

I stare at my phone. She doesn't reply.

I want to see our photo, I want to get back that energy of doing something together. She listened to my ideas and opinions and I don't think I was imagining that I was a good team player even though my school reports always say

'Natalia is not a team player.' We had that feeling and then it slipped away and I want it back.

It's 7.30 a.m. and I have how many hours to fill until it's not too sad to go back to sleep again and then start another day after that, and another, and then go back to school having done almost nothing all school holidays, other than doing a great impersonation of a dead person.

I check the news and there's nothing about Yin that I don't already know.

I put on some music, I take out my suitcase, I put on the crown I made for the photo shoot. I'm clearing out my schoolbag, old mandarins, tampons spilled out of their box, no less than seven chapsticks, and I find the piece of paper I pinched off Petra, her creepy list of Doctor Calm's victims. Reading the list of the girls' names, their ages, how long they were held for, has not gotten any better.

The words 'Cold Crimes' are written at the top of the paper, in my handwriting. I don't even remember doing that, it's scary the amount of things I must do on autopilot like those people who wake up and they've crashed their car into a tree without even realising.

I search the term on my laptop, and it transpires that *Cold Crimes* is a supremely ugly website for true crime enthusiasts and I don't know why, but my heart starts beating fast immediately.

The front page is a hot mess—there are forum rules and information, lists of members and announcements, trending discussions, case folders, urgent cases, current legal trials and missing persons.

According to the sidebar there are currently 990 members online. At least half of them sound like conspiracy theorists and the other half sound like police trying not to sound like police.

I am sick to my stomach but I keep clicking, reading, clicking, reading.

Number one under 'trending discussions' is the brand new forum devoted to Doctor Calm.

When I open it there are threads upon threads about the police profile, various suspects, how the name Doctor Calm came about (according to Dtctv86 one of Doctor Calm's victims cut her finger and he told her that he's a doctor), summaries of supposed victims and linked cases and, at the bottom of the second page, the question: *Why has Yin Mitchell not been returned???*

I scroll through conspiracy theories about Yin's father and the Chinese government, child brides, and a cover-up involving police at the highest level. The majority of people think that Yin must have figured out who Doctor Calm is, recognised his voice or accidentally seen his face, and when I read that, I can picture it. I can see Yin pulling at a mask, seeing the monster and dooming herself.

The forum seems to grow as I'm reading it, spawning more and more comments and information. There's so much more available here than I've ever heard in the news reports.

BoardShorts77 suggests that Yin went willingly with a 'much older boyfriend'.

Catsrfriendz thinks that Yin has been the victim of a global child-porn ring.

MaxwellSmarts provides a supposed map of the GPS positions for Yin's phone on the night she was taken but then everyone piles on him for lying and he gets banned.

I find out the reason that the police cleared the guy on the CCTV in the convenience store is because he was interstate on the night Yin was taken.

I find out there was a scandal at Balmoral in the 1980s when one of the teachers married a student three months after she completed Year Twelve.

I find a list of reported sightings of Yin that spans from Tasmania to China.

Piratemajid114 says that aspects of Yin's kidnapping remind him of a cold case from forty years ago and links to a podcast episode.

I'm torn between thinking the world is one sick place and taking heart from the fact that so many people care about Yin's case, that they actually care about catching Doctor Calm or finding her alive. Who are these people? How do they have so much time on their hands? Why do they care? Is Petra one of them?

I imagine Chunjuan and Stephen reading this site and feel sick all over again.

Bugs crawl under my skin and my head is weird and empty like I might be getting a cold again and Mum won't stop trying to make me talk and I have to get out of the house.

I almost make it out unseen but then Mum tries to derail me when I already have one leg out of the side door.

'Where are you going?'

'Chloe's house.' The lie comes as quick and easy as snapping my fingers. I know I'm not invited to Chloe's house despite all my gentle hints. I'm still surprised she met up with me on the holidays—she's so hell-bent on remaining mysterious at all times. Would it hurt her to invite me over?

'But—I thought we could have lunch together. I was going to suggest we go down to Sushi Nara.'

Sushi Nara is my favourite and very chi-chi and expensive and Mum knows all of these things, so it says a lot about her need to keep me within her sight, but we can't have everything we want in life, can we mother.

'I'd love to Mum, but Chloe is spinning out about her project. She desperately needs my creative guidance.'

Mum's eyes narrow so maybe I overdid that a little bit.

'But…' she says and no one can put so much expression into one word and on one face than her, except maybe Liv. 'I thought we could spend some time together.'

She's terrible when she works from home, always procrastinating in the most blatant ways. I simply must not enable her and I have to make these bad bugs go away, somehow. 'I'm sorry, Mum, I'll try not to be too long. Maybe we can do girls' night tonight?'

She nods and I try not to seem too much like a bird flying out of the cage and I open the back door and I'm free.

Of course I have nowhere to go at all because South River is an inherently boring place, that's why people pay so much to live here, so that their boredom is assured for the rest of their lives and also so they don't have to see nasty poor people in non-designer clothing.

I traipse to the reserve under skies that threaten rain and the playground is deserted and the oval is fenced off to coax the grass back so that as soon as summer hits the sun can fry it all back to dry husks.

I run on the cross trainer, I do crunches on the tilted bench, I dip on the bars and thank the lord that no one is here to see me use the public exercise equipment. All of that takes up around five minutes and then I'm alone with the bugs and my bad thoughts and the memory of my dream.

I sit in the big whirly teacup and tilt back to look at the clouds. I've even done all the homework I was assigned for the holidays instead of saving it for the last minute so it turns out Mum is probably right, I'm not myself right now.

The glum grey sky whirls into a spiral as I turn the teacup steering wheel faster and faster and my thoughts wander off into the washing machine spin cycle distance and then Yin is there again. She's on the other end of the phone and she's saying:

'I can see if Milla can get a spare ticket?'

She's off to see some amateur symphony orchestra at the university recital hall with her classmate Milla, who plays the French horn and is also in the junior wind ensemble. They are friends who hang out on a Saturday even though it's only four weeks into Year Seven and Yin says nothing about the fact that we were supposed to go to the mall to buy me new swimming goggles and as much makeup as Mum will let me wear because she's already forgotten that we always hang on the Saturdays that our families aren't dragging us off to do something else.

I blink blink blink my way back into the cold metal present and my fingers itch and twitch to go back to the *Cold Crimes* website and my phone is out of my pocket before I even know what I'm doing. I scroll through some of the same stuff I read at home, then I click through to the Doctor Calm forum, that black internet spiderweb that infiltrates my brain like a weed.

The top thread is about a tabloid article published in the last few days: 'Secret Suspect Tops the List'. It's behind a paywall but someone has copied and pasted the full text of the article into a comment.

The journalist has read a confidential police document, the 'Echo Files', that names the top twelve suspects in Yin's abduction. Strangely, one of the suspects agreed to be interviewed anonymously by the journalist.

> 'Steve' was jailed for eleven years in the 1990s after pleading guilty to eight violent attacks on young girls and women during an eighteen-month period. The former gymnastics coach and father was convicted on aggravated rape and sexual assault charges after holding the victims at knifepoint in their own homes.
>
> Steve admits that he is a key suspect in the hunt for Doctor Calm, but claims that police have wrongly accused him. He says that he was grilled by police for ten hours the day after the

abduction of Yin Mitchell, and that his home in the Melbourne suburb of Stockton was searched.

'Whenever there's one of these types of crimes, the police come calling,' says Steve. 'They search my house and I answer their questions. But I did my time. I was completely rehabilitated after I was in jail, I raised a new family. I started my own business, I made something of myself.'

Good for you, Steve, I think. What a fucking great member of society you are. Congratulations on making something of yourself after you ruined eight people's lives. The report goes on to say that he remarried and had more children, but what would you even do if he was your dad? Could you still love him after you found out about his past?

I'm so disgusted I have to lean over the edge of the teacup and spit onto the tanbark.

My heart starts thumpety-thumping all over again.

There are pages and pages of comments after the article, and people are still commenting even now. You can't top these true crime nerds for detail and going the extra mile, and it makes sense how Petra of all people got sucked into this world.

There are replies with the precise details of Steve's convictions: locations, victims' first names and ages, charges. Details of which prison he served his term at. Someone has provided a blurry photo of a man, well-built, wearing a tracksuit. It's hard to see his face, but he's good-looking, sporty, not at all what I expected.

Thump thump thump.

I'm about to abandon the thread when I see a new comment: Aceventura★666 thinks they've cracked 'Steve's' real identity. As evidence they have posted a scanned original court document, and right there at the top is the name of the accused: Samuel Pulpitt. I scan the document but it's sixty pages long and full of incomprehensible language and I'm not my mother the lawyer so I quickly give up.

I re-read the article.

Samuel Pulpitt. The name burns a bright scar in my brain.

I start searching, trying every combination of words possible using the details from the comments.

Samuel Pulpitt gymnastics coach/Samuel Pulpitt Doctor Calm/Samuel Pulpitt suspect/Samuel Pulpitt 1996 convictions/Samuel Pulpitt sex crimes/Samuel Pulpitt Warrawood/ Warrawood rapes 1990s/Warrawood Milltown crimes 1990s/Gym coach sex crimes/Pulpitt prison sentence release/ Pulpitt gymnastics/Pulpitt rapist court case/Serial criminal Warrawood Milltown…and on and on and on.

Somewhere along the line there's a click in my brain and I return to the original article where they describe 'Steve' outside his Stockton home that has been searched dozens of times over the years and Stockton's not so far from school, so then I google 'Pulpitt Stockton', and I find Samuel Pulpitt in the Australian Business Registry, located in Stockton, and then I click on the next search result which happens to be the plain old telephone directory and all of a sudden my heart is leaping out of my chest and I have this: Pulpitt, S. 316 Mewling Road, Stockton.

What the hell.

What the hell.

Could it really be him?

There's a phone number, so I could just call and ask, but what if he has caller ID and then he has my mobile number?

I'm so pumped full of adrenaline that I might fly off the play equipment and shoot into the sky. I'm so sick of doing nothing. I'm so sick of sitting still

'Samuel,' I boom, scaring a nearby pigeon. 'I'm coming for you.'

I get a reply from Chloe while I'm on the train but I don't read it because I am a laser now, every part of my being from my heart to my fingertips focussed to a pinpoint of energy that says: Samuel Pulpitt of Stockton, I'm coming to get you.

Chloe has been spending her holidays in productive ways and she would approve of my sleuthing and I don't need a European trip to be exciting because I am finally doing something for Yin and all the other women and girls that have been hurt at the hands of men. I keep reading on the train. Pulpitt's oldest victim was thirty-three and the youngest fifteen. It's hard to believe you could do things that horrible to eight girls and women and only get eleven years in jail.

Eleven years versus always being scared, always looking behind you.

My fists itch to hit someone.

I get off at Stockton station and follow the blue line on the map towards Mewling Road. I am exactly like Senior

Detective Hillary Burns from *Devil Creek* in that my outfit is terrible and also I can be an ice-cold bitch. I imagine I'm an assassin on the way to my target, a Wingdonian assassin with extra-sensory perception perhaps, who can fry man-brains to a crisp with one point of her finger.

Houses in Stockton are welcoming and well-kept, even if they aren't nearly as fancy as those in South River. There are trampolines in several front yards, natives growing on the nature strips, four-wheel drives in driveways.

What will I do when I get there?

On the train I thought about writing a letter about Pulpitt's crimes and sending it to everyone on his street, or putting up posters around the neighbourhood so everyone could share in making his life hell. I guess I can still do those things if I want to but I need to keep moving to feel all right.

What will I do when I get to the house?

I'll just look. I'll see for myself what the house of a sicko looks like. Maybe it will tell me something. Maybe if I look at it I will get a sense of whether Pulpitt has anything to do with Yin's abduction, maybe I'll just *know*.

The Mewling Road sign informs me that it is named for one of the town's earliest councillors.

I am faint.

My boots make clomping noises on the footpath and I try to bring back that fizzy Detective Burns Wingdonian assassin feeling.

I pass two apartment blocks, a small park, and the local primary school. The kids have decorated the front fence with welcome messages in different languages, and there is a convicted sex offender living within walking distance from where they play so isn't life wonderful.

And then, quicker than you'd think possible, I'm at number 316.

A narrow house, weatherboard, pale green, more rundown than some of its neighbours. A moulting paperbark tree on the nature strip, a beaten-up silver station wagon parked out front.

I keep walking past, on the other side of the road, while I figure out what to do.

The article said his house had already been searched. It's not like Yin is in there, right now, that's not possible.

On my return stroll I check out the red side gate, the front window. The curtains are drawn. There's a caravan parked in the backyard, and a thick vine taking over the carport.

My mind is cold, clear.

I imagine reaching quickly into his letterbox, to see if there's anything there.

I imagine knocking on his door and getting a glimpse into his house.

I imagine sneaking a look into his windows, seeing what's in his backyard. I picture climbing in a window, getting a knife from his kitchen and using it.

As I stare, a man comes out the front door and shuffles down the driveway, past the wheely bins. He's looking at me.

'You! I see you!' He makes it to the letterbox and uses it to keep his balance. 'Girl, I see you! I know why you're here.'

I squint and it's him. Paunchy and balding and much older than I expected. Samuel Pulpitt. He's not a muscly gym coach anymore but an out-of-shape old man.

'Yeah?' I call back. 'Why am I here then?'

'You don't think people have been gawking at me, spying on me all the time? I see through you.'

I can't believe he is standing right here in front of me, less than ten metres away with only a thin strip of road between us.

'I know who you are!' I make sure my voice is deep and strong. 'You're disgusting, a rapist and a criminal.'

His mouth flaps open and shut, out of breath from walking up his own driveway. Power surges through me.

'Do your neighbours know that there's a predator living next door? What do you think they'd do if they knew?'

'Listen, I went to jail for that. I did my time. It was a lifetime ago.'

'You ruined lives. Those women will never forget what you did to them.'

'Oh, you've asked them personally, have you? What you're doing now is equally disgusting, you spoilt little brat!' He coughs from the effort of insulting me. 'This is my house, my life, my privacy!'

'How can you say that?' I'm outright shouting now, shouting my throat raw. I am a rage bomb, a firework going off, a nuclear mushroom. 'What you did is unforgivable and you should pay for it for the rest of your—'

Out of nowhere my breath deserts me, my voice trails off. I'm breathing just as hard as he is.

'Oh, I see.' Samuel Pulpitt leans harder on the letterbox. He's wearing a tracksuit with stains down the front. 'You're her age, aren't you? The Mitchell girl. Do you know her? Is that it?'

A shiver runs through my whole body. 'No.'

'Is that why you're so upset?'

I try to move my feet but I'm frozen. 'You're wrong. You're delusional.'

But maybe it's me that's delusional. The man in front of me doesn't fit the police profile at all and he's not the sinister abducting machine that the media has painted. He's old and sick and pissed-off.

'Why don't you search my house, if you're so convinced?' Pulpitt says but my feet have finally come unstuck and I'm not convinced at all.

I run and run, as fast as I can.


When I reach the train station I'm still shaking all over and my shirt is plastered to my back and my throat hurts and my hands hurt and it was not fun being a detective or assassin and I feel grubby all over.

Even though it's the middle of the day, there are still quite a few people on the platform and they're all staring at me but not in the good way, more in a what-is-wrong-with-her way. I walk right to the end and find a bench, sitting with my head in my hands.

If Samuel Pulpitt isn't Doctor Calm, that means someone else is. There are probably hundreds or thousands or tens of thousands of men out there who hate girls and want to hurt them and the world keeps going around and nothing changes. And what can we do? Make a photo, chase a suspect, read the news.

My face is either freezing cold or boiling hot—I can't tell anymore.

I'm so so tired and term is about to start on Monday and I'll have to face everyone and put my game face on and it's as if I haven't had a holiday at all. Yin will have slipped from everyone's minds a little bit more, and by the time exams and the formal come around she will have slipped completely, and by the time we're in Year Twelve and going on to live full and interesting lives she'll be a puff of dust in the distance, still only sixteen years old.

The tracks hum and I shuffle to the edge of the platform as the train arrives, the robot voice chanting over the PA and then the train comes in fast and loud, squealing metal on metal.

There's a moment of danger when the train pushes hot dragon breath around me and I'm dizzy and it would be nothing to let myself fall forwards, off the platform and into space. All I have to do is take another step forward, then another. It would be that easy.

The lurching spreads all the way through me as the train streaks past in a rush of sound and wind. I haven't moved, of course I haven't, because I don't want to move, I don't want to fall, I want to live, I know that. I really want to live. Seconds feel like hours and I walk towards the nearest carriage door. All I can think is: *I can't go on like this.*

✦

On the train I find the quietest seat and read Chloe's message.

*Yeah. I talked to a cool artist. Thanks for inviting me.*

She doesn't apologise for leaving the opening without saying goodbye and quite frankly I don't need her to, I just need her to keep replying to me. I don't know if I'd describe Genital Gerard as 'cool' but maybe it's an art thing. I read and reread her words, trying to discover more of their tone and mood, but they stay the same.

Mum sits at the dining table with her laptop open in front of her, reading glasses on, a cup of coffee beside her, in an example of the most normal scene you could conjure up in our household.

'Did you have a nice time at Chloe's?' She flips her glasses to the top of her head. I think she knows I lied.

'Great,' I say. Our potted palm needs watering, no one has stacked the dishwasher since yesterday, and nothing has changed at all in the world. I met a sex criminal, I yelled at a rapist and still everything is exactly the same.

'I hurt my hands.'

I hold them out towards her. I've grazed both of my palms, close to my wrists.

'Oh, sweetie, how did you do that?' Mum gets up straight away.

'Tripped and fell over.' I have the vaguest memory of stepping off the gutter near Stockton station and flying, sprawling across the asphalt and bouncing up again.

'Upstairs,' says Mum and I follow her to their ensuite,

where she washes, disinfects and bandages my hands. Her touch is cool, her presence soothing.

'Mum, can we do delivery tonight?' I ask.

'Sure,' she says and she lets me wear her slippers and dressing gown because somehow hers are so much softer and more comforting than mine.

# Chloe

## DAY 58

I start Term Four locked in a toilet cubicle, the mature and reliable technique I used heavily in my first few weeks at Balmoral. Looking down at my hands, I can literally see the work I did on the holidays: paint under my fingernails, irritated patches from the glue, a tiny cut from my scalpel. I had to take a 7 a.m. bus here this morning, dragging my clunky artwork with me, and I'm already exhausted.

The illusion of bathroom calm holds for one moment, but then I picture the bell ringing at the end of form assembly and thousands of girls spilling into the corridors, funnelling up towards the Great Hall for all-school assembly. The entries for the school art prize, including mine, have been hung in the main corridor along the outside length of the Hall.

Everyone that enters the school will see them.

I spent the weekend in a frenzy of collaging, making a frame around my photo that hopefully gives some context to the piece. Adut recommended I look up a German artist called Hannah Höch, who used collage to comment on gender issues and criticise the government. It was just the reference I needed, so I put my doubts aside and went for it. I've used newspaper snippets about missing women, shreds of *Devil Creek* episode descriptions, excerpts from one of Mum's crime books and a dozen tiny cut-out clones of me in my school uniform, standing or crouched, looking inside at Natalia.

I've called the piece *Someone's Watching*, because the words seemed like they held a few different meanings.

My phone buzzes. Three guesses who that will be.

*Where r u*

*Your photo is getting some love*

I wash my hands and leave my haven. The corridors are still full so maybe the first bell hasn't even rung yet. I make my way to the main corridor and try not to think about vomiting all over my shoes.

To my surprise there are already quite a few girls looking at the paintings and sculptures and hanging costumes. Many of them hold the green voting forms for the students' choice award. It's a bigger deal than I thought it would be.

Natalia and her friends are easy to spot, clumped at the end of the hallway. Somehow I don't think of them as The Blondes anymore. I wonder if she told them that we hung out on the holidays.

'Chloe! Yours is so good!' Lisbeth appears next to me. 'It's very intense.'

'Oh. Thanks, Lisbeth.'

I feel a rush of affection for her.

'I never thought I'd say this, but Natalia almost looks like an angel.' Lisbeth glances around. 'And I know she's not.'

She looks guilty, as if she's said something really mean.

I smile. 'I know what you mean. Maybe she could be a fallen angel?'

'Yes, you're so right!' I'd forgotten that when Lisbeth gets excited, her curls actually bounce up and down, for real. She's so sweet, it's ridiculous. I missed her on the holidays. 'Hey, maybe I'll see you in the quad at lunch today?'

'I would love that! And I'm definitely going to vote for you, Chloe. You can count on me.'

Lisbeth drifts away and Natalia pretends she doesn't see me coming towards her but I know she does. I wonder if she expects me to apologise for disappearing from the Park ARC exhibition. I don't feel like apologising, even though I probably should. She did completely neglect me that night, but it ended up being helpful.

There's a semicircle of space in front of my photo. Sarah, Ally and Marley say hello, which is about the most I've ever gotten from them. Sarah and Ally are both deeply tanned.

I stand next to Natalia and dare to look. It's one of the biggest pieces on the wall.

'What do you think?' It occurs to me that the photo is an exposure of sorts for her as well. Maybe she's more comfortable with that than me, though.

'I had no idea you were going to do this extra stuff.'

Natalia leans in to inspect my collage. An eternity passes. I was so rushed getting it done that I didn't have time to judge if it worked. I'd rather Natalia tell me the truth than lie. I still think she looks great and otherworldly in the photo, even if the lighting isn't perfect.

'Of course I'm insanely jealous that you're so talented,' Natalia says eventually. Her face and voice are uncharacteristically flat.

'Are you sure you like it?'

Light slants through the high windows, striking Natalia's face at an odd angle. She's pale, and there are blue marks under her eyes. She doesn't look like someone coming off the back of two weeks holiday. Then again, I probably look equally pasty after spending all my time in Dad's shed.

'It's great. I like it. I look good for a dead person.'

'Or asleep,' I remind her. 'Hibernating attractively.'

'I wish I could believe that,' she says.

Sarah pushes Ally into position and takes a photo of her looking at me looking at Natalia, which is so many levels of meta I can't even figure it out. I'm still not convinced that Natalia isn't mad at me for leaving the exhibition opening early. If the others weren't here I'd ask her straight out.

The bell rings and Marley sidles up to me. 'I feel very disturbed, Chloe,' she sighs, with a hand on her heart and a smile on her face.

In fourth period English we troop down to the main corridor and view the exhibition as a class. Mr Purdy wants us to use the artworks as writing prompts, which I'm pretty sure is a convenient way to keep us busy so he can play Solitaire on his iPad.

'Devices away!' he shouts. 'I want you to try writing by hand. It's good for your brains.'

'Can I do a graphic novel?' calls out Teaghan.

'No.'

Mr Purdy always wears brown suit pants that are too tight. It means that when he's standing in front of us, with his legs apart and his hands on his hips, we all have to look away.

Audrey raises her hand. 'What about poetry?'

Purdy is more irritated by us than he should be. 'Sure.'

'No fair.' Teaghan slams her folders down.

I ignore my entry and spend my time looking at the other work in the exhibition. A Year Eight girl has made some surprisingly good felt toys, mushrooms and fungi and moss. The Year Nines have obviously been working on still life recently, because there are several paintings of flowers, vases, jugs and fruit. Up the far end is a mannequin dressed in an amazing Marie Antoinette-style costume made from recycled rubbish by a Year Eleven.

I sit down in front of Bochen's entry—her pencil portrait of Mercury Yee. Bochen has rendered Mercury's face with painstaking detail in orange and blue and pink, showing her sucking on a bubble cup with her mouth twisted comically to the side. Her style is exaggerated and realistic at the same time. The drawing must have taken hours and hours to complete. She's incredibly talented.

I write a few stiff lines in my notebook and then cross them out. They're so bad I would rather cut off my hands than have anyone read them. I am not in the headspace for creative writing.

'I don't get it,' Petra says to Audrey. They're directly to my right, ignoring me and looking at the felt mushrooms.

Audrey is lying on her tummy, already scribbling furiously. 'What are we supposed to be writing about?'

Audrey waves her away. 'Express yourself, P, I don't know.'

'Excuse me, Chloe?'

Bridie and Sunita crouch next to me.

'I want to write about your photo,' Bridie whispers, 'but I was wondering, what does it mean?'

I answer truthfully. 'I'm not one hundred per cent sure.'

'Is it meant to be scary?'

I let out a breath. How am I going to explain the book covers and *Devil Creek* and the other things and how it didn't turn out precisely as I wanted it to?

'I want to write about it too.' Sunita has her pen poised over her notebook, ready to take notes. 'Is it about Yin?'

'Not really.' But that's not totally true either. It isn't about Yin directly, but it does have something to do with her. Sort of.

'I think it's a story where two schoolgirls get murdered,' Sunita says. 'So the title *Someone's Watching* means that there's a guy we can't see and he's about to attack them with a knife.'

'I guess?' I don't want to reject her idea, especially as this is the first proper conversation we've ever had.

'Sunny, that's completely wrong. Look, she's already bleeding, so he's already attacked them.'

Sunita writes in her notebook. 'Shhh, babe, I'm feeling it.'

I notice Mr Purdy looking at us, so I keep my voice low. 'If you look closely you can see the red's actually feathers. It was more about the colour.'

'I'll have to look at it again.' Bridie seems disappointed by my response. I rack my brains for something Ms Nouri might say.

'It's not my meaning that matters anymore. The point is what happens when you look at my photo. It's yours now. You get to make your own meaning.'

Sunita stops writing for one moment. 'That is literally the one of the deepest things I have ever heard, Chloe.'

'Thanks,' I say, and they retreat.

Next to me, Audrey is on her third page of notebook, filling the space up with lines and lines of words, but Petra is getting more and more restless. By the amount of deep huffs coming from her direction, I'm guessing she likes creative writing about as much as I do.

Eventually she puts up her hand.

'Mr Purdy, I don't get it. What themes are we supposed to be writing about?'

Even though you can tell he doesn't want to lift a finger, Purdy comes over. I cover my mostly empty page with my arm, and turn away.

'Why does there have to be a theme?' Purdy says. 'Break some rules. Let your imagination run wild.'

'I've tried, and I can't. I don't like any of them.'

Both Petra and Purdy sound more annoyed than you'd think anyone would be about a minor task.

'Year Tens,' Purdy raises his voice and both his hands. 'The exercise is very simple. How about less whingeing and more independent thought?'

'How can he say that?' Petra says, low and furious to

Audrey. 'Who does he think he is?'

'Work independently, ladies,' whispers Teaghan, doing her best deep-voiced Purdy impersonation, 'and let me get back to watching my porn.'

## DAY 59

Tuesday morning is quieter, but girls I don't even know are still coming up to me in the hallway to compliment me on my photo.

It's regular, standard-issue Balmoral, just with one major change, as if we've slipped into a parallel universe where people know my name.

I have a spare for second period, so I go to my usual table in the library. Petra is already set up there, tackling statistics, by the look of it. Thanks to art dominating my holidays, I figure I'm at least a month behind in my maths homework.

'Room for me?'

Petra looks annoyed to be interrupted but nods and continues hunching over her books and poking at her calculator.

I sit down and begin the Chapter Ten exercises but it's hard to concentrate. Petra is restless when she studies; she crosses and uncrosses her legs, scrunches bits of paper, sighs a lot, drums her fingers on the table.

After a few more minutes of my mind sliding over maths problems and not landing anywhere I catch Petra sneaking glances at me.

I put down my pen. 'These graphs are killing me.'

It's an excuse to talk—in fact the only good thing about stats is drawing nice neat diagrams on clean, checked graph paper. Petra looks tired. We haven't bumped into each other at our lockers yet this week.

'How were your holidays?' I ask.

She looks away so I barely catch her words. 'I went home.'

'Where's home?'

'Karraton. The country.'

If I didn't know better I'd say she's upset about something. We've built up a tenuous connection since the notorious self-defence class, but none of that is there today. I try to think of a topic that will interest her but I fail and return to my calculations.

A few minutes later Petra packs up her things abruptly and leaves without saying goodbye.

I pedal as hard as I can on stats, trying to make up for my neglect. Mrs Wang has been trying to talk me into doing Advanced Maths next year, but I'm not sure.

If I could, I'd do all humanities and absolutely no science or maths for the next two years, but Balmoral want us to choose subjects that will get our university entrance scores scaled up, even if we're not interested in them. I'm already worried our careers counsellor won't let me study Art next year unless I commit to applying for a Visual Arts course at uni, which isn't an actual option.

With about fifteen minutes of period two left, Mrs Berryman gives me a heart attack by appearing right next to me, out of thin air. Secret librarian skills.

'Chloe? Ms Nouri has asked to see you.'

'Now? Why?'

'Not sure, love, but she wants you to go up to her office.'

Mrs Berryman should swap places with the school counsellor or nurse, she's that nice.

I gather my things and pretend that it's not unusual that Ms Nouri wants to see me.

My heart thumps a little faster. Could it be something to do with the prize? Surely the judges haven't made their decision already.

As I make my way to the third floor I run through my favourite fantasy, a blatantly unrealistic daydream where Ms Nouri tells me that her art-dealer friend likes my work and wants to give me a giant pot of money to go overseas to make art and find myself.

Ms Nouri's office is barely bigger than a broom closet, and she shares it with two other art teachers. Once you've crammed in three desks, bookshelves, a portable heater, three oversized handbags and a collection of lumpy statues, there's barely room to move. Funny things are going on with my insides.

'Chloe, take a seat.'

Ms Nouri is alone in the office and I perch on a spare chair. There are art books, sketchbooks, stacks of paper, jars of pens, posters on every available surface. A framed photo of Ms Nouri and her wife and their little boy is tucked on the shelf nearby and I try not to look too nosy.

'How are you doing?'

'Good.' It's hard not to sound nervous.

Ms Nouri taps her big teacher's diary with glitter-storm fingernails.

'I have something difficult to tell you, Chloe.'

She hasn't looked at me properly until now. She looks worried.

'A decision has been made to remove your artwork from the exhibition. After receiving a complaint, Mrs Christie has decided this is the best course of action, to prevent others from getting upset.'

Ice runs through me. It's very similar to the feeling I had when Sam went missing at the mall. It takes a few seconds for me to get any words out.

'What kind of complaint?'

'I didn't field the complaint personally, so I don't know every detail. Mrs Christie indicated that the person was distraught.'

'My photo upset them?' I ask, trying to make sense of it. Ms Nouri has spent the entire year telling us art is supposed to make us feel something. 'I don't get it. Why didn't I get called into the principal's office?'

'It was thought best that I discuss it with you. Break the news to you gently.' Ms Nouri attempts a laugh and sounds nothing but bitter. It dawns on me that Mrs Christie has made her do this. 'I can still accept the piece as your final project, though. Your grade won't be affected at all.'

I think of all the guidance Ms Nouri gave me, the suggestions, the extra attention. Maybe she had been doing that for everyone, though. Here I was thinking I was someone special.

'What do you think?' The ice floes melt, and all of a sudden I flood, turn to water. 'Do you think I did something wrong?'

My cheeks are wet, my eyes spilling over. I don't care about dignity anymore.

I spent every bit of my money I had. I endured awkward exchanges with Natalia. I barely went outside all holidays.

Tears fall onto my school tights, soaking my legs.

'I'm in a difficult position, Chloe. I can't talk as freely as I'd like.' Ms Nouri rolls her chair closer and pats my shoulder. 'I can tell you though, that you've done nothing wrong.'

'But I'm disqualified from the prize.'

'Yes.'

It's true that Balmoral isn't for people like me. They let you think for a moment that it is, that you're on equal footing to them, and the whole time it's not true.

I knew I'd never get that prize or money. I shouldn't have bothered.

'You didn't tell Mrs Christie what you think, though. You didn't tell her you think I'd done nothing wrong. You—'

But I'm hiccup-crying too hard to get the words out so I stand up, wipe my face.

'It's so unfair.'

'My hands are tied, Chloe.' Ms Nouri fusses about on her desk, finds an envelope and hands it to me. 'Please understand that, I want you to—'

I leave without saying more, I can barely see or think. I crush the envelope in my fist.

Ms Nouri's office door slams shut behind me and then I'm face to face with Marley and Ally, who are huddled against a wall nearby, looking intently at Marley's phone.

They've been waiting for me. No longer strangers or enemies, but not friends either.

'Chloe? Are you okay?'

I march away from Ally's worried voice.

'What's happened? Chloe? Talk to us.'

She calls my name until I turn the corner, already searching for a place to be alone.

After nearly crying in the middle of Japanese, I skip PE completely. I've never been able to leave a scab alone so it makes sense that I have to see for myself that my photo isn't there anymore.

The corridors are empty, but when I pass the Great Hall I see Natalia already standing in front of the space where *Someone's Watching* used to be.

'You're quick,' I say.

I wonder how much longer it's going to take before it's the talk of the year level. Or maybe I'm flattering myself that anyone beyond us will care.

'I have eyes everywhere.' If I thought she'd hug me in commiseration, I'm wrong. Natalia is preternaturally still.

We contemplate the bare wall. Who would have thought that white space could say so much.

'Where is it?' she asks.

'I don't know.' This surprises me. I don't think it was in Ms Nouri's office. It's big enough that I would have noticed. 'I have absolutely no idea.'

'Tell me exactly what Nouri said to you.'

I swallow over the nervous lump in my throat and try to remember the whole blurry awful conversation.

'She said someone put in an official complaint about our photo, uh, they were distraught, and Mrs Christie made the decision to take it out of the exhibition. I got the impression that Nouri might not agree but was forced to go along with it.'

'Distraught?' Natalia's voice is steely. 'What a joke. Who do they think is distraught?'

A great weariness takes over me. My limbs are heavy, my head heavier still. I think about Sunita and Bridie and all their talk about dead bodies and blood, and I can't figure out anymore if I've done something wrong. Was it too much? Was it the wrong message?

Natalia's phone chimes. She checks it, puts it away.

'Okay, we need to go.'

'Where?'

'Right now.'

Her fingers close around my wrist and she walks me, fast, towards the closest door that leads outside.

'Where are we going?'

'Shush. Thinking.'

'Who was that?'

Natalia doesn't answer, but it soon becomes obvious as we round the outside of the tuckshop and cross the small lawn to the portable that serves as the Year Ten common room. There are so many reasons not to go to the common room—it's cold, the carpet smells, it's cliquey—that I can barely remember what it looks like inside.

Marley lounges on the steps, Ally is doing some sort of risky parkour move, standing on the handrail and clutching the windowsill.

'She's in there.' She jumps down.

Natalia storms up the stairs, checking to see I'm with her. And something very obvious becomes clear to me.

Natalia is not still, not calm or relaxed or resigned. She's wound up, waiting for the right moment, muscles coiled like a panther. She's a weapon about to be unleashed.

I follow her across the common room, to the corner where a group of boarders—Brooke, Petra, Audrey, Jody and others—are sitting on couches.

Natalia slows to a saunter.

'Hi guys!' Natalia's voice is friendly bright. 'Mind if I sit down?'

Instead of waiting for them to make room she muscles into the group, forcing herself into place right next to Petra. I hover a few metres away.

'How are you going, Galbraith?' Natalia slings her arm across the back of the couch and Petra cringes away from her. 'Been up to anything interesting lately? Like, sorting your pencil case, or…ruining someone else's hard work perhaps?'

The group finally catches Natalia's tone, because they start melting away, until it's just Petra and Audrey.

Petra doesn't say anything. Audrey looks intently at her feet.

'I'm trying to figure out why you would do this,' Natalia continues to Petra conversationally. 'Is it because you're a bit of a jealous bitch? You can't stand that Chloe's not only smart but creative too? I mean, you get good marks, right, but there's something robotic about you, isn't there?'

'Tal—don't, I don't need you to—' I say, even as I'm wondering if she's gotten it right. Why would Petra do this to me?

'Or perhaps it was me that offended you? Oh, that Natalia, she's always looking for attention, she thinks she's so hot. Is there something about *me* that bothers you?'

Natalia has never looked more of an evil little pixie, with a mouth full of knives and eyes that can slash.

I have to ask. 'Petra, was it you?'

Petra looks up at me, stricken. I remember her fidgeting in the library this morning, and all of a sudden I don't need her to answer.

'Why wouldn't you say something to me directly? I wasn't trying to upset anyone.'

I was trying to pull on a thin thread of meaning from deep inside and convince myself it was worth something, that it was significant enough to show.

'The photo is disrespectful, Chloe!' Petra blurts out. 'Even if you didn't mean it to be.'

'I definitely didn't mean—' I try to interject but Petra is bursting with things to say.

'You haven't been here as long, so you don't know what it feels like. You're making fun of something awful that's happened to us. Death is serious, death is forever…I don't know why you of all people don't see that, Natalia! The whole thing is really tacky.'

That word takes my breath away, even as I was starting to feel sorry for Petra, being pinned down by Natalia's force.

Tacky.

Tacky is tracksuits in public, second-hand school blazers and fourth-hand textbooks, sneakers from Kmart, saying *haitch* like my Morrison friends do. Bringing your basic sandwiches to school, your family not having a car, living in the wrong suburb, never having the right jeans. Like filth, like smudges on white surfaces. Tacky.

'How dare you act like you even care.' Natalia puts her face close to Petra's. 'You think you're better than everyone else, always being so good and so holy, the way you sit back and judge everyone.'

'I don't.' Petra's voice trickles out.

'Only a suck like you could have talked Mrs Christie into this. Did you get Daddy on the phone? I guess he does donate millions to the school. Everyone knows why you're always dux, why you get so many prizes…'

Audrey finally gets the courage to look up. 'That's too much, Natalia.'

Natalia doesn't listen. She pushes herself up and away. I stand there for a moment, waiting for more words to come, but when nothing happens I follow Natalia out.


No one can see you if you sit low on the banks of the oval, in the far corner of the school grounds, close to the outer fence. The grass is lush and soft there, and a cluster of tree ferns and wattles keep the sun at bay.

No one can see you let your face finally crumble, soften around the edges and slide off into misery.

No one can see you, but you can see others: the cars driving down the side street, student specks crossing from the main building to the PE centre, from the music building to the boarding house, back and forth.

You can hear the bells for the end of lunch and the beginning of fifth period.

You can text Katie in peace, begging her to bribe Tim to come pick you up after school so you don't have to carry this thing on the tram or endure the stares or overhear the whispered gossip.

You can see Lisbeth's progress as she power-walks across the oval, looking around like she's committing high treason.

'Oh, it's true,' she says, when she sees *Someone's Watching* lying on the grass next to me, collected from one of the impassive secretaries in the main office. Mrs Christie has managed to execute her ban without even seeing me, or even asking me to explain my artwork, or give my side of the story.

'I'm so sorry, Chloe.' Lisbeth drops down next to me. 'I think it's very unfair to make you remove your photo.'

'Thanks.' She's the first person to say a simple 'sorry'.

'Maybe you're not in the mood for this, but I got you a spinach-and-cheese from the tuckshop.' She hands me a paper bag. I don't mind that Lisbeth sees my puffy eyes and red nose, but I don't want Ms Nouri or Mrs Christie or any of the teachers or anyone else to see how much I care about this.

I peek at the pastry, but I can't stomach it. 'How did you know where I was?'

'Sunita saw you walking this way.'

It's impossible to keep a secret around here, apparently.

Lisbeth smoothes her school skirt over her knees. She wears her uniform extra long. 'What happened?'

'Petra complained about my photo and Mrs Christie banned it. Ms Nouri told me in second period.'

I think of our creative writing task in English class, and how Petra was right there next to me. She had every opportunity to say something, to talk about it with me, and she didn't. I don't understand why she would go against me, straight to a teacher.

'What have you been doing since then? I didn't see you at recess.'

'Trying not to cry, mostly.' I scrunch the napkin. 'And getting into fights.'

Lisbeth's eyebrows shoot up.

'Natalia made me come with her to the common room to confront Petra, and then it got pretty heated. Natalia was practically yelling, saying that Petra's dad gives all this money to the school and that's why Mrs Christie took her side.'

Natalia's twisted face sticks in my mind, making me uneasy. I would almost have sympathy for Petra, but then I think about how messed up it is that she could ruin everything for us so easily, with no regrets. I'm right in the middle of a giant pile of steaming Balmoral drama, which is exactly where I didn't want to be.

'It is actually true that Petra's dad donates a lot of money to Balmoral's building fund,' Lisbeth says. 'You know the Galbraith wing? Where the new science labs are?'

It never occurred to me to connect the name of the Galbraith wing with Petra. I'm beginning to wonder if I understand anything about this school.

I sigh. Part of me did want to slap Petra when we saw her in the common room, but the other part of me wanted to run away and hide.

Lisbeth picks the daisies around her feet, pulling them into a little bunch. 'Has anyone told you yet about Natalia and Yin?'

'What about them?'

'They used to be best friends. The bestest friends you could imagine. In Junior School, like maybe in grades four, five and six, they did *everything* together.'

'I didn't know that.'

I try to remember if I ever saw Yin and Natalia even say hello to each other. Yin was in such a tight three with Claire and Milla, and so deep into senior orchestra, that it's hard to imagine her and Natalia having anything in common.

'They even had this special secret language they would use. No one could come between them.'

I don't know what to do with this information. It puts a twist on everything I know about Natalia. I think about what it would be like if something happened to Katie or Liana. I don't know how I would react. Maybe I would go around yelling at people and poking them in the eye.

'It's hard to believe, isn't it?' Lisbeth says. 'In Junior School we'd always say YinandNatalia as one word, but as soon as they got to Year Seven…'

'What happened in Year Seven?'

'Everything changes when you get to Senior School. I mean, I used to be friends with Teaghan, can you believe it?'

I shake my head.

'We used to do bible study together, but Teaghan strayed from the path. I did try to save her…'

'You do know I'm a massive atheist, right?' I'm not sure

I should be risking one of my only Balmoral friendships, but honesty seems important right now.

'Of course, Chloe. I've matured a lot. I can be friends with non-believers.'

Lisbeth picks up my photo and dusts it off. She takes off her blazer and lays the photo carefully on top of it.

Something dawns on me.

'Hang on, Lisbeth, are you wagging class?'

'I am. I should be in Maths right now.' She looks equal parts terrified and pleased. 'It's my first time, but it turns out to be quite easy, especially if you have chronic sinusitis. Mr Scrutton thinks I'm in sick bay.' She pats me on the arm. 'I'll stay for as long as you need me, Chloe. And I'm going to pray for you extra-hard tonight.'

'Thanks Lisbeth.' I'm in danger of tearing up again. I may be a heathen but I know praying is her way of showing she cares and I'm grateful. 'Don't go overboard. Just one little mention will do.'


Mum is on the night shift so I deadlock the front and back doors and give in to Sam's demands to paint his nails, toes and fingers. I was so busy on the school holidays that he is super thirsty for my attention. We had to send him on a council holiday program for the first time in ages, and I'm full of guilt.

Sam chooses a Disney soundtrack playlist and instead of complaining I sing along. It blocks any thoughts I might have had about messaging anyone or hopping online to vent or rant or see if anyone even cares about my photo.

I paint Sam's fingernails alternating blue and red, with silver stripes down the centre of each nail. Superhero nails, sort of. He's so excited he can barely sit still, and I keep smudging the stripes. I sincerely hope the kids in his class think they're as cool as he does.

My phone beeps and I lean over to see who it is. Mum, plus three unread messages.

Mum—feeling sorry for me obviously—authorises takeout for dinner using her credit card.

Lisbeth forgot what chapters we were supposed to revise for Japanese—easy. I text her back.

Katie wants to sneak into the dodgy pub next to Meridian—definitely not.

Natalia wants to discuss 'our next move'—hard no.

I'm caught between being hurt that Natalia didn't confide in me about Yin, and feeling terrible that I made her pose like that. Her reaction makes more sense now. I hope I didn't traumatise her.

I can see from my notifications that Bochen has sent me a Facebook message too. Every message makes my head hurt even more.

'And then Louis gave me a go only the batteries were almost flat so I only got five minutes but do you think Mum would buy me one? Not the old model, the new one.'

Sam has been erupting words, an unending monologue, for at least an hour now. I'm trying, but I can only keep focus for so long before my mind wanders, going back to the same few sore scenes. Petra shunning me in the library. Ms Nouri's office. The common room.

Petra's right. I've been at Balmoral for less than a year and clearly I don't understand anything or anyone. I could finish her sentence for her: you haven't been here as long, and by the way—in case you haven't figured it out yet—you still don't belong.

'Why don't you put it on your list for Santa?' I say, even though Mum has been trying to break that particular news to him for two years now. Sam's not ready to let Santa go.

I look at his too-long hair and his grimy pyjamas and worry about whether everything lovely about him will be lost when he becomes a teenager. I've no intention whatsoever of leaving the house tonight when I could be home, where I belong, with one of the best people I know.

'I could and I suppose it's not that far away when you think about it and do you think maybe there'll be a sale before then—'

When I slot the brush into the bottle of polish, I accidentally topple the neighbouring bottle, sending a pool of sticky red across the couch cushion.

'No!' I'm up in a flash, righting the bottle and dithering. I blot the puddle with my sleeve, only to realise I've just ruined my favourite hoodie.

'Fuckety fuckety fuck!'

'Swears, Chloe!' Sam is halfway between disapproving and impressed.

My jumper comes off in a huff.

'Why are you so upset?' Sam asks, and it's a good question. My eyes are prickling again. I screw all three nail polish lids on slowly and perfectly until the tears subside.

I will not cry any more because I'm sick of red eyes and having a raw nose because Mum is too tight to buy the good aloe tissues.

'I'll give you a foot massage, that always makes you feel better.'

'You can't, Sammy, your nails are wet.'

I'm angry, boiling hot, but I don't know if I even have the right to feel that way, so I am just stuffing the feeling deep down in a very healthy, sustainable way.

'Watch me do a headstand then, I've got much better.'

'Your nails!' I say, but Sam doesn't hear me, or he ignores me, and he has his blue toenails up in the air and his sticky fingers squishing into the carpet before I can stop him.

Dad calls late and I know that Mum must have told him what happened. Sam has emptied himself of every thought he's ever had and is asleep on the couch.

Dad speaks in a low voice, and I know from the clink and echo that he's sitting on his porch with a beer, watching fruit bats whirl around overhead.

'Chloe, I'm so sorry, mate.'

There is a clot in my throat that won't let me speak. I fiddle with the pens in the mug on my desk.

'It's senseless, love. You made a beautiful piece of art that meant something.'

'But what did it mean?' I don't speak loud enough.

'These people.' His voice is soaked in disgust. 'They can stuff their exhibition up their you-know-what, because we're going to have our own party anyway.'

'Really?'

'I'll organise it with your mother. Wine and cheese and the whole lot. I think I've got a beret somewhere.'

'Do you think you and Mum can get along for one night?'

'You'd be surprised. Your mum calls me sometimes, when she's in the mood. She's not always pissy with me.'

'Okayyy,' I say, because it's weird to think about them talking and not shouting. 'I'd like that. But no one wears berets anymore. They all wear these fisherman beanies.'

'I can do that.'

'Dad, I think you were right all along. I should go back to Morrison. I want to transfer back.'

A pause in which I'm sure he's knocking back beer.

'That's fine if that's what you want, love. But why don't you let the dust settle a bit? Do you think you can tough it out a little longer? It's not worth messing up your exams if you don't have to.'

I say yes, because maybe I can ride it out. Because if I'm being real, I don't want to go back to Morrison, I just don't want to stay at Balmoral either.


Much later, when I'm going through my school diary to see if I have anything due tomorrow, I find the envelope Ms Nouri gave me tucked into the cover. Inside is a photocopy of an interview with Bill Henson, titled 'I'm comfortable with the fact my pictures disturb people'.

Ms Nouri might not have stood up to Mrs Christie, but her message is clear.

I read the interview slowly and marvel at how focussed Henson stays on his work, how little he cares about what people say. How does a person grow an iron skin like that? How do you feel that amount of certainty? Do you have to be a middle-aged white man to feel that way?

I usually don't care too much about other people's opinions. If they want to think my body is too big, they can. If they find me too quiet in class, whatever. But this is different. The photo means too much to me.

I showed too much of myself, and now, to my surprise, it turns out I do care what other people think.

# Natalia

**DAY 59**

Dad picks me up from outside the gym where Marley and I have been taking the class that has you dancing along having a good old time and then suddenly dropping to the floor to do push-ups and crunches until you want to hurl all over your mesh-panel leggings.

'Does Marley need a lift?' Dad cranes his head.

'Nah, she likes to walk. It's barely a block.'

'We should take her…'

'Dad! We're not babies anymore.'

That shuts him up, but in actual fact I am personally relieved that I don't have to walk the narrow streets in the dark. Marley, on the other hand, loves this time of night.

'Good workout, honey?'

I fiddle with the aircon, directing the jets right onto my sweaty face. My body has been full of adrenaline and secrets since I went to that pervert Pulpitt's house, and then that got mixed into a sludge with anger at Petra, but now stomach-crunching until my abs burned has somehow restored my feeling of reality, of being back in my body instead of in a nightmare.

'I had a crap day so I suppose it helped.'

'Crap day? Anything I need to know about?'

'I'll tell you at home, I just want to flop for a second.'

I put the radio on loud, Dad turns it down a notch, and we race down the slippery dip of Windermere Avenue, flanked by the biggest, richest, oldest mansions, the kind that have tennis courts and swimming pools and British-sounding house names. I wonder what crimes have happened behind the closed doors of these houses that no one knows about.

When we get home Dad makes me sit at the breakfast bar and pick coriander leaves off the stalks, which definitely counts as child labour.

The benches are littered with gaping spice packets and sticky spoons, the food processor is out and awful ancient Bob Dylan is on the sound system and there are one-and-a-half empty wine bottles and I realise that Dad shouldn't have been driving the car. Mum is going to crack it when she sees the mess and Faith doesn't come again until Thursday.

Dad pours himself another glass. He puts rice on to boil and commences chop chop chopping a giant pile of vegetables. Steam gathers around us and fogs up the back windows.

'You in the mood yet to tell me about your day?'

I shift on my stool, nearly kicking Dylan Thomas, who wends his way around my legs.

'What do you think about censorship, Dad?'

'You'll have to be more precise, honey.'

'Censorship of art.' I scroll on my phone for pics of Chloe's art piece, which I also think of as mine. 'Remember that art project I helped my friend with at the beginning of the holidays?'

He nods, even though he has no idea. Mum keeps track of me and my schedule, but he has only the faintest idea on any given day. I show him the screen.

'Is that you, Tal?'

He reaches across the bench and grabs my phone with his greasy cooking hands.

'I don't like seeing you like that. Where were you? Why would you agree to that?'

I grab my phone back and wipe it on my top.

'Forget it's me, Dad. God, can you just try and be normal for a second? Chloe is trying to make a point about the portrayal of young women or something. And then this dweeb complained about Chloe's photo, saying she was offended or whatever, and Mrs Christie banned it from the exhibition.'

Even just talking about it makes my hackles rise. I pretend not to feel it most of the time, but Balmoral is a stifling, suffocating blanket, as bad as the boarding school in *Picnic at Hanging Rock*. It's not only that Petra thinks she's got the moral high ground, but also that the school agrees with her, that they don't care about the things that matter to us.

When something real and raw like Chloe's photo comes along, they push it away. As if we don't know what bad people can do.

'Is that what happened?'

'Chloe worked so hard on this for her major art project, and so did I, and it was only up for less than a day before one person—one person!—complained, and they've taken it out of the exhibition. And Chloe isn't eligible for the art prize now, which is totally unfair and she deserved to win—'

'I'll call Gary after dinner—' starts Dad.

'NO.'

I march over to the wall and flip on the fan before the smoke alarm starts beeping.

'I don't want you to call *Gary*, Dad. I want you to tell me what *I* should do about it.'

'Huh.' Dad gives it actual thought. The kitchen is an utter mess around him and he forgot to put an apron on and has turmeric smeared down his front.

'So this photo is an important personal statement, right?'

I nod.

'And you've been silenced from making this statement.' You can almost see his mind rewinding to his radical university days, as he likes to call them. Apparently even Gary was a socialist back then, which is impossible to believe.

'I think a petition is a good place to start.' He slides spring onions into a pan. 'Get the support of your fellow students first. And try to get some teachers to sign.'

'Dad, please. That's not going to happen. The teachers don't care about anything but keeping their jobs.'

'Yeah, fair point.' He bats the onions around the pan with an egg flipper. 'Still. You can ask, to make your point. Make it obvious what you're doing and if anyone questions you, say you're exercising your democratic rights.'

'But what about an actual protest? Hanging a banner over the school, or staging a walkout…or a sit-in. Or a hunger strike?'

'Let's cross that bridge when we get to it.' Dad's eyes are shining and it's not just chilli and steam and wine. 'First, create awareness around the issue. It might be enough. Your posse will help you, right?'

I roll my eyes. *Posse.*

'They might.' I already know awareness won't be enough to fix this, not at Balmoral. Something more extreme is in order.

'Maybe ask Sarah? I haven't seen her over here for a while. Are you two still tight?'

'Dad, just because I asked you for your opinion doesn't mean you get to mess with my social life.'

He holds his hands up in surrender.

'Okay, point taken. My only condition is that you don't get yourself suspended. Know your limits and try to exercise some judgement.'

'Sure. Judgement.'

Dad takes the coriander off my hands. 'Did I tell you I'm taking a few weeks off?'

He didn't.

'Your mother is stressed out of her mind with that Baker-Hill contract,' he says. 'I'm going to stay home to cook and be around for her. And you, of course. Give you lifts, help you with your homework.'

Mum is always stressed out over some project so it's not an excuse. I look at Dad's tired face, the pan smoking on the stove behind him, and I feel bad for ever doubting him, for wondering about the nights he comes home late, for thinking the police might be onto something.

I want to ask him about the case, what the police asked him and why, but I can't.

One day he'll have a stroke or a heart attack or an ulcer from too much work and I wish he could just say he's taking time off work for himself, because he needs a break too.

> We are alarmed by the censorship of Chloe Cardell's artwork, *Someone's Watching*, and are dismayed by the restriction of free speech in our school. Balmoral's motto, *Sapientia et Libertas*, encourages its students to think independently, which we believe Chloe Cardell has done.
>
> We demand that *Someone's Watching* be put back on display and that it be rightfully considered for the Balmoral Art Prize.

Sarah thinks that I should put the petition online, but I disagree. Anyone can click 'like' or join a group, it doesn't mean they believe in it, they just want to do what everyone else is doing and be seen looking like they care. What I need is to look people in the face and know for sure that they think that Nouri and Christie and Petra are wrong and we are right. I need them to agree with me.

So, I'm going old school with this: a paper-and-pen petition, something that Christie and the School Board might understand. Dad helped me with the wording and it made him tragically happy.

I use the photocopier in the library and get a surprising amount of encouragement from the librarians who are all secret anarchists except when it comes to the Dewey decimal system. But they laugh when I ask them to sign and say it's not their place to get involved. I stick petitions up on every corridor, and then I go around with a clipboard and I talk people into signing and I am a proper campaigner.

I hit up our year level first, at morning recess, starting

with 10Q, Chloe's class. It's not easy. I have to convince everyone you can't get in trouble for having an opinion.

'You were in the photo right?' says Teaghan. Because Teaghan signs, Brooke and Ella do too. 'Looking scary and dead.'

'Thank you for your support,' I say because I am a born diplomat and I'm genuinely surprised that Teaghan still talks to me after we replaced her with Ally in eighth grade. 'But I'd do this anyway even if someone else was in the picture because I don't think the school should infringe our civil liberties.'

I can tell they don't believe me and I wouldn't either and I don't actually know anything about civil liberties, but I don't waste time worrying. I've gone into what Dad calls the zone, which apparently happens to him sometimes when he's playing golf or drinking aged whiskey.

All I'm focused on is the numbers; the more signatures the better. Chloe was so dejected yesterday, like a stray dog that had been kicked one too many times, and I wonder if I can be a good friend, a better friend, the best sort, and whether that will make up for anything.

The international students decline to sign the petition, except for Bochen, who listens carefully.

'What do you do with it?' she asks.

'I'll give it to Mrs Christie, and if that doesn't work, the School Board.'

'No government?'

'No, never,' I say and she signs.

I count and I've hit ten pages of names and addresses. Ten! I'd count actual numbers of signatures but I can't afford to slow down for one second.

Chloe's not at school and I can't tell from her messages whether she's really sick or just moping. I'm hoping to surprise her with an avalanche of signatures by the time she comes back to school tomorrow and she will weep tears of joy and tell me how amazing I am, both as a muse and a future prime minister or CEO or general all-round boss bitch and she will be right.

I race to every class as soon as the bell goes, so I can use the seven minutes in-between periods to get signatures.

At lunch I convince Marley and Sarah to cover the bottom corridors, while Ally and I roam the top levels. It is a testament to our collective boredom that they agree without a single argument.

Ally and I have amazing success with the Elevens and Twelves, who are grumpy about their assessment tasks and sign easily. I don't think about how the entire school probably feels sorry for our year level and I don't care if some are pity signatures.

We work our way down to our floor again and come across Petra sitting in an empty classroom with some minor fellow geeks, playing chess of all things and it's like we're out on the savannah and I'm a cheetah and she's an antelope. Dinner time, little antelope.

'Tal, no,' murmurs Ally, and tries to reverse out the door, tugging on my sleeve. I pretend I haven't heard her.

Petra is minus her twin Audrey and looks scared when she sees us. I can actually hear Ally whimpering behind me.

'Hi everyone. We're petitioning Mrs Christie about the unfair censorship of Chloe Cardell's artwork.'

'Chloe who?' one of the chess players asks.

'If you care about freedom of speech, then you should sign it.'

I place the clipboard down on the table and hold out a handful of pens. The geeks avoid eye contact.

'Who's organising it? Is it Amnesty International?' one of the girls asks Petra.

'It's me!' Is it that hard to believe?

Ally—I could kiss her—joins in. 'It's a student-led thing. We're being involved citizens, or something?'

'We just don't think that one person's opinion should override what the rest of us think.' I stare right at Petra when I say this, and to my surprise she meets my gaze.

'Why are you doing this, Natalia?' asks Petra. She's not being defiant, she seems genuinely puzzled. Realising her hand is hovering, she puts the chess piece down on the board.

'Do you think it's fair?' I throw back. 'That one person thinks they're so important and so right, that they're going to make everyone else suffer?'

'I'm not suffering,' whispers a girl to her neighbour, confused.

'Is it that you think you're above us, Petra?' I can't help raising my voice and banging my hand on the table. I'm on a roll again; pure lightning runs through my veins. 'Are your precious little feelings more important than Chloe's hard work and talent?'

Petra has gone super-red in the face, and I can see she's surprised because I'm one hundred per cent right and she can't deny it.

'Individual rights should be balanced against what's best for the group,' she has the nerve to say. 'And if I'm so cold-hearted, then why am I the only one who thought about how upset the Mitchells would be if they saw a photo mocking the whole idea of kidnapping up on the school wall?'

This is enough to take my breath away, for real. I understand for the first time what seeing red means. Who was it that let Chunjuan snot on her shoulder?

'Mocking? You don't know *anything* about how the Mitchells feel. Why do you get to decide what's right?'

Petra clears her throat.

'I didn't decide. Mrs Christie did. But do you want to know what I think?' Her voice is low but there's total hush in the classroom so it rings out. 'I think you're using Chloe for attention. And you're using me as an excuse to be angry.'

She's in tears which is just a cheap ploy to get her nerd friends to turn against us. I open my mouth to respond but she gets in first.

'You think no one remembers Junior School, but I do. So I don't get why you're defending that photo! Or why you would do it in the first place. Where's your heart?'

That is like a punch to the face and I'm actually reeling backwards but I try to control it, try to wipe any expression off my face and stay strong. I'm so mad and frustrated I can barely see.

'My heart is *broken*...' I start, but a torrent of tears threatens to overtake me and I won't let anyone see me like that.

I pick up my clipboard and leave and Ally rushes to catch up to me, saying nothing, but sticking to my side.

It is completely unacceptable that Mrs Christie is not in her office when I have a million signatures to hand over, collected scrupulously over the last two days. Who can blame her, though, it must be hard to admit that everyone at this school thinks you're wrong wrong wrong. She's such an egomaniac it would never occur to her that someone might ever stand up to her.

'Try the staff room,' offers the receptionist through the annoying little window that makes her look like she's selling drive-thru hamburgers.

I narrow my eyes to indicate my disapproval and whirl away, and the queue behind me shuffles up.

In a case of the most rotten or perhaps the best timing ever, Petra and Audrey walk across the open space in front of me, arm-in-arm. I brighten my face when I see them, smiling like I'm an entrant in a beauty pageant and holding up my impressive stack of paper. Behold my wrath and quake before me et cetera, the Queen is here to carve new factions in the kingdom and reign supreme. I zoom the petitions through the air while Audrey sneers and Petra looks away.

The doors to the staff room are almost as busy as reception, swinging back and forth every few seconds spitting out teachers or sucking them in, but the teachers have looks on their faces that say *don't interrupt me*, probably on account of not having had enough coffee or sleep or not having had sex in the last two hundred years.

Every time one of the staffroom doors swings open you get a tantalising glimpse of the interior. Everyone knows that the teachers are always getting drunk in the staffroom and that's why they never let students look inside although I guess 8.30 a.m. is a little early.

'Natalia, can I help you?'

Finally Mr Scrutton takes pity and lingers in the doorway.

'Mrs Christie is supposed to be in there.'

'Let me check.'

The doors slam in unison, and the posters on the wall opposite flutter. As if the universe is trying to mock me, there's a big poster publicising the art exhibition. The exhibition cocktail evening is tonight, which means I only have today to get Chloe's artwork reinstated. I don't have time to play cat-and-mouse with Christie.

'No luck, I'm afraid, Natalia.' Mr Scrutton stands in the doorway, keeping it ajar with one foot. A microwave dings somewhere in the den of iniquity. 'Have you tried her office?'

I'd like to answer his very obvious question but my attention has been taken by the noticeboard just inside the staffroom, near the open door. Student photos are pinned up with notes underneath, warning of chronic asthma, allergies, epileptic seizures, diabetes and more. Yin's face is among them.

'Is everything okay? Anything else you need help with?'

I try not to get busted staring at the noticeboard. Mr Scrutton is not too bad as far as teachers go.

'Everything's fine!' I sound so fake he must be able to tell. Under Yin's photo it says 'Shellfish—anaphylaxis. Moderate asthma—ventolin.'

I'd forgotten about Yin's allergies until now. I remember the time Yin accidentally ate a dipping sauce with minute amounts of fish sauce in it and her eyes and mouth swelled up instantly and Chunjuan had to stab her in the thigh with an epipen. What if Doctor Calm doesn't know about her allergy? What if she told him and he didn't take her seriously?

'It's been a stressful year for everyone.'

'Uh huh.' My eyes want to return to the noticeboard. *Drop it*, I tell myself sternly.

I thank Scrutton and get away from the staffroom, the petitions heavy in my hands. I wonder if Yin had her epipen and ventolin with her when she was taken. What if the reason she hasn't been returned like the others is because there was an accident?

*Drop. It. Natalia.* This time I rap myself three times on the head with my knuckles, as if I can make each word sink in.

I walk slowly across the foyer, sunk in thought.

Two maintenance men in blue overalls carry a large orange-and-green balloon arrangement across the space, the balloons skimming the low ceiling.

I know where Mrs Christie's office is, everyone does, so when the receptionists aren't looking, I scuttle down the short corridor to her lair and put the petitions right in front of her door, where she can't miss them. Because I'm clever, I also take a photo of them, so she can't say afterwards that she never saw them.

I send the photo to Chloe with the message: *We need to talk about tonight.*

She doesn't reply but when I go to get my books for fifth period she's waiting in front of my locker.

'So you are at school today!' I remark. I must say that I've seen her look better but I guess that's what happens when Balmoral tries to crush your dreams.

'Ally showed me the petition.'

'I didn't count for sure, but I'm thinking we might have over four hundred signatures. At least.'

'It's nice that you're trying to do something for me...' she starts.

'No no no no—' I jump in, 'Not trying, I *am* doing something for you. And there's more, that's what I wanted to talk to you about. I have a spectacular protest planned for the cocktail evening tonight.'

'Natalia,' she says.

'We're going to stick it to the man, or the woman I suppose, in this case. Christie needs to know that we won't bow to her fascist—'

'*Natalia*. Look at me.'

Chloe holds her head at the temples like her brain might explode any second now. I'm no expert, but she seems unusually stressed. Her eyes are sliding about like she knows something I don't know.

'I appreciate you doing all this, but I need you to stop.'

The look on my face must say it all because she continues.

'I don't want to fight anyone about this,' Chloe says. 'Not Mrs Christie and not even Petra. Audrey came and found me this morning, and she thinks Yin's disappearance has brought up Petra's grief over her aunt who passed away not that long ago.'

'What? That makes no sense. Yin has nothing to do with Petra's aunt. She deserves everything she gets!' My finger goes up in the air. I am ready, more than ready, to debate this. 'Firstly, we both know that Petra fired the first shot and anything we do is just matching her dirty move. If she didn't want to fight, she shouldn't have taken us on.'

Chloe opens her mouth to interrupt me, but I roll right on.

'Secondly, you didn't do anything. I, on the other hand, did go in quite hard because there was a principle at stake, right? And I'm trying to defend you, because, let's face it, you're not doing anything to defend yourself.'

Chloe looks outraged at this, but I'm almost there.

'Thirdly, this has been going on for a long time. You forget that I've known Petra since Junior School. She has always gone overboard about every little thing.'

Chloe crosses her arms in front of her chest. 'Why does everyone always bring up the fact that I didn't go to Junior School?'

I'm very confused for a second. 'What? We don't.'

Chloe draws up to her full height which, truth be told, is slightly intimidating.

'You don't get anything,' her voice is strangled, 'because you're rich and beautiful and you've got all the confidence in the world. You don't know what it's like to be an outsider or a target, you don't know how easy it is to bring someone like me down. I tried, and I failed, and I just want to go away and be quiet now.'

I stare at her. This conversation is starting to resemble a runaway train, a train full of sentences that make no sense at all. What does she mean about confidence? She's confident.

'No petition. No protest. No attacking Petra. I mean it.'

'Attack? Come on, Chloe.'

We fall silent for a moment, staring at each other, and there's a sense that we're strangers and don't know each other at all. It's embarrassing to be carrying on like this in the corridor where everyone can see us.

'Is this our first fight?' I ask. If she only knew what I'd planned for tonight, she'd see what a stroke of brilliance it's going to be.

Chloe bites her lip, looking very uncertain. 'You're not listening to me, Natalia. Maybe it's because this whole thing is tangled up with how you're feeling about Yin.'

My vision blanks for one second, blanks with a red curtain. When it comes back Chloe is tenser than ever.

'I feel terrible that I asked you to pose like that, now that I know you used to be fr—'

I hold up my hand to halt her. Yeah, I can do that because I'm rich and beautiful and that's one of my superpowers.

'Not you as well,' I say, and walk away.

'I think it's a little strong.'

Dad fails to do a head-check before changing lanes, which is hypocritical of him because he's always at me about it when he takes me on a driving lesson and this is why I don't listen to him about many things.

'You said I had to decide the best approach on my own. Using judgement.'

'That's right and, respectfully, I'm telling you, I think the language you've chosen is too strong. There's a difference between making your point and being inflammatory. You could have just said *bring Chloe's photo back*.'

'That's got no flair, Dad. Boring.'

I turn to look at my placard resting on the back seat.

*STEALING STUDENT VOICES SINCE 1910*

Take that, Balmoral knobs.

The school is so proud of its august history that I think it strikes exactly the right note. I am very satisfied with my sign. It took me at least an hour to paint those thick black letters when I could have been doing a million other things like watching music videos or stalking Samuel Pulpitt's adult children online.

I'm wearing all black and I've got a roll of gaffer tape ready to slap over my mouth. I was going to use my school scarf to gag myself, until Dad pointed out that might be in bad taste. And I took his fatherly feedback on board, because I'm not a monster. My small rectangle of tape will be very tasteful.

'Any word from the principal?'

Mrs Christie had plenty of time after lunch today to respond to my impressive wad of paper and she did not get off her arse to do anything, so if anyone is to blame for tonight's public spectacle, it is her.

I sit up and pretend I possess Mrs Christie's giant mono-boob and prissy mouth. 'I imagine she would say: *We don't negotiate with terrorists*.'

Dad tries not to smile at that, but his cheeks twitch suspiciously.

When we get to school I make Dad park as close as he can, so he can see the main doors clearly. The entrance lobby is lit up but it's abandoned and there aren't many cars in the front car park.

'Okay, what's the plan, kiddo?'

'Enter the building, find a place to situate myself for the duration of my peaceful protest. Engage in passive resistance.'

'And leave if you're asked to by the security guard or teachers,' finishes Dad.

He makes me pose quickly by the side of the car with my mouth tape on, holding up the placard, taking pics with my phone. I have the good sense not to send any to Chloe. Maybe later, when she's calmed down, I can show her, and she'll say, you were right, Natalia, I was afraid to grab the attention and acclaim that I so clearly deserve.

It is maybe a tiny bit possible that perhaps I overreacted a small amount when Chloe brought up Yin, because of course someone told her how close we used to be. It's not ideal, but I am admittedly a notorious and interesting person that others talk about.

'Remember, if they try to expel you, I've got your back.'

'Comforting, Dad.'

I trudge towards the main doors, thinking about how Dad is almost certainly having his second mid-life crisis and I'm only enabling him and Mum would definitely not approve—if we had told her about our plan, that is.

I manage to wiggle my sign through the school doors.

My breath comes in little snorts and it's hard to tell if it's because I am beginning the very slow process of freaking out completely or if I'm still adjusting to breathing only through my nose.

A sandwich board announcing the Arts Sparks cocktail evening has been set out in the lobby, beside the fugly towering balloon thing that I saw the workmen lugging around earlier. I peer down the corridor and can see a few students and others milling around right at the end.

'Ahem.'

Two Balmoral mums sit at a table about ten metres away and I literally did not realise they were there until now.

Their table holds matching glasses of champagne and a full bottle of champagne on standby, which seems quite keen for a cocktail evening that starts at 6 p.m., plus an array of school merch and some amateur ikebana and raffle tickets. Their expressions are set somewhere between puzzled and disapproving and they're sporting the Balmoral Mum uniform of tailored asymmetry, chunky jewellery and patterned scarves—Old Girls for sure. Women who never got over the glory days of their time at the school and still hang their entire identities on being Old Collegians and making sure their own daughters repeat their very same experience at Balmoral. So very very sad.

I tilt my chin in a haughty manner and glide to my chosen site of peaceful protest next to the hideous balloon monster. I hold the placard in front of me and set my gaze to forward.

The mums exchange murmured assessments of my behaviour.

The doors squeak open, letting in a rush of outside air. Dad flashes his headlights at me in what I suppose is encouragement or solidarity or whatever and I hope isn't a warning. Cars gather around him as the car park fills.

A family walks past, slowing slightly to read my sign. The girl smiles and takes a photo, the parents do not.

'Honey, are you supposed to be there?' One of the mums calls out. 'You're Kasha's daughter, aren't you?'

I flip my placard to reveal the other side.

*FREEDOM TO EXPRESS NOT FREEDOM TO SUPPRESS*

They read my second message and fall back into their chairs, more murmur more murmur more murmur. One takes a pic of me, the other taps at her phone.

The doors open again; more people arrive, more eyes slide sidewards. No one seems confident enough to fully acknowledge my presence.

I'm used to breathing through my nose by now, but my arms are getting tired from keeping my sign at chest level. Very occasionally someone gives me a confused nod. A Year Eleven flashes me the peace sign.

'Is this performance art, Natalia?'

Nouri appears magically by my side and almost gives me a heart attack.

'PLOH-TESS,' I say through my tape.

'Right.' Nouri smiles and waves as more parents and Old Girls and students arrive.

She lowers her voice. 'I'll consider this as going towards the grade for your project. It's thematically consistent with what you've already handed in.'

I nod and definitely don't appear too grateful. It didn't occur to me before she said it, but yes, while I deserve a medal for this, a B+ will also do.

Nouri moves away quickly, as if she doesn't want to be associated with me. The gaping loneliness of the activist fills me. Chloe should be here to see this.

A grey-suited security guard wanders into the lobby, stares and retreats. She soon multiplies into two security guards. I smize at them. And then, inevitably, Vice Principal Mackenzie marches into sight.

'Natalia, good evening. Would you mind explaining what you're doing?'

I shrug, raise my sign, and try to convey that my whole deal for tonight is silence.

'Who are you here with this evening?' It's a pity Mrs Mackenzie has such a pointless job because she could be quite nice if everything about her life was different. 'I'll need you to speak now, Natalia.'

I roll my eyes and peel off my mouth tape. That sounds simple, but it's basically ten times more painful than getting my bikini line done.

'Oh my god.' I wince and roll the tape into a ball. When I recover feeling in my lips, I talk. 'I'm protesting, miss. I'm exercising my democratic rights.'

This makes her frown. 'One moment, please, Natalia.'

No doubt she has gone to call Mrs Christie on her batphone and receive orders about what to do with me.

I take the opportunity to tuck my sign under my arm and

sprint down the hallway towards the exhibition, pretending to be a secret agent while I do it. Now that most people have arrived for the evening, maybe I can stand in the blank space where Chloe's artwork should be hung. Speeches are going to be every kind of awkward tonight.

I wedge myself into the spare stretch of wall.

At the end of the corridor is a table of drinks and canapés. Parents and students stroll up and down, passing comment on their daughter's work (the best), their daughter's friends' work (a nice attempt) and their daughter's enemies' work (a toddler could have done that). I seem to be winning more than a few indulgent and condescending smiles so I keep a permanent scowl on my face so everyone knows how serious I am about fighting the power.

When I'm not demonstrating my political credentials I crane my neck, trying to see who has come tonight. I see Brooke and Bochen and some of the other boarders including that nasty supremacist Jody and wonder if Petra has the gall to be here when she has ruined everything and is clearly anti-Art.

The front doors thump heavily. Even though the entrance is a good thirty metres away I swear a gust of air races up the corridor. A trick of the sunset sends rosy light angling through the glass doors, filling the lobby with dusty sparkles.

Standing in the distance is a still figure dressed in a silk blouse, tailored pants, pale shoes. Familiar blonde hair, spun gold in the sudden beam of light.

The sunset glow smooths out her skin, turns her into an angel with a halo. When she spots my Marcel Marceau act among the paintings and collages and drawings she grows even more still.

Viewed as if from another world, barely glimpsed.

A cord that connects her to me and me to her.

Mum?

I stare. Fair and golden and good parental angels don't belong in the school corridor outside the Great Hall when they're supposed to still be in the office working on the Baker-Hill contract.

She marches towards me, and the closer she gets the clearer it becomes that I'm not seeing things.

I smile quizzically in what I hope is a disarming way and raise my hand hello, but Mum doesn't smile.

Students and parents and teachers melt out of her way and I am about to be incinerated, Dad too, for my unruly behaviour, my spectacle-making, my refusal to know when to stop, for being too much.

But Mum's expression isn't warpath, it's soft. It's soft like ice-cream and sorrowful and full of pain. There's compassion on her face, and regret and fear and there's only one thing that could give her that face. I saw it when Grandad died and here it is again.

My face gets it first, my lips snarl, and then the knowledge rolls down my body in a sickening oily wave. Somewhere, in some other part of my brain, I register a Dad-shaped smudge coming through the front doors, but I don't pay it much note because—

It's Yin.

Not good news.

They've found her, but not really her.

An emptiness, a shell.

They've found a body.

I know I know I know what tsunami is about to crash over us, not just me but the whole year level the whole school rippling outwards, crashing into every worried person in this city.

I push off the wall and run.

Mummy.

I get so close I could reach out to her and the realisation hits my legs and my knees melt to nothing. Her mouth an O, her arms out, but I'm too far away still and I feel the hard floor and the bite of carpet for only a millisecond before darkness comes.

# Chloe

## DAY 62

The story unfolds on our TV screen in gritty blue pixels, as if it's another shaky scene from *Devil Creek*. A windswept reporter in a parka stands in the foreground, while behind her there are police cars and people in dark clothes and hi-vis vests.

'The body of sixteen-year-old Yin Mitchell was found around 4 p.m. yesterday by a park ranger in the Broken Ranges State Park in Melbourne's far west, cementing what has been suspected for a long time: that this is a homicide investigation.'

I can't help drawing in a sharp breath, even though this has all been mentioned in the morning news. It looks so unremarkable, this scrappy paddock, the run-down picnic facilities.

'Should I turn it off?' Mum squeezes my hand, hard, and we lock eyes. She let me stay home today, even though classes were still on. Attendance was optional, not just for Year Ten but the whole school. I wonder how many girls showed up.

'If I don't find out the details now, I'll look online later anyway. I want to know what happened, otherwise I'll just be making things up in my head.'

'I can't believe it's come to this.' Mum looks as shaky as I feel. 'I don't know how I would go on living if anything happened to you or Sam.'

The reporter goes over the timeline of Yin's abduction, accompanied by computer graphics showing dates and places. When it's laid out so clinically like that, this ending seems inevitable, but there are no words for how unreal it all feels.

Arnold curls warmly over my feet. Just over two months ago, Mum and I sat in this very same position and watched Yin's abduction unfold like a bad dream. Sam isn't here this time. Dad has taken him to soccer practice and he's having a sleepover at Dad and Jarrod's house.

'Several pieces of evidence have been removed from the site today, and the police will continue their search tomorrow. Broken Ranges State Park is popular with hikers and rock climbers. Police are calling for anyone who has witnessed any suspicious activity in the area in the last six months to please contact them via the Operation Panopticon hotline.'

A police detective appears on the screen to talk about something to do with the post mortem and forensics and bringing the killer to justice but suddenly I'm full of too many awful details so I switch the TV off myself.

The exhibition and the art prize seem inconsequential now. The argument I had with Natalia doesn't matter either, none of it's important. I swear I'll never complain about homework and acne and bad marks and not finding the right jeans ever again. I swear I'll never be anything but patient and nice and loving towards Mum and Sam. And Dad too.

'Have you heard anything from Natalia today?' asks Mum. I told her that Natalia and Yin were childhood best friends, told her about what had happened at the photo shoot. Mum said it sounded like Natalia was experiencing the after-effects of trauma.

'No.' I almost messaged her this morning, but something stopped me. 'What do you think I should do?'

'Send her your love and thoughts,' Mum says. 'Let her know you're thinking about her. And then give her time.'

# Natalia

**DAY 63**

When I finally let someone into my dark bedroom, it's Liv.

'Don't expect good conversation.' I immediately go back to my bed and get under the doona.

Liv follows me under there. 'Not here for the conversation, just the snuggles.'

I pretend to complain and push her off but her skinny arms are tattooed tentacles and I eventually give in and let myself sink against her. I don't know how she can look so sharp and hard but in reality be so massively soppy.

Once I give in to her, something inside me breaks and I cry again for the millionth time since Mum interrupted my protest to tell me the news early, before anything was officially released, before it hit the news. Which seemed cruel and unnecessarily humiliating at the time, but was probably a good idea.

Liv waits out several waves of tears and also has the good sense not to mention that I've barricaded myself in my room for almost two days, with Mum leaving increasingly elaborate tray meals outside my door.

My bed is awash with scrunched-up tissues and old Balmoral yearbooks that I've been flicking through on repeat repeat repeat. I have my phone and my laptop somewhere here on the Good Ship Natalia, but I'm sick of the outside world and want to float only on my bed, which is cut off from the mainland and surrounded by an ocean of my very own snot and tears.

If only I was still friends with Yin. If only I had realised what I had when I had it. If only I could remember our last conversation. If only I had called her out of the blue that night and shifted the course of history. If only we still had slumber parties and I'd been there to protect her.

'You're into drugs,' I dig my chin into Liv's collarbone. 'Can you get something to make me stop crying?'

'It's better to let it out.' My sister sounds like a bona fide adult. 'Plus you're one of those annoying people who looks good when they cry. You should have seen me after Mel and I broke up.'

Liv acts out how grotesquely she wept and it prompts a smile from me, a smile that makes me immediately guilty for feeling anything except the worst ever, when Yin is where? In a metal drawer in a morgue that looks like the one on *Devil Creek*?

The tears leave me now, adios until the next round comes and grabs me by the throat and shakes me down. Periods of calm followed by one thought—*I can't believe she's gone*—and then the earth shakes and the rocks fall and the rivers burst their banks and I come close to throwing up my own stomach, followed by all my major organs.

I've been having nightmares about what Yin's last hours or minutes might have been like, how scared she was, how much she saw, did she know this was the end, what was the last thing she said, was she in pain and on and on and on.

'Look at these...' Liv has wonder in her voice. 'I can't believe you kept them all.'

Neither can I. I'm sure I should hate Balmoral but instead I have religiously kept every single yearbook from prep through to last year's. The Junior School ones are thin and simple, but the yearbooks from Year Seven onwards are glossy, full-colour books.

'Hey look, it's us.' Liv shows me the page. We're at Sports Day, in matching polo shirts, with ribbons pinned to our fronts. Me, a baby Grade One, Liv a big girl in Grade Six. We're wearing these puffy old-fashioned bloomers that are just glorified underpants and my little infant legs look like sausages.

I screw up my face. 'Embarrassing.'

I find my Year Seven yearbook and Liv and I leaf through it together. Our House Concert that year was set on a cruise ship, and there's a photo of me in a sailor costume dancing with a mop. The Year Twelve formal minus Liv, who refused to wear a dress and wasn't allowed to come unless she wore one. Bad poetry from nice girls. Class lists. Debating reports. A tedious essay from Mrs Christie extolling the virtues of the Lord.

'I was looking for answers, I think.'

'About you and Yin?'

'Yeah.'

I show her the photo of Yin in Junior Orchestra, how she's smiling so hard her eyes have disappeared, clutching that clarinet like someone might want to rip it out of her hands. She started learning it because she wanted to graduate as quickly as possible to the saxophone, but instead she fell in love and I bet she wanted to marry that clarinet.

Claire and Milla are in the photo too, Milla with her French horn, Claire on timpani drums. Every year, every time there's a photo of Yin, either Claire or Milla are in it. I guess Claire and Milla are feeling what I'm feeling now, but maybe even worse, if that's possible.

'You never know, you and Yin might have come back together again, in Year Twelve, or even later in uni,' Liv says. 'That happens sometimes.'

'Not now it doesn't,' I reply and burrow my head on Liv's shoulder as another wave takes me.

# Chloe

**DAY 67**

'Chloe, can I talk to you?'

I'm lost in my own thoughts when Petra speaks to me at our lockers. It's a shock because I know she's been actively trying to avoid me all week. Lisbeth told me she saw Petra stashing her books in Audrey's locker, which is right at the far end of the corridor.

'Sure.'

A mottled flush decorates Petra's throat and ears. I wait, because I don't want to make this too easy for her.

'I want to apologise for going to Mrs Christie with my concerns about your photo. I thought at the time that I was doing the right thing. I didn't think she'd disqualify you...'

'Didn't you? What did you think she'd do?'

'I mean, I didn't think it through that well—but I felt very *strongly* that—'

'If you didn't think she'd do anything, then why would you say something in the first place?'

Petra's lip trembles and I force myself to lower my voice and tone slightly. She's already had Natalia yell at her and it didn't do too much good. And if what Audrey told me last week is true, Yin's disappearance set off a grief ripple about her aunt, so maybe I should be showing a bit more compassion.

'Don't get me wrong,' I tell her, 'I don't want to hold a grudge, but this isn't even a proper apology yet. I currently don't care why you complained. Do you know how hard I worked on that photo?'

Petra has no idea how much it took from me to put myself out there like that, to take a risk, to submit an entry to the prize. I wouldn't expect her to understand. She's been bred for lifelong, all-round excellence.

'Okay...' Petra takes a big shaky breath and I can almost hear the cogs of her brain working. 'I'm sorry that I got you eliminated from the exhibition and the prize. It must have been disappointing for you...'

'It was.'

'Especially since you worked so hard on it. So—for all your hard work to go to waste like that—and—I can see why you hate me.'

'I don't hate you. Honestly, Petra, I don't.'

Petra gets a panicked look on her face and waves her hand down low, shooing. I turn and see Audrey and Brooke slink away. Girls are trickling into the corridor, so the bell must be close to ringing. Or maybe none of us are in our classes. Most of the Year Tens have been coming in this week, but the days don't have their normal structure. Small groups have been sent to counselling sessions, movies have been playing in the Great Hall for anyone to attend, candles are being lit with the chaplain.

I haven't seen Claire or Milla or Natalia all week, and Natalia still hasn't replied to my message.

'I know you thought you were doing the right thing.' I've spent some time over the last few days trying to put myself in Petra's shoes and not being that great at it. 'I was trying to do the right thing too, in my own way. But I'm sorry I upset you with the subject matter of my photo.'

She dares to look at me. 'Really?'

'I've been wondering if I did the right thing. Maybe I should have thought about other people's reactions more. Audrey said—' I have no idea if this is a no-go topic or not so I tread lightly, 'that Yin's abduction might have brought up some family stuff for you.'

Petra sighs; I see her whole body inflate and then deflate completely.

'I know that's Audrey's theory…and maybe she's right. But. But.' Petra grapples with something unseen. 'I'm not a good person,' she whispers eventually.

'Let's go outside.' I grab Petra's arm and take the doors outside to the breezeway. We lean on the waist-high balcony, looking down to the quad where the Year Sevens have been constructing a mandala out of flower petals. One breath of wind and the whole thing is going to blow away, which I guess is the point.

'Why aren't you a good person?' I ask.

Petra doesn't look at me. 'Because…because I was always envious of Yin. She was first clarinet, I was second. We took all the same subjects and she always got slightly better marks than me. And everyone likes her—liked her—but I secretly thought of her as my nemesis. Even though she was *so* nice to me, so generous. She used to lend me her notes all the time, like we weren't rivals.'

She falls quiet.

I try to understand what the problem is. 'So you felt guilty when she went missing?'

'A little.' Petra wipes her nose and I see that she's been silently crying. 'I know logically that I have nothing to do with what happened to her, but I wish I had been nicer to her, accepted her friendship more. I can't believe the things that used to matter to me.'

'I get it,' I say. I do. It's hard not to pit yourself against other girls in the hothouse environment of Balmoral. 'It makes sense.'

'Thanks, Chloe. You're the last person I would expect to listen to me.'

'It's done, right? Let's try to move on, if we can. You might have to ignore Natalia for a while. She's going through a lot, I think...'

'I know.'

We're both quiet. I had no idea I would do this but I step forward and give Petra a hug.

'It's been awful,' she says. 'The whole thing.'

'I know,' I say, and we separate. I'd feel embarrassed, but there's been more hugging in the last three days than in the whole year combined.

'I keep waiting to wake up and find out this has all been a nightmare.' Petra extracts a tissue from her blazer pocket. 'I knew what the chances were. Statistically speaking, you know. That whole thing about ninety per cent of kidnapping victims being dead within the first twenty-four hours isn't a particularly accurate statistic, it's more complicated than that, but it's not far off.'

Something occurs to me for the first time. There's something familiar about what she's saying. 'Petra—did you write the email about what to do in the case of an abduction?'

She flushes all over again. 'Please don't tell anyone. Not even Audrey knows.'

'I won't. You must have been worried to send that around.'

She nods, her eyes wide. 'I was so scared. I just wanted to do something useful.'

# Natalia

Every bone in my body is screaming get away get away get away but somehow Mum and I pile in the car and follow Stephen and Chunjuan's champagne-coloured Audi down the highway and into an area of the city I've never seen before.

'You don't have to do this,' says Mum as we park our car and my heart goes pitter-pat or more like BANG BASH BANG and I think I've figured out how cows feel before they get led to the big chopper.

'You don't either,' I say back, but neither of us stops moving as we get out, put our jackets on and join the Mitchells at their car because we were asked to do this and it wasn't our family that lost a member and there are some things you can't say no to.

The BBQs and wooden tables that I saw on the news and in the papers are everywhere around us. The scrubby trees too, the dodgy public toilets and the trail signs.

Even though it's not that cold today, Albert and Nelson have so many layers on they look like round puffballs on

314

sticks, robins before the winter. Stephen hands them knobbly supermarket bags and they heft them onto their shoulders with seriousness. They give me a solemn squeeze each, even though it's been years since they've seen me.

We all look so grim we could be in one of those Polish arthouse movies Nanna used to watch before she got dementia and switched to game shows.

Chunjuan holds out her hand and I take it. Her face is unmovable, her hand firm and strong.

We march off into the park, followed by Albert and Nelson. I look behind and realise that it's just us; by some prior arrangement or discussion Stephen and Mum are waiting with the cars. We walk along a green corridor and into a piece of nothing bush, the most desolate place you've ever seen.

A police officer shows us a barely-there track, and we shuffle through waist-high grass until we're in a clearing of sorts.

My legs don't want to move, but I drag each foot forwards.

'I'll show you what to do, it's not difficult,' reassures Chunjuan as we reach the edge of a taped-off area.

My head spins, everything goes black for the longest blink of an eye, there are stars, and then the clouds and the swaying grass right themselves.

This is where Yin's body was found.

I take a deep breath, look down at the clods of dirt and tell myself I have to do this. I try not to think too much about Yin lying on this cold, sodden ground. When I posed for Chloe I think I was trying to understand what it might have felt like.

Together Chunjuan, Albert, Nelson and I unpack the plastic bags.

Chunjuan lights a small fire in an old cooking oil tin with the top cut off. She shows me how to fold up sheets of red-and-gold paper and we start burning them.

Albert and Nelson, solemn as priests, lay out paper plates with a pile of mandarins and a packet of biscuits. I wonder how much they understand about what happened to Yin.

We light thick sticks of incense and then push the ends deep into the dirt where they stand up like miniature trees.

Chunjuan, Albert and Nelson kneel on the earth, press their hands together, bow their heads. I get down and copy them.

Smoke spirals, minuscule pieces of black ash fly about, sticking to my face. My knees are damp almost immediately, my fingertips are hot from burning the paper. Wind shushes through the grass, rippling across us.

A thin animal sound comes from Chunjuan, the barest trickle. She cries softly. She cries louder.

And then the wailing starts.

Chunjuan wails like an animal in pain, a baby keening in a cot, like someone facing a black, dark void.

Her face is a tortured mask. I've never seen anyone in so much pain, and still she wails.

Albert and Nelson shift next to me.

I look down and they're holding hands. Their faces crumple, they stare at their mum and they look so confused and scared.

Chunjuan needs me. She wanted me here and she trusts me to know the right thing to do.

I help Albert and Nelson to their feet, brush them down and take their hands, one twin on each side, and we retreat to a safe distance and we wait and we wait and we wait. I gather them close around me, being the safe grownup for them, their arms circling my waist and my hands stroking their baby-fine hair.

Back in the car, I shake my head when Mum asks if I want to talk about it.

Stephen practically lifts Chunjuan into the passenger seat. Albert and Nelson seem to be doing better.

I'm chilled to the bone. Numb. I watch the boring grey nothingness of the suburbs race by and think about how Yin's story ended in the most depressing place ever.

Mum gets us takeaway tacos and the sweet tang of cola rushes through my body.

When we're getting close to home I finally reply to Chloe's message.

I write more than I usually do. I say thank you for thinking of me and sorry it took me so long to reply and how shit and strange my day was. I ask her if she's coming to the memorial service and tell her that I'm not sure if I will be able to get any words out. I say sorry for fighting with her the other day and say I wasn't myself.

I write so much in this one text I don't know who I am anymore and for sure she's going to wonder too.

# Chloe

**DAY 68**

My hands shake with nerves, but I let the edge of the scalpel bite into the paper and then drag it downwards. Angling the blade this way and that, I carefully cut Natalia's body out of *Someone's Watching*. It's painstaking work, trying to get close to every line and detail. A few times I flinch, thinking I've cut off her finger or a curl of hair, but my blade stays true.

I've taken over the entire lounge room floor.

I lift paper Natalia out of the scene, exhaling with relief, and lay her down on a fresh canvas prepped with white gesso. An old nail-polish brush is exactly the right size to carefully apply glue to her back and stick her down in her new home.

I turn over the original photo and paste white construction paper over the hole. I pick off half of my collaged frame, leaving the remnants to speak louder.

After that awful conversation in Ms Nouri's office I thought I would give up art for good. But then Yin's body was found and it was like the earth fell out from under everyone. Death is the worst kind of silence, and I don't want to be silent.

I can't explain it, but my gut tells me this is the right thing to do.

The result is two companion artworks with identical dimensions.

One an empty room with a white silhouette of a missing person at the centre. The other a large white expanse interrupted only by the black-and-white image of a floating girl.

As if she knows I was thinking about her, my phone vibrates, and it's Natalia. She only messaged me back yesterday, after a week's silence, so I wasn't expecting a call this soon. I turn down my music before I answer.

'You sound surprised,' she says.

'No, not surprised.' I am surprised.

'Okay, nervous then. Like you don't know what to say to me.'

If I thought tragedy was going to bring a new, softer Natalia, I was wrong. 'How about pleased? Pleased you called me.'

I hear her snort.

'No, it's weird. I'm the one being weird,' she says. 'I woke up this morning and realised I'd sent you an essay yesterday.'

It takes me a moment to realise that she means her text message. 'It's not weird at all. First the—the—' my throat practically closes up, it's impossible to say 'gravesite' and I don't even know if that's the right phrase for a place where a body isn't placed respectfully and intentionally. 'The park sounded intense. And now you've got to get through the memorial tomorrow. It's a lot.'

There's a public vigil for Yin tonight, on the steps of Parliament. It might have even already started. I overheard a few Balmoral girls say they were going, even though there's no official school presence, it's more for the city itself. I never thought about how a whole city might need to grieve. The memorial tomorrow is going to be enough for me; I can't imagine mourning among thousands of people.

'Thanks. I called Ally too much in the first few days when I couldn't do anything but lock myself in my room and cry. That poor girl had to listen to me ugly-crying for hours.'

'I'm so sorry,' is all I can think to say.

It's not enough, but I have no idea how to behave. Talking openly about our emotions is not something I thought I'd find myself doing with Natalia, but I make myself do it.

'And I'm sorry I didn't appreciate your petition enough. And your protest, too.'

'You heard about that?'

'I did…Bochen sent me a photo.'

Natalia standing in the school lobby, all dressed in black and holding a sign, with a fierce look on her face. I guess any gossip about her protest got lost quickly among the awful news.

'What are you doing, Cardell?'

'Right now?'

I look at my work spread across the floor. Mum has taken Sam out for dinner so I can have some peace and quiet. I've commandeered every spare surface in our kitchen and living areas. I wasn't in the mood to trek across town to the studio at Dad's house. Streets, train stations, bus stops, parkland—ever since Yin's body was found they all seem like they could be hiding bad men, all over again.

'Don't get worried, but I did something to our picture.'

I hope this doesn't seem callous to her, that I'm making art while she's been visiting the place where Yin was found. 'I had a revelation. Or I think I did. I've pulled it apart.'

In bed last night I was thinking about something Lisbeth said—that it was horrific to find out what had happened to Yin, but it was a relief that the wondering was over. It made me think more about the limbo that we've been in, everyone at Balmoral, but especially our year level.

I remembered something Natalia said when she first saw my folio, about how the girls on crime novel covers always look like they are in-between places. That's exactly where we've all been for the last few months. In-between hope and despair.

I try to explain my new angle, but Natalia gets impatient. 'You're making no sense. Send a pic.'

I do that, and then she's quiet for way too long.

'Are you mad that I cut it up?'

'No,' Natalia replies immediately. 'It's good. I don't have any words at the moment, Chloe, but it's good.'

'It's about the in-between places,' I tell her, 'and the girls in them. I remembered what you'd said. The real world, and other places too.'

The white canvas with the floating girl used to mean a place we couldn't imagine. Doctor Calm's house as it appeared in the police sketches, or another dimension we couldn't fathom. And now we know the white expanse means the end; peace, we hope, or rest.

'Cut out of life,' says Natalia flatly, and then she's quiet. I stay on the line and we breathe in unison for a while, letting stillness hold us together.

'Please come tomorrow, I need your face in the crowd,' she says after a while, and then she hangs up.

## *Natalia*

**DAY 69**

I've already been awake a few hours or maybe I never even went to sleep at all when Liv knocks on the wall adjoining my room and the spare bedroom that she's been methodically transforming into a messy hovel.

She knocks and knocks and you bet she won't stop knocking until I knock back: I'm alive, I'm okay, I'm here. We knock good night and we knock good morning and you can say a lot with a knock apparently. I'm already dreading when she goes back to her own apartment and things supposedly return to normal.

My eyes close again but then my bedroom door clicks and Liv is there with her woolly blanket clutched around her like a couture cape.

'You still want to do it?' she says. 'Let's do it early before Mum can stop us.'

We creep downstairs, avoiding the two creaky steps and it would be like midnight feasts or Christmas morning except that today is Yin's memorial service and the whole of Balmoral will be there and I have to speak.

There's no point to our stealth because when we get downstairs Mum is already in the kitchen drinking carrot juice in her pilates gear and Dad is pan-frying mattress-sized slabs of French toast which is basically their entire relationship summed up in one neat scene.

Mum is silent while Liv swirls an old sheet around me and fastens it with a butterfly clip but I can see her starting to twitch when Liv runs an extension cord from the kitchen and plugs her clippers in. I sit at the table and push aside the thick orange envelopes they've been sending my schoolwork in, which I have been studiously ignoring.

Liv buzzes the clippers once, twice, to check they're working properly and both times the sound makes me jump.

'You know you can't change your mind once she starts, darling?' Mum says.

It's early in the morning and I'm grumpy and my eyeballs are dry and what I need to do is something extreme.

'You are aware that hair grows back, aren't you, Mother?'

'There's no need to be snide!' she says in an overly wounded tone but then Dad swaps out her carrot juice for a steaming cup of coffee and it miraculously shuts her up.

Without further ado, Liv gathers my hair into a ponytail, the whole honey-blonde enviable lot that everyone is always complimenting me on including uninvited strangers, and shears it off with Mum's sewing scissors.

'Ta-da!' She holds it up and blonde wisps drift over the parquetry floor.

Mum yelps as if her arm has been cut off and Dad moves in to cuddle her. They've been unusually lovey-dovey the last few days and it has been the cause of much retching between Liv and I.

I have zero regrets when I look at the blonde clump in Liv's hand. I am colourless, expressionless, drained of spark or fire or anything normal.

'Your beautiful hair,' Mum whimpers from the kitchen.

'Enough of that patriarchal crap!' I say loudly. 'You make me sound like Jo in *Little Women*.'

'YOUR ONE BEAUTY!' Liv says melodramatically as she starts buzzing. The clippers bite at my nape and they are oh so hungry. Mum's sneakers pad out of the room.

I fix my eyes on the back window, focussing on our wattle tree, which is starting to bloom, and the grey sky that might bring a storm big enough to cancel the memorial service and strand our car on flooded streets so it's a pity but we won't make it after all.

Buzz buzz buzz. The blade is firm against my skin. I imagine harvesters driving over fields of wheat leaving clean stubble in their wake.

'Do you want to practise your speech?' Liv asks over the drone.

I don't dare shake my head. 'No. I got it.'

I try to forget the fact that my sometimes-unreliable sister is wielding a blade centimetres and in some cases millimetres away from so many things I need, like ears, eyes, scalp. She mows behind my ears, temples, right over the top, around my crown.

I close my eyes and the ticklish drift of hair eddies around me, but there are black things behind my eyelids, toothed monsters and dark deeds.

The clippering goes on and on and then Liv stops, all is quiet, her hands come away from my dome and she walks around me.

'I think I'm done.' She goes to find a mirror.

'Yes,' I say when she holds it up in front of me.

I have one centimetre of dark blonde fuzz covering my round head. My ears protrude slightly. My face leaps out, and every blue vein and dark shadow on it. I look tired and washed out and younger than before.

I look stripped bare. Finally my outsides match my insides.

# Chloe

I shuffle into the bluestone building with everyone from my form room. It's the first time I've visited the church in the city where Balmoral holds its most pious events. They shipped us in on buses, like we're on an excursion.

The church is forbiddingly gothic, circles and arches and ironwork everywhere, and it's not difficult to imagine medieval murders and monks and intrigue in its walls.

It's strange to remember Yin here, when this wasn't what she believed in, if her refusal to pray during school assembly was any indication.

Yesterday the newspapers printed a photo of Mrs Mitchell at the State Park with Albert and Nelson. Yin's mum's face is contorted with grief, her hair flies in the wind. You can't see the kids' faces because their heads are bowed over incense and offerings. There's no sign of Natalia; you wouldn't know she'd been there at all.

The photo is crisp, moving, beautiful, the perfect capture of a fleeting moment. You could even call it art. But is it right to take a photo of a mother in her private grief? Did

Mrs Mitchell want to be seen in that state? Why is it so easy to override what girls and women want, what they might decide if they were given any control?

Inside the church everything is shadowy and stale and hushed. Dark. Not glorious at all.

A huge photo of Yin dominates the lobby.

It's a better photo than the ones they used in the newspapers and on the TV. She's standing outside among trees, maybe on school camp, laughing and looking off camera. The sun hits her face; she looks relaxed and happy.

I never knew her properly. Not like that.

There are piles of tributes at the foot of the photo. Flowers, cards, more photos, soft toys.

Milla stands next to the photo and easel, holding a massive basket of lilies. Claire stands nearby with an identical load.

I take my flower and lay it down among the many, and have one quiet moment with Yin, concentrating on her memory.

I hope you understand my photo was for you, I think. You and other girls like you, and all of us for having to live in this shitty world where people don't value our lives.

# Natalia

## DAY 69

The thing about churches is that they're designed to give you religious vibes, with those high ceilings and stained-glass windows and hard benches. If the light hits the windows just right and sends shards of light beaming into the church then you can't blame people for thinking about stairways to heaven and all the other stuff.

But churches do none of this for me, ever, and definitely not today.

I am full of terror and it is very hard to hide that amount of scared with my usual tricks.

There are hundreds of Balmoral girls crammed into the pews, and any other spare spaces they can find to stand, and the air is cold against my hands and bare neck. The cross hanging up high looks judgey; the priest or father or whatever he's called is a dinosaur in a black robe.

I turn around in my front-row pew and sneak a look across to the standing-room-only section at the back, thinking of all the times in history you could find big groups of girls gathered. Witch hunts, denouncements, concerts.

I see Sarah and Ally and half of Marley's obscured head, but I don't see Chloe. I try to take everyone back in time, put them in tartan pinafores and hats with ribbons but my trick doesn't work today.

Suddenly the priest is calling my name.

There's a rustle and a murmur because everyone expects Claire and Milla to speak at the memorial service but no one expects me, and there's also my new haircut and I'm already sick of everyone making a big deal out of it.

The walk to the lectern is long and I hope I only feel twitchy instead of visibly twitching.

I don't look up as I pull the microphone down towards me.

My voice starts croaky when I wanted it to be pure and strong.

'Yin was my best friend for a long time, even though our friendship changed in the last few years,' I begin, reading from paper that's already wearing thin on the folds.

I look over at Chunjuan and she's a mess of tears and snot and puffy eyes and she might be breaking Stephen's hand she's squeezing it that hard, but at least she's not wailing like an animal and she's also looking me straight in the eye, nodding. She trusts me, she trusts me, she wants me to do this.

I take that look and I turn it into a reason to do this properly, to not turn away from the task, to do something real for a change.

'Everyone knows that Yin was incredibly smart and a whiz at the clarinet, but the thing that stuck our friendship together was how silly and funny and imaginative she was.

She was a good mix of adventurous and sensible and she would rarely turn one of my ideas down.'

I see Claire look at Milla and smile and it makes me think that maybe I did still know Yin, that she hadn't gone and gotten a personality swap any time in the last four years.

'She was a loyal friend, and when you told her a secret you knew that she wouldn't tell anyone, even when it was a juicy one that would have messed with several people and got everyone talking.'

This gets a gentle laugh but I don't look up because I can't stand the thought of how many people are watching me right now.

'She was a much nicer person than me, because she always saw something good and beautiful and worthwhile in everyone. And she was a better person than most of us here because she had goals and was already working towards her future. If she got obsessed with something, you couldn't stop her from living and breathing it and she would talk about it until you needed her to stop.'

This is where it gets hard. I gulp down everything and try to stay strong. I imagine I'm drawing calm from my friends. I don't want to break down in front of this many people.

'This is why I know she would have gone on to do amazing things with her life. And this is why she is the wrong person for this to have happened to. This is why it's so unfair.'

I can't even speak of the anger I hold deep down for the man who did this. I know that you're supposed to be forgiving in churches.

I lift my head and look out over the bobbing heads and see that everyone is with me. Some girls are crying, some look in shock. Some are practically climbing into their friends' laps and burrowing into shoulders.

Claire nods at me from the front pew. We talked properly for the first time since Yin's disappearance, in the empty church before the buses arrived. I wanted to make sure that she and Milla were okay with me being the one to speak.

'I won't ever get over this. I won't ever forget Yin.'

My voice wobbles and I sound truthful. I sound like I'm telling everything and I am telling almost all I can. I feel naked enough with my lack of hair and all the truth. But there's more that I hold back for myself and Yin only, the bits of us that no one else will ever touch or hear about. And I have to do that to survive, I have to keep the precious parts of our friendship for me, for us.

I breathe in deeply, look up at the high ceilings and there, among the rafters and stained-glass windows, I find something new.

It was Yin who found other people to hang out with first in Year Seven.

She was in a form room with Claire and Milla, I was in another. Yin tried to get me to join up and make a group of four with them, but they were all into music and I wasn't. There was a terrifying lag of a week when I had no friends at all, and then I hit it off with Ally and the rest is history, history with a bad ending.

Maybe I was a bit cold to her for a while, but it was because I could tell she wanted to move away from me and towards other people, and I was immature and didn't know how to cope.

Something lifts off me, something releases.

I still feel sorrow for her, but now, I'm also sorry for myself. For everything I've lost.

There's a few more things typed on my crumpled bit of paper, but I'm done.

Part of me was hoping I would sense Yin's presence here, that there would be light and colour and whispers somewhere out there, but there's cold emptiness and that's okay. All I want to do is go home and lay out the entire contents of our suitcase on my bed and spend the afternoon with her.

# *Chloe*

hi chloe

quick question: are you interested in being part of a group show? my friends and I are putting on an exhibition at my friend's warehouse. call me. we'd love to have you be part of it.

Ax

'Chloe! You called!'

'Uh huh.' I'm on the line, but I'm nervous as all hell. Adut and I have exchanged a few emails but this is our first time speaking on the phone.

'I'm so pleased you got back to me. Hang on.' I think I hear a tram bell in the background, air whistling all around. 'Sorry, I'm getting off the road and putting my headphones in…How are you doing, Chloe?'

'Good, thanks.'

I realise Adut doesn't know much about what has been going on. When I told her about my art project I made it sound like an intellectual thing, I didn't mention what had been happening at school. She has no idea about church services or grief counselling or anything.

'Are you interested in the show? It's nothing intimidating. I'm part of a collective and we put them on every few months.'

'I don't think my work is good enough.' I may as well say it right out. 'Won't it look too basic compared to everyone else?'

'Listen we had a meeting last night and we got talking. We're always thinking about how to improve representation in our shows, you know, identify who doesn't get traditional space and then give them a platform. And we realised that we've never included a teenage artist, which is kind of...we should have our eye on that, right?'

'I don't know...Is there time for me to make something new?'

I'm not sure I want to show my photo of Natalia anymore, even in its new incarnation. Everything has been so bleak lately, and now it seems too dark and lonely. I'm glad I finished it, transformed it, but it's time to move on.

'For sure. I'll email you the timelines. And it doesn't have to be photography. We're open to anything you want to do. How do you feel about that?'

'Nervous,' I admit.

'Don't worry, I'll help you. We can discuss what you might want to put in. Your work will show where you are right now. Where you are is where you are, and it has every right to be seen. Don't you think?'

'You're messing with my head a little, to be honest,' I say and Adut laughs loudly and genuinely.

The sky is purple-dark, scattered with the kind of stars that give you hope. We're halfway through spring and surely it should be warmer than this. Katie, Liana and I lie on Liana's trampoline and look up at the universe. There are so many people in Liana's house that this is the only place we can get any privacy.

I tell them about Adut's invitation and how I'm not sure I should have said yes. I still have a bundle of schoolwork, I still have to see out term four.

'Whenever you talk about your art these days, babe, your face scrunches up,' Katie demonstrates, in case I don't get what she means, 'like, *stress face*. It never used to be like that.'

'Remember when I started my YouTube channel and all of a sudden I hated doing my hair and makeup?' Liana sticks her legs in the air and flexes her feet. 'Two videos a week? Too much pressure, man.'

I sigh. They're not wrong. 'I know I need to get the fun back. I just don't know how.'

Adut said everything she could to take the pressure off and followed up with an encouraging email, like she's the nicest person in the world, but still.

There's a round of screams from inside the house. We all lift our heads up in alarm. The glow from the television is visible through the glass doors. Liana's dad, brothers, nieces, nephews and cousins form animated shadows in front of the rugby match.

'They need to calm down or someone's going to have a coronary,' Liana remarks. She'll only watch women's sports, that's her rule, meaning she lies outside on the trampoline a lot on weekends.

How can I keep art fun but still handle this burning need to say something?

I've been thinking about Natalia's art pieces, the seventies models with their mouths scratched out. I know she thinks they're sloppy and a lazy joke, something she did at the last minute to hand in, but they still spoke to me, somehow.

And the conversation I had with Petra about her chain email has stuck with me too; how she was so scared she wanted to do something to warn us, to help us, to increase our chances, to cope with the uncontrollable fact of Yin being missing.

'There actually is this new thing I want to do, that has me kind of interested...' I shift about because Katie's head on my leg has made it go to sleep. 'It's kind of an extension of what Natalia and I did. I want to do a new photo shoot, with these girls I know at Balmoral—'

'Do it!' says Katie.

'You don't even know what I'm going to say yet.' I jiggle my leg, making us all bounce. 'It's about choosing how you show yourself to the world, like being in control of how others see you. I think.'

'Are you going to use Natalia as your model again?'

'Maybe. I mean, she also makes a good assistant. Her visual sense is great, she's just too disorganised to do her own thing.'

'Ha!' says Katie. 'I can relate.'

'Get her on the phone.' Liana slides my phone across the bouncy fabric. 'Do video. I want to actually meet her.'

'Now? Nah, she's got a lot to cope with at the moment.'

'Yeah, exactly,' Katie says. 'Maybe she wants to think about something different for a change.'

I'm surprised, but I call her anyway.

When Natalia's face appears on my screen I say, 'How are you going?' because the memorial service was only yesterday.

'Average,' she says. 'Where are you?'

I sweep my phone around so she can see the stars, the trampoline, the Fifitas' overgrown backyard. 'With some friends.'

'Hello, Chloe's friends.' Natalia sounds and looks tired but at least she answered my call.

Liana calls out, 'You're so pretty!'

I bounce my way off the trampoline, heading for somewhere quieter, more private. I stand in the back corner of the garden, where moths gather around the security light.

'Do you think you'll be back at school this week?'

'Not sure…How did I do yesterday?'

'You did well. It was nice to hear more about Yin, from a different perspective. It was really sad, of course.'

I can see tiny hints of what looks to be Natalia's bedroom, whenever she shifts about. 'I'm sorry I didn't tell you that I used to be friends with Yin.'

'It's fine,' I say and it is. In the last week I've thought more about how hard things must have been for Natalia since Yin went missing, all the hanging on and waiting.

'Why did you call me?' she asks.

'Just to say hi. And Katie and Liana wanted to meet you.' I leave it at that. She looks even more shattered than I expected, so my new idea can wait until she comes back to school.

'You're so strange, Cardell,' she says and I know her well enough by now to take it as a compliment.

# Natalia

**DAY 73**

The only time that Dad and I talk about anything real is in the car, I don't know why, that's just the way it is, the words come easier when you're sitting side by side, when you can pretend the view is fascinating and you're not talking about something earth-shattering.

'How are you feeling?' Dad taps his fingers against the steering wheel as he drives.

'How do you think?'

About as good as if I was being boiled slowly in a giant metal cauldron over a slow-burning fire or if I was a little baby deer walking through the forest on my own and there were wolves nearby. And I'm wondering if the psychologist is going to make me lie down on a couch or if that's just something they do in movies, only I can't bring myself to ask Dad that so instead I say:

'What was the deal with your nervous breakdown?'

Dad flinches for real, takes his eyes off the road, briefly. 'I'm surprised you even remember. You were so young.'

From one answer-dodger to another I say, 'I was young

enough that no one told me what was going on and no one has talked about it since so that's why I'm asking you now.'

Dad throws an exasperated hand up at the driver who has just overtaken us and then cut back in and then he can't avoid answering any longer. He's already sweating so much that he has to wipe his forehead with the back of his hand.

'I wouldn't call it a breakdown, I guess I'd say it was a fairly serious episode of depression.'

'Why were you depressed?'

'There's not always a reason.' Pause to think. 'I had a chemical imbalance in my brain, for sure, and I needed medication to fix it. But it was also more complicated than that.'

'In what way?'

He sighs loudly and I can tell he's having trouble keeping his patience and let me tell you I'm having patience issues at having to drag it out of him sentence by sentence. Does he think it's easy for me to ask him these questions?

'It was complicated, because I was under a lot of stress at the time. Business was bad and I was working punishing hours and not taking care of myself, and I had no tools at all to manage my stress.'

'Huh.' I think about the medicine cabinet. 'Do you still take medication?'

'No. It got me through a crisis period and then I focussed on my lifestyle and therapy and after a couple of years I could manage without it. I still have to stay balanced though, you know, exercise, eat well, meditate.'

I snort. 'Just because you keep your gym bag on the back seat doesn't mean you actually do any exercise. Come on,

Dad. I don't think you take care of yourself as much as you think you do.'

'I hear you, Natalia. You're right, I should keep it in mind.'

Dad eyeballs me seriously. I wish he wouldn't take his eyes off the road so much.

'You should do more than keep it in mind. I know you don't always feel good. I do have eyes, you know.' My voice sounds ever so slightly choked.

'I don't want you to worry about me too much, but there's no miracle cure for depression, you know?' He's quiet. 'It's more a matter of managing it as best I can. I do have rough patches still.'

All I remember about Dad's depression is that he stopped working and stayed home a lot and didn't do any of the normal things I was used to. And he cried more than usual and lost his temper more than usual too. And I wonder if that's not how I've been these past few months. Like him. The thought scares me.

'How do you not drown in your emotions?' The questions burst out of me. 'How do you control your thoughts when they're going everywhere?'

How do you know when your brain has gone too far, like it's gotten too weird in there?

'What kind of thoughts?'

Dad sticks his indicator on, and when it's safe, he pulls over by the side of the road.

'What kind of thoughts?' he says again.

'Everything,' I say.

He waits. I don't want to say.

'Like, is there anything anyone could have done to prevent what happened to Yin? What did she go through before she died? Was she scared? What was she thinking about? Did she think about her family, or me even? Did she hate me?'

I stop, because I'm starting to get worked up, the tears creep in from the corners and threaten me. I don't tell him my strangest thoughts, just the more normal ones.

'That's a lot to cope with, hon,' Dad says. 'But they're all very reasonable things to think about. I think it's especially hard because they haven't caught anyone yet. There's no closure.'

I put my head down on the dash in front of me. 'My brain is so tired. I'm so tired. I can't get a break.'

'You've been so strong.' Dad pats my hair gently. 'I know you're exhausted.'

'What do I do?'

'I can only tell you what works for me. Sometimes I distract myself if I'm overwhelmed, and sometimes I go into the feelings, talk to someone about them. Both things work, at different times. And I keep people close around me, even when I'm not in the mood.'

I lift my head up. 'Does that mean you think I should go back to school this week?'

Somehow I'm stuck on going back to school, even though there's no real dread in it. I don't mind seeing that complainer Petra, I'm not scared of any of the teachers, and Claire and Milla and I made our peace at the memorial service.

'Not if you don't want to. Take all the time you need. But maybe a bit of routine might help. Doctor Radcliffe is going to talk to you about all of this, and I'm always here for you. You're absolutely not on your own.'

'I already hate Doctor Radcliffe,' I say with all the passion I can muster.

'I know,' he says and I suppose he probably does know. He finds a park close to the doctor's fancy consulting rooms and switches the engine off. He reaches out and we hug extremely awkwardly over the gearstick.

'Love you,' he says quickly.

# *Chloe*

**DAY 77**

Natalia's house is overwhelming—lush cream and beige everything, carpet that's pillowy underfoot, abstract art on the walls—but at least her bedroom is relatively ordinary, if you ignore the fact that she has her own en suite bathroom.

It's awkward at first, of course, in the way that it's always awkward when you first go to someone's house. Natalia hasn't been to school for weeks, and the last time I saw her was standing up at the pulpit for Yin's memorial service.

The light is good in her room, and it's the archetypal teenage girl's bedroom—bed, desk, wardrobe, ruffles, posters, lamps—which is exactly what I want.

Natalia shows me on her laptop how easy it is to find out where someone lives. We sit at her desk and gape.

'How did you found out this guy was a suspect?'

'He was mentioned in this thing called the Echo Files, under a fake name, but then these web sleuths found out his real name.'

She takes me through the steps, his crimes, the court documents, the phone directory.

'And then I went to his house,' she says.

I'm so shocked that I hit her on the arm, harder than I intended.

'Ouch! Abusive, Cardell.'

'What the hell? Are you joking?' But I can see from her face that she's not. 'When? Why? What happened?'

'Shh, calm down. You're the first person I've told.' Natalia snaps her computer shut. 'I need you to be more chill, Chloe.'

I inhale deeply, summoning the type of fake inner calm I use when Sam is being a brat. Natalia wears a deep scowl so I tone it down. 'When was this?'

'School holidays.'

'Why did you do it?'

Her eyes dart about; she swivels back and forth on her computer chair. 'I just wanted to do something. I felt an unbearable itch that I needed to scratch.'

I try not to let any dread creep into my voice.

'What happened?'

She puffs out her cheeks and lets a long whoosh of air go.

'He was there,' she says. 'He saw me scoping out his house and he confronted me. I've never seen a creepier man in my whole life, and that's saying a lot.'

'Did you talk to him?'

'We yelled insults and accusations at each other a bit and at first it felt good to tell him how evil he is, but then I woke up and realised the madness of standing metres away from a predator and a convicted criminal and I got out of there quick smart.'

She looks pale even talking about it.

'And when you saw him, did you think that he could be Doctor Calm?'

'No.' She fiddles with the edge of her desk. 'I don't think they're gonna find him, are they?'

You'd think the reward or Yin's death would have ramped things up a bit, made things happen, but it doesn't seem that way.

'I don't think so, or maybe not for a long time,' I admit. 'And so that means he wins, and in a way we lose.'

Natalia watches me silently, her eyes deep and dark as rock pools. It's hard to know what she's thinking.

My phone beeps. 'It's them. They're almost here. They took the wrong tram.'

Natalia rubs her hedgehog hair.

'I've been thinking about not wasting my life,' she says eventually. 'How we have to make it count. Maybe that's how we win.'

Bochen and Cherry arrive in a flurry of bags and perfume and exclamations over how nice Natalia's mum is and how hard her street was to find. They carry their shoes in their hands, because there's nowhere to leave them at the door, and bring a bag of vacuum-sealed bubble cups. I can tell Natalia hates her herbal jelly drink but she drinks it anyway, to be polite. Maybe some of the things I've said to her have gotten through.

I show them some reference shots, some famous, others maybe not so much. The famous ones are Ai Weiwei flipping the bird at famous monuments around the world, and most controversially, sticking his finger up at the Gate of Heavenly Peace in Tiananmen Square.

'I like the spirit of rebellion,' I say. 'I want to capture that.'

'You know he's a friend of Bochen's parents,' Cherry says cheerfully.

Bochen shoots her a dirty look. 'Not friends. Perhaps they are in the same scene.'

'Her parents are artists.' Cherry is oblivious to Bochen's discomfort. She points. 'She's supposed to be an artist too, she's meant to be going to the Central Academy, but she's a bad girl so they send her here.'

Bochen grabs Cherry's finger and squeezes it to shut her up. 'Don't ruin my reputation. What's the next photo?'

'It's a video.' I cue up Cao Fei's *Cosplayers* video on Natalia's computer. The video starts with young cosplayers acting out action or fantasy sequences in a range of busy city environments. Gradually, though, they're shown hanging out in the city like normal teens, riding the subway, walking down the median strip of a busy highway, looking out at water, bored. Eventually they're shown at home, still in their costumes and doing mundane things like scrolling on their phone or eating dinner in front of the TV.

It's a combination of how they would like to be seen in their best fantasies, together with the bare reality of their lives.

'Do you recognise any of those places?' Natalia asks Cherry.

Cherry gives her a pitying look. 'I'm not from Guangzhou.'

I turn away so Natalia doesn't see me smirk.

When we get going on the shoot everyone starts to get along a lot better.

I've asked Bochen and Cherry to bring their own costumes and direct us on how they want to be portrayed. It's a lot more loose and random than what I did with Natalia, but I'm hoping it will capture something truthful.

Bochen wears a tiger onesie, stripes and ears and tail and all.

'I'm a lazy tiger girl,' she says. 'I'm too lazy to do my homework, I'm too lazy to think about the future, I sit in my bedroom and do nothing all day.'

Natalia sets Bochen up on her bed and piles textbooks and stacks of paper around her. She finds her old Nintendo Playstation in a box under her bed. She brings up donuts and dirty plates from the kitchen and we arrange them around the bed as directed, along with our empty plastic cups.

I was worried that she was being kind of withdrawn once the others arrived, but Natalia is surprisingly meticulous when it comes to creating the set and she seems to enjoy being in the background for a change.

I start clicking and Tiger Bochen slumps on the bed with the Playstation controls in one hand and a half-eaten donut in the other. She looks hilarious.

'Feels so goooooooooooood.' She pretends to cram the donut in her mouth.

'We got it!' I say, after I've shot enough. I have no idea what Adut is going to think of these photos, or the other proper grown-up artists, but I'm having enough fun not to care. Yet.

Cherry has spent most of Bochen's shoot locked in Natalia's bathroom getting ready and when she emerges she is in full Snow White costume, Disney-style, with blue bodice, yellow skirt, puffy sleeves and bobbed black hair. The sanitised pretty movie version, not the disturbing Grimm's version I've always liked.

'I look pretty, don't I?' is the first thing she says and I immediately go into freefall about how we're going to make this work. Natalia wears her scepticism plastered right across her face.

Cherry and Bochen tip out the seemingly dozens of bags they brought with them; plush animals of every colour and size and condition tumble out onto Natalia's bed.

'We got a bulk deal,' Bochen explains.

Cherry pulls a giant pair of plastic novelty scissors out of the last bag.

'I'm Snow White,' she says, 'if Snow White hated all the animals and chopped their heads off.'

Natalia looks like all of her Christmases have come at once.

For Cherry's shoot we set up in the spare bedroom that Natalia's sister has been staying in. Plush toy carcasses pile up around the room, mixed in with Olivia's mess of black clothing, piles of novels, cigarette packets and old coffee mugs. Fairytale Cherry sits in the picturesque bay window holding up a severed rabbit head triumphantly. She is truly, truly scary. I don't know how I missed this fact at school.

The more Cherry smiles the scarier she looks.

'Don't mess with the princess,' she keeps saying.

Bochen is almost asleep in a pile of leftover toy limbs, while Natalia holds up a circular gold reflector to get the light on Cherry's face. She's biting her lip in concentration, working her arms hard to ping the light just right.

I take a moment in between clicks to check on Natalia, her dark under-eye circles, her bare head. She doesn't look like she's been eating much, but her focus is strong, the misery isn't hanging over her so thickly as before. She might have even laughed a few times.

I'm going to find a way to do the photography elective next term. And maybe we're all going to be all right.

# Natalia

I finally go back to school and it's not the big deal I thought it would be. The thing about the Balmoral prison schedule is that you have to keep marching to each class at the appropriate time and sit still and not talk and wear the regimental uniform of the regimented and that leaves no time for drifting, no time for wandering off in your head and slipping off the face of the earth.

By lunch it's apparent that spring has sprung at least for one day and there is actual blue sky and swords of sunlight piercing the atmosphere. Instead of skulking in the quad like we did last term we bleed out onto the oval and you couldn't make grass this green in a factory.

Our year level loll about in small groups, sunbaking, gossiping, filming each other, making daisy-chain headpieces and other childish pastimes, I kid you not, and exams and final assessments are so many weeks away and not a bother at all and the official memorialising is over which means we can be sad on our own timetable now.

In a satellite city clump by the trees are Audrey and Petra

and Brooke and the other boarders. Chloe wants me to shake hands make up with Petra, but I won't. Milla, Claire, Lisbeth and the good girls sprawl near the goal posts, Sarah poses next door, Marley is asleep, Ally sings to herself.

Bochen and Cherry and Mercury and some other international students have pooled their food and laid out a picnic and there is unspoken respect between Bochen and Cherry and me now because those girls are wilder than you'd imagine.

Somewhere in the middle, pretending she is nowhere in particular at all, Chloe is sunk like a happy stone in the grass.

We made it. We survived.

There's still a Yin-shaped gap in the world, there always will be. A Yin-shape in the clouds, in a passing shadow, in the shape of a tree.

She's here, I know, or if she's not, I'm going to pretend hard that she is. Here in my head, not easily forgotten. Wherever she is, I hope she has the curly hair of her dreams, the hair she always wanted instead of the straight hair she got. I hope she lives out every career she ever considered, I hope she gets to play clarinet all day long, hell, I hope there are only hot available clarinet players in her village.

Nothing will ever be the same, but I allow the sun to sink into my body, let myself be optimistic for a change.

I weave my way from the tap near the tennis courts, through the scattered girls, my filled-up water bottle in my hand. How easy it would be to pop the top off it and sweep my arm like a powerful wizard drawing an arc of magic, shooting surprise splashes of cold water over these relaxed bodies, these brave girls.

Making us scream, making us feel more alive.

# Acknowledgments

*The Gaps* took seven long years to write and was a difficult book to get across the line. I started writing it, unexpectedly, during a residency at Peking University, which was supported by Asialink Arts and the Malcolm Robertson Foundation. Asialink provides significant cultural exchanges between Australia and Asia, and my residency in Beijing was a life-changing opportunity. Thank you so much to Liu Hongzhong and David and Karen Walker for their friendship and support on this trip, and to the Australian Studies Centre at Peking University for hosting me. Much gratitude also to Zhang Bochen and Zhan Chunjuan for interesting conversations and lending me their names.

I wrote *The Gaps* with the support of the Victorian Government, through Creative Victoria.

Many thanks to my early readers, writing cheer squad and unofficial career advisers: Andrew McDonald, Myke Bartlett, Chris Miles, Alison Arnold, Bronte Coates and Marisa Pintado. I'm so grateful to Wai Chim, Nina Kenwood, Robert Newton and Lili Wilkinson for taking the time to read my book and support a fellow writer.

I have worked at the independent bookshop Readings for

more years than I can count, and I couldn't have a writing career at all without the understanding and friendship of my wonderful colleagues, all of whom absolutely believe in the power of books and can deliver carb-loading and amateur psychotherapy in the same session.

Thank you to the amazing team at Text; they're a passionate, hard-working and professional bunch and I'm so fortunate to have them championing my work. I'm extremely grateful to Imogen Stubbs for designing such a gorgeous and fitting cover. Special thanks to my editor Samantha Forge for her calm manner, excellent insights and careful attention. Thank you to Vanessa Lanaway for her meticulous proofreading.

Finally, my family and friends have always understood my strange ways and showed a keen interest in my writing. Thank you Mum, Dad, Jacqui and Carly. Big kisses to Grant, and unlimited heavenly doggy treats to Minnie, who faithfully kept me company for so many years.